THE CURSE OF KULDHARA

Also by Richa S Mukherjee

I Didn't Expect to be Expecting
Kanpur Khoofiya Pvt Ltd
Excess Baggage

THE CURSE OF KULDHARA

RICHA S. MUKHERJEE

HarperCollins *Publishers* India

Black Ink

First published in India by Black Ink 2022
An imprint of HarperCollins *Publishers*
4th Floor, Tower A, Building No. 10, Phase II, DLF Cyber City,
Gurugram, Haryana – 122002
www.harpercollins.co.in

2 4 6 8 10 9 7 5 3 1

P-ISBN: 978-93-9440-720-6
E-ISBN: 978-93-9440-728-2

This is a work of fiction and all characters and incidents described in this book are the product of the author's imagination. Any resemblance to actual persons, living or dead, is entirely coincidental and does not intend to hurt the sentiments of any individual, community, sect or religion.

Typeset in 10.5/14 Utopia Std at
Manipal Technologies Limited, Manipal

Printed and bound at
Thomson Press (India) Ltd

MIX
Paper
FSC FSC® C010615

This book is produced from independently certified FSC® paper
to ensure responsible forest management.

This one is hardly a mystery.
Dear Anirban (Banu), thank you for listening, loving, placating and holding this temperamental writer while never questioning why you had to wait in the dedication queue till book 4. For this and so much more, I'm never letting go. Remember what papa said – Ab bhag ke kahan jaoge?!

A NOTE ON THE SERIES

I grew up thinking detectives were city slickers, wearing trench coats, smoking pipes or then mad geniuses with dishevelled hair and odd quirks. There's another earthy, homegrown kind living in small towns with big dreams, who neither have the luxury of indulging in apparels nor whims. Through Prachand Tripathi, the kind, oily haired detective and this series of books, I want to take you on adventures through the streets of Gwaltoli and beyond where each book offers up much of what life is, a mystery, a negotiation, full of surprises and a barrel of laughs. Let's get on with it shall we?

CHAPTER 1

'They're coming. I can feel it in my bones,' said the old man,' his bulbous eyes gleaming. 'They are coming. I see it.' He extended his arm into the dark night, beyond the glow of the dwindling fire in front of him. As if in connivance with the ominous prophecy, the cold wind stirred the sand from the Thar Desert into the eyes of the four men squatting by the fire. They huddled and glanced around nervously.

Rocking back and forth, their eyes fixed on the old man, one of them pulled hard at his chillum, the embers dancing around the pipe. Thick smoke blew out of his nostrils as he pulled his shawl closer. 'Who? My goats that ran away? That was two weeks ago. And your enchantment to herd them back didn't work. My wife hasn't let me back into bed ever since,' he said.

The old man shot the pedant an irritated look.

One of the other men laughed and shook his head. 'Oye, bawlo! He is talking about the daktar saab who is returning from the city with special medicine for the loose motions. There's a bad bug going around.'

'Silence!' the old man raised his arm. The garrulous men cowered under his gaze.

'This is no trivial matter. The tides of upheaval are headed for this village. Strangers will arrive and bring with them death and chaos. Everything will change. Everything!' he roared, causing the men to huddle into a human block of quivering mass and bones.

The old man stroked his long white beard, continuing to look into the distance where a bleak outline of a ghost town was visible. No moon, no stars and a cloudy night, yet it stared back, defined by an eerie glow that blurred the details and rendered it monster-like, shapeless, amorphous and vigilant.

'Baba, is it them? Are they angry? Are we in trouble?' the devotee who had lost his goats inquired with folded hands.

The old man shook his head. 'I can't say, Daulatram. But I sense that they are restless.'

'It has been quiet for a while. Ever since the last disappearance,' another man said. 'Little Chameli left for school unescorted and happened to wander into ... into the ruins ... and never returned.' He repeated the story he had heard often, as if to validate it and elevate it from the status of mere paranoia.

The last man, who had held his silence all this while, spoke up. 'Others are afraid to say it, but I am not. Why fight our destiny? Those ruins are cursed, and so are we. If Bhutaari Baba thinks some danger is coming, I believe him. We must spread the word so that people can be warned.'

'No!' the old man, who was popular as Bhutaari Baba amongst the locals, said in a firm voice. 'Not yet. I shall try and speak with the spirits first.'

Daulatram pulled at the chillum, wondering what direct or trunk-calling system the mysterious but acclaimed Bhutaari Baba possessed. And if he was such an accomplished tantric, why were his eyes so full of fear and foreboding? That's when an invisible hand tugged at his turban and flung it into the darkness.

Without waiting for his companions or any residual spine-chilling prophecies, Daulatram ran screaming into the night, faster than any of his absconding goats.

CHAPTER 2

Prachand Tripathi decided to have a word with his mother. Despite being a patient man, his resolve had come untethered. And with good reason. The credibility of his beloved Kanpur Khoofiya Pvt Ltd (KKPL) was at stake. Just when his lifelong dream of running a respectable detective agency was finally coming to fruition, his mother's preposterous commercial ventures were threatening to undo all the years of his hard work. But, before he could summon some courage to challenge the formidable achar-making queen of Gwaltoli, there were other matters to traverse.

'What do we have here?' he asked aloud, trying to navigate his faithful scooter Champa through a crowd that was blocking the path between him and his ancestral home, Awadh Niwas. Sensing something untoward, he ran ahead, leaving Champa in the company of a mutt that was sniffing her rear tyre with much interest.

When it came to calamities in Gwaltoli, it was protocol to shake heads vigorously, cluck tongues, sympathize without taking any concrete action and analyse the series of unfortunate events. One helpful bystander would even take on the mantle of directing non-existent traffic. Contrary to these norms, Prachand noticed that there was something unhurried in the general manner of the crowd before him, sipping tea from impossibly tiny kulhads of chai from the tiny tea shop nearby. When Prachand finally managed to push through to the front, he found some men digging a hole. Blaming his lack of observation for missing the catastrophe on hand, he turned to a kurta-clad gentleman to his right. 'What happened here, Bhaisaab?'

The man shrugged. 'They're laying pipes.'

Prachand sighed. Indians had reached the moon, brought polio to its knees and built the largest statue in the world, yet here were his neighbours, watching a road being dug with the kind of fascination that should be reserved for epoch-making events. Shaking his head, he walked back to Champa and drove around the suitably entertained bystanders.

While normal folk had dogs, cats and foul-mouthed parrots perched outside their doors, the Tripathis had made a small enclosure for their high-maintenance cow, Hirwa. Prachand shot his favourite pet a doleful look as she swished her tail and stared back at him.

'Do you know you're being exploited in the name of commerce, my dear sakhi?' he said to her. Hirwa mooed with bovine insouciance. All she cared about was food and the deference with which she was treated in the neighbourhood.

He swung open the creaking teakwood doors that led into the aangan of Awadh Niwas, which hosted not only the best papads and achars in the locality but was also the high-octane processing hub of a small-scale enterprise: Hirwa ke 'Khoofiya' Utpaad.

Owing to the success and media attention from the last few cases, now that her son's investigative enterprise was well known, the jugaad queen Rachna Tripathi, Prachand's mother and head of the popular women's WhatsApp group Gwaltoli *Gilehris,* had zeroed in on a business opportunity and was now packaging and selling *gau mutra* and *kanda*. Understandably, Prachand was not in the least pleased with his precious agency's name being infringed upon in this manner.

'Ma, it isn't ethical,' he had tried to reason with her.

'Stop being Satyavadi Harish Chandra.'

'You know this is wrong,' the ever-conscientious and staid Prachand Tripathi had said. 'Didn't you and *Pitaji* give away this stuff for free earlier? Why should we turn into opportunistic vultures now?'

'It would be unnatural not to, Prachand! We have Laxmiji herself beckoning us with an opportunity. Should we squander it?'

'I doubt Laxmiji would beckon us with anything that comes out of Hirwa.'

'Stop being a smart mouth. You know what I mean. Fame and popularity are transient. People are still curious about the Kanpur Khoofiya success story,' she quipped. 'So what if I have to discuss your cases with every customer? It's exciting and I'm going to make a few *annas* while I'm at it.'

'Pitaji doesn't like it either.'

'Pitaji is fine as long as I give him spare supply for his freeloader friends.'

Prachand noticed his offense crumbling. 'What of Hirwa? This must be putting a strain on her.'

Rachna Tripathi gave her son an incredulous look. 'That cow cannot be *made* to do anything. Thank the lord that these are by-products. Imagine the drama if we needed milk from her! Her tantrums would be worse than Ammaji's!'

Prachand capitulated, resigning himself to the fact that Kanpur Khoofiya Pvt Ltd's future lay somewhere in the biogas industry. Vidya Tripathi, who was shelling peas, smirked from one corner of the *aangan*, watching this familiar exchange between her husband and mother-in-law.

Though Rachna Tripathi didn't have Prachand's approval, Vidya grudgingly appreciated her mother-in-law's entrepreneurial spirit. The saas-bahu didn't see eye to eye on matters concerning the homestead. Vidya being absent from daughter-in-law duties, given her position as partner and finance head at Kanpur Khoofiya Pvt Ltd, was the common bone of contention but the women had developed a necessary respect for each other, avoiding mutually flammable issues. The latest one after three years of marriage was the '*pota-poti kab khelenge aangan mein*' variety.

'AAAAAAAAAK-GARRRRRRRR-THUUUUUUUUU!' Vidya's reverie was broken by a guttural, unearthly sound emanating from the bathroom. It drew a quick response from her mother-in-law who often resorted to loud muttering behind her husband's back.

'The doctor has advised him against this habit. It will scrape and bruise his throat, but who listens to me? Let his *phepdaas* land in the sink, what do I care! All the men in this house are the same. Hacking, sneezing and coughing like they have microphones embedded within,' Rachna Tripathi said.

She bustled past Vidya and picked up her shiny brown purse. 'I'm off for my *kirtan,* Vidya. The flour shop will deliver ten kilograms of atta. Bimla Chachi is stopping by to drop off my blouse and the kheer is on the stove. It should be ready in about ten minutes.'

Vidya observed the retreating figure of Rachna Tripathi and turned her attention back to the peas, hoping Prachand would return from his ablutions sooner. It was turning out to be a listless Sunday. As she counted the money her mother-in-law had left for her haute couture arriving from the famous house of Miandad tailors two lanes away, she started thinking about her own finances.

Much to her consternation, Prachand was still as gullible as a mewling infant. And the smidgen of popularity had brought with it never-ending requests for 'favours' and 'help' where no one seemed to want to pay for anything. Even the women's committees, of which she was a key member, often egged her on to ask for favours from her husband on their behalf, which frustrated her. Every random person seemed to be related to them and she, holding the reins of the business's finances, had to work twice as hard to keep the revenue stream going, especially now that Prachand had started spending some time at Tripathi & Sons, the family's leather manufacturing and retail shop, in a bid to please his perennially surly father.

She sighed loud enough to startle Hirwa. They exchanged a look. Even the cow seemed to understand that Kanpur Khoofiya Pvt Ltd needed a leg up.

CHAPTER 3

Yatish Bhatnagar sat behind a rotund mountain of a man whose derriere barely fit into the plastic Nilkamal chair used for guests at Kanpur Khoofiya Pvt Ltd. His childhood friend's detective agency now felt like home. The two-room office with its floral curtains, sparse furniture, multicoloured pictures of Bholenath and impeccable orderliness, thanks to Prachand, always smelt of incense sticks. People from all walks of life would walk into this pious haze daily, armed with their sometimes insurmountable, and often minuscule, problems. Missing papers to missing spouses, feuding families to fake promises, these doors offered a cost-effective solution to all maladies.

Yatish cracked open a few plump peanut shells kept in a crumpled newspaper cup, licking the delicious salty masala with his finger. The cracking drew a look of admonishment from his friend who sat across the client. The peanuts were set aside with alacrity.

'Bansal Bhaisaab, this case is a bit complicated. Not only do you want me to pull out your family's property records, but I'll also have to travel to Allahabad to ascertain the ownership status. I try and avoid cases where the jurisdiction works against the investigation,' Prachand told his client.

'But you are the famous Prachand Tripathi! You can do anything.'

Prachand shifted in his chair, always uncomfortable with voluminous praise.

'That's not true. I will give it my best shot, but accessing records and working around the government machinery isn't easy. I can't promise anything till I do some preliminary work.'

'Wonderful! You just start. Now, Mr Prachand, the cost?'

If praise made him squirm, fee negotiations had him gunning for the nearest exit. Prachand thought of Vidya, his straight-talking and confident partner who had no qualms negotiating or driving a hard bargain. He wished that the meeting had been moved to another day.

'My wife, who manages the estimates, is not in right now. But I think the initial figure, excluding accommodation and travel, would be close to thirty thousand rupees. I can get you an exact number by tomorrow.'

'Oh ho!' Bansal Bhaisaab shook his large sweaty head.

'Is there a problem?'

Bansal Bhaisaab looked up with forlorn eyes. 'My daughter is going off to college. That's why I am trying to generate funds through this contested family property. It's all for her. I don't have much money right now, but I promise, as soon as ...'

Yatish had an insane urge to lob a bunch of peanuts at the man's head. He could predict the sequence of events from this point. His poor friend was so gullible, perennially wedged between his good heart, his constant philanthropy and his abhorrence for unscrupulous cases, no matter how well-paying they may be. Vidya Bhabhi was adept at chasing away schemers and freeloaders like Bansal, but today Prachand was easy prey.

'Yes, Bansal Bhaisaab. I understand. Let me speak to Vidya and see what I can do. Just leave your file with the details right here.'

Bansal Bhaisaab, satisfied with the outcome of some stellar acting, left post-haste.

'*Kambakht*! *Lalchi lomdi*!' Yatish spluttered.

'You might want to treat this as an office for once, instead of acting like you're sunning yourself on the ghats of Bithoor, Yatish.'

'Prachand Da, you're giving me an earful for eating peanuts in front of a client. But can you predict what Vidya Bhabhi will do once she finds out that another client is attempting to wheedle his way out of a fee? Can't you see that his penury is fake?'

Prachand smiled. 'I can.'

Yatish looked at him quizzically.

'He might have turned up with a sad face and a crumpled shirt, but I saw what I needed to. I saw him removing a watch before entering; I'm guessing it was an expensive one. If a man has money to indulge his planets, wearing *neelam* and *pukhraj* rings, he clearly has change to spare. The diary he kept on the table had a member's parking sticker peeking out. It's from the Mansarovar Club, which only admits extremely affluent businessmen. Bansal Bhaisaab is clearly not a beggar.'

Yatish smiled. 'I forgot I was in the company of Kanpur's most famous detective and the smartest man I know.'

Prachand shrugged. 'Titles mean nothing, Yatish. What matters is kindness. Titles disappear, but kindness lives on.'

'And these are the kind of *satsangi* statements that get you into trouble.'

Prachand laughed. 'Let me just call for some snacks. A bad client at the end of a long day stokes my appetite.'

'The air we breathe stokes your appetite,' Yatish said. Prachand smiled affectionately as his friend called out to Chotu, a young and eager apprentice who, when not in school, would hang around for juicy titbits and odd jobs.

Chotu didn't respond. 'Oye, *baudam*! What are you doing? Didn't you hear me?' Yatish called out again till he realized that Chotu was standing at the window. 'How is it dark so early in the evening?' he mumbled.

As if on cue, the lights went off, plunging the room into semi-darkness. The wind picked up outside, making funnels of dust on the side of the road. 'Strange weather,' Prachand said, walking to the window. Yatish followed him.

Chotu's eyes bulged. 'Bbbb ... Bhaiyya ... two black cats just crossed the threshold. And the flowers I water outside, the ones that face the sun? They were facing the other way today. My dadi told me nature can sense things that we cannot perceive.'

'So?' shrugged Yatish. 'Are you an eighty-year-old chachi to believe in such nonsense?'

'It is not nonsense, Bhaiyya. Some trouble is brewing. Don't mock the signs.'

CHAPTER 4

'I suppose my feelings aren't important. That Bipin Kumar deserves a comfortable silk *dhoti* and I get a tattered cotton one? Just because I'm playing Ravana! That is hierarchical and mythological discrimination!'

'Why are you so quick to take offense, Kesari Ramji? You are our veteran actor. Why would we sideline you?' said Prakash Srivastava, the director and playwright, placing a hand on the agitated man's shoulder.

'Offense! I'll tell you what's offensive. The indignity of having two crater-like holes in my dhoti, which a child can effortlessly put his body through. And to top it off, being used as a guinea pig for all these make-up people you change every two days. My eight-year-old granddaughter could do a better job!'

'These are lean times, Kesari Ramji. We're all adjusting.'

Kesari Ram stood up in a huff. 'I'll be adjusting till I reach my funeral pyre,' he muttered. 'And I'm not about to do any more song and dance. You please send this pesky nausikhiya away. He can take his new-fangled idiocy and go home.'

'Kesari Ramji, we must move with the times. It's an experiment. Ramlilas have always had song and dance. This boy is only trying to offer better entertainment and get viewers back to this dying industry. Isn't it refreshing to have women play the female characters than having to wear those dreadful, itchy wigs?'

'I look great in a *ghaghra*!' he pouted. 'And its infinitely more preferable to pretend to be a woman than an acrobat. That boy asks me to kick high in the air when I have prostrate issues already. Have I earned all this respect over the years only to have the audience look under my dhoti while I prance about on the stage?'

The *nausikhiya* in the spotlight, young Bhushan Tripathi, was unfazed by the hostility. In his head, he was a pioneer, a trailblazer. And much like his brave ancestors, he was prepared to take the heat that came with it. He just needed to stay focused and deliver the first-ever Broadway-style Ramlila that Kanpur had never seen. Most people had received the idea with incomprehension or a slack jaw, but Prakash Srivastava had shared in this fantastical dream and was trying to bring it to fruition. The cast and crew remained convinced that both men had lost their marbles.

Bhushan was scribbling on a sheet of paper when he felt a hand on his shoulder. A spectacle of hair and teeth stared back at him.

'Oh, Chachu!' He took a deep breath. 'You scared me!'

Dinanath Tripathi sat down heavily. Technically, he should have been a happy man. But reality and expectations are almost always a long boat ride away from each other. From a time when his elder brother would have hung him upside down for even contemplating life beyond working at Tripathi & Sons to being allowed to take a stab at acting in his free time, things had turned for the better. But the timing had been unfortunate. At fifty-four years of age, despite his passion, the roles for an enthusiastic, lanky man with a balding pate were limited. His happiness knew no bounds when his youngest nephew offered him a role in his play. But it was short-lived happiness.

The opportunity to play the role of Jambavan, a wise and revered character in the Ramayana, seemed like a fair offer. But the glamour of being on stage wore off quickly once it hit home that he would be playing a bear who had three lines in total. His nephew, in fact, seemed to be adding *ghee* to the fire by making them all burst into song and dance at the drop of a hat.

'Why am I always the first to finish make-up and costume on rehearsal days, Bhushan? Do you know how hot I feel under all this hair?'

Bhushan looked at the long snout of the modern-day Jambavan. He could only imagine the expression underneath the hirsute surface. Feeling a surge of pity, he said, 'Yours takes the longest, Chachu, which is why they finish it first. Don't worry. The weather is getting better already, isn't it?'

Chachu Tripathi continued ranting. 'I just hope Bhaisaab doesn't find out. I boasted to him that I've snagged a big role. If he finds out that my dialogues don't last beyond the length of a bathroom break, he will tell me to get back to the shop.'

'Will some samosa chaat appease the great Jambavan?' a woman's voice floated in.

Both men turned around to peer at the smiling face of Vidya Tripathi. Prachand and Vidya would often drop by during practice sessions.

Bhushan smiled and Dinanath Tripathi stood up to hug her affectionately. She cowered in his hairy arms and scratched her face. 'Chachu, your hair.'

He looked at her solemnly. 'I know you can't tell, but I'm making a sad face. Do I really look nothing like myself, Vidya? Will no one even recognize me?'

Vidya chuckled and pulled out a tiffin box. The heady aroma of *papdi chaat, samosa chaat, dhaniya ke aloo and rabdi* wafted out as the crew members walked by, sniffing and eyeing the food longingly.

'Thanks for the snacks, Bhabhi,' Bhushan beamed. Vidya smiled affectionately at the former lead singer of the Kanpuriya Beliebers who had left the band on the principle of not compromising on his dreams by singing at child-naming ceremonies, weddings or *jagratas*. Rumour had it that he was once locked in a room for a whole evening by some mischievous children. That's when he had sworn off the tedious life of an entertainer. She was proud of him for not having forsaken his dream and having found another way to channelize his creativity, even if her father-in-law had branded him a directionless and certified loony.

'We haven't seen you and Bhaiyya at rehearsals for a while. Too much work?' Bhushan asked.

Vidya grunted and set her plate down. 'Work? We don't have time for it. With Prachand helping out at the shop, where is the time for taking on more work? I have so many ideas to help the business grow, but what good is that?'

'Why don't you speak with Bhaisaab?' Chachu suggested.

'How's that going for you, Chachu, having had so many years of practice?' Vidya ribbed the old man.

Chachu Tripathi cleaned some *saunth ki chutney* from his chin and laughed. 'Not well. But I'm sure you'll do a better job. Besides, I feel that a big opportunity is heading your way. Don't worry. Listen to the wise Jambavan!'

CHAPTER 5

'When my daddu was alive, we lived like kings. We lacked nothing, be it food or friends. The *choupal*, especially in our locality, was the talk of the town. Every evening scores of acquaintances would turn up to chit-chat, for heated debates or just for hookah and snacks. Those were the days!' said Dinbandhu Tripathi, the resident angry old man of Awadh Niwas.

He seemed to be in a good mood, which was a phenomenon as rare as a street devoid of a cow, goat or a shop selling chaat in Gwaltoli. The reason was swishing in a steel tumbler sitting next to him. He took a sip of his drink, took a long drag of the hookah and passed it on to his eighty-eight-year-old amma who had more tobacco in her lungs than air on any given day.

'How has anything changed since then?' Rachna Tripathi sensed an opportunity and dove right in. 'I still need to buy big sacks of grains to accommodate the bottomless appetites of your friends. Things aren't getting cheaper, you know, but our philanthropy continues. *Ghar mein nahi hai daane, amma chali bhunaane!*'

'*Aaiiin*?' Ammaji straightened up, straining to hear. '*Hamau ka thoda bhoon ke dei deo*.'

'Na, na, Amma. No one is frying anything. Rachna is a bit excitable today.' Dinbandhu Tripathi settled his mother and gave his wife a scathing look.

'When will you learn, Rachna? My daddu used to say, "*Jab daant nahi tab doodh dayo, jab daant diye toh ann bhi dei hain*."'

Rachna Tripathi, who was grinding the masala mix for her famous *mirchi ka achar*, muttered to her brother-in-law, 'I wish the Almighty would make him shut up and stem this philosophical tide.'

Dinanath Tripathi scratched his soft beard. 'I'm pretty sure Dada would manage to be angry even when silent.'

'What are the both of you talking about? Did you even understand what I just said?' Dinbandhu Tripathi inquired suspiciously.

'Of course, Dada. That was beautiful!'

This seemed to appease Dinbandhu Tripathi. 'Oh, I have an infinite supply.' Rachna Tripathi groaned imperceptibly on hearing this.

'You see, I keep telling Rachna, everything will be fine. Now Prachand is also helping out at the shop, his business is taking off, you have snagged a prestigious role in a play ...' here Dinanath Tripathi coughed discreetly '... my only real concern, as always, is that youngest *suputra* of mine.'

His wife jumped to her son's defence. 'Bhushan is doing okay, isn't he? He is studying and directing such a big play. That's commendable!'

'Huh! 41 per cent isn't commendable! First he wants to mimic some firangi boy and sing at weddings. Now he wants to do some firangi song and dance and taint our traditions. Will he ever find any sensible purpose in life?'

'Pitaji, what I am doing is revolutionary,' said a thin yet defiant voice from the other end of the *aangan* as Bhushan walked in with his brother and sister-in-law.

'Revolutionary!' His father's voice lost its geniality. 'Why don't you try evolutionary things first? Like finishing your studies, getting a normal job that doesn't involve making people prance around the stage like langurs.'

Prachand decided to step in. 'He has promised to improve his grades. But you really should drop in to see one of the rehearsals. This little man here is in charge of an entire production, and such an important one.' He drew Bhushan closer for a sideways hug.

Rachna Tripathi handed them glasses of buttermilk. She spat around Bhushan's face as he protested and cleared some saliva from his eye. 'As long as that white haired boy's ghost and his music have left his body, I don't care about the rest. He was positively possessed!'

Dinbandhu Tripathi grunted. 'My opinion won't change,' he said and looked at Bhushan. 'You should learn from your brother. Yes, he wasn't able to live the IIT dream, but he was successful in what he chose to do and is now helping me with the business. Till you have some clarity in your head, why don't you join us?'

'I don't agree.'

All eyes turned to Vidya who had just placed her empty glass on the ground. Respectful, but never one to mince her words, she continued. 'Distractions can be disastrous.'

Prachand looked at his wife with a puzzled expression.

Vidya raised her eyebrows. 'You know what I mean. With half your attention on the shop, KKPL is suffering.'

Ammaji belched into the awkward silence that followed.

Dinbandhu Tripathi sat erect with furrowed brows while Ammaji tried to wrest the hookah from his clenched fist, anticipating a long debate. 'So, this is what has been brewing,' he said, wagging his finger.

Prachand sighed, feeling the familiar sensation of bile rising up his throat. 'Don't misunderstand her, Pitaji. I don't mind helping out. Really. I just need to be more efficient with my time.' He then turned to Vidya and said, 'Don't worry.'

'But I am worried, Prachand. Yatish and I can't run the agency on our own. Plus, I have had to spend more time at home, so ...'

Rachna Tripathi was quick to take offence. 'Just because I choose to spend a few hours with my Gilehris every now and then, it's a problem? Vidya, of all the people, I never expected to hear this from you!'

'Ma, don't get me wrong!' Vidya pleaded.

As expected, waterworks, more grumbling and accusations were hurled like missiles. Amidst this hectic parley, Prachand's phone rang. He had to walk out and stand next to Hirwa to distance himself from the commotion. He tickled the cow under her ears as she nuzzled into her most favourite person from the Tripathi clan, the only one who seemed to be in possession of his mental marbles and didn't scream and shout.

'Am I speaking with the famous Mr Tripathi?' a cheerful voice inquired.

'I can't say much about the fame, but the identity is correct,' Prachand replied, humouring the stranger on the phone.

'The modesty is admirable! How rude of me. I'm Paramveer Khattar. I'm calling you with some exciting news!'

CHAPTER 6

Ever since the call, Paramveer Khattar was the subject of intense curiosity. As was de rigueur, Vidya and Yatish spent some time online researching their potential client.

'Now I know why his name sounded familiar,' Yatish clicked his fingers. 'His father is *the* Dharamveer Khattar, the political bigwig from Jandharma party who is forever involved in some scam or the other. Complete crook!'

'The court has pronounced its verdict I see,' said Prachand from a corner of the room where he was cleaning a photograph of his favourite Bholenath.

'The judicial system has found him guilty time and again. The fact that his clout helps him get out of jail doesn't prove his innocence,' Vidya said with a shrug.

'And yet, notorious or otherwise, we have nothing to do with the father. It's the son who is coming to meet me,' Prachand said with a twinkle in his eyes. 'Hence, relevant information would be truly appreciated.'

'Paramveer is the face of the party. It seems that he is being primed and shall receive a ticket to contest in the next elections,' Vidya explained.

'Interesting.' Prachand settled into his chair as Chotu planted a cup of tea in front of him. 'I wonder why he's coming all the way from Punjab to meet us.'

Vidya smiled, looking at the expression on her husband's face. She knew his mind was whirring away. Lack of clarity always disturbed Prachand, and he wouldn't rest till he had access to all the facts.

'His ancestors were from Punjab, but his family shifted base to Rajasthan a few years ago,' Vidya said, 'They are in Jaisalmer now.'

'A clean slate is important for great political ambitions. The move seems to be driven by a desire to distance themselves from controversies and start afresh in another constituency. The family heft would still carry. A smart move,' Prachand surmised.

'He has proven that he is smart by choosing us to solve whatever troubles him!' Vidya said and peered at her husband. 'Prachi, I hope you're not upset with me about speaking up at home?'

'I'm not upset. And I know you meant well, Viddu, but I was going to have the same conversation, only at an appropriate time.'

Vidya scowled. 'Which essentially means never. Instead of a thank you, I get a lecture. Nicely done, Mr Prachand Tripathi.' She switched off the computer screen and headed out.

Prachand called out after her. 'Viddu, what about the estimate you were going to work out for the client?'

Vidya turned around with a mock smile. 'I shall do so at an appropriate time.'

Later that day, Paramveer Khattar sat with his legs suspended as Jhuli whistled and swabbed the floor under his feet.

Prachand called out to the young lady crouching on the floor. 'Jhuli, can we do this later?'

'Arey Bhaiyya, Bhabhi tells me to finish the cleaning and mopping first thing in the morning. Just two more minutes and then I'll get chai for all of you.'

Prachand smiled apologetically, realizing that it was difficult to have a conversation with a contracted abdomen.

'Please let her clean up,' Paramveer Khattar gestured reassuringly and then used the same hand to flick his luscious, wavy hair away from his broad forehead.

Vidya observed the fair, almost brown-haired man sitting across the table in a crisp white shirt, his ears dotted with tiny diamond studs. He could easily be a model, she decided, imagining party posters and banners with his face beaming down amongst a sea of notorious-looking folk.

The sudden mention of a movie made her tune back into the exchange between Prachand and Paramveer Khattar.

'A movie you said?' Vidya inquired.

'Oh yes, very much,' Paramveer Khattar nodded. 'We have a young and supremely talented writer-director who has written a new script centred around you. Your celebrity case in Mumbai might have fallen out of public consciousness, but you certainly sparked the imagination of the common folk. We want to rekindle that memory and build on how the audience relates to you and your sense of aspiration. The film will be shot in Rajasthan and you will be hosted by a member of the royal family.'

As Vidya's eyes bulged with excitement, Paramveer Khattar opened a slim briefcase. With a swift movement, he placed back some small vials that fell out.

'It's a story set specifically in the region. *Khooni Haveli ka Khooni Rahasya!* If you are okay with the script and our offer,' he said, handing over an envelope and a white folder, 'we would need to work out some permissions and legalities. After that we would very much like for you to come to Rajasthan and oversee the shoot, to offer suggestions for authenticity. That will make all the difference. I think real, gritty stories and interesting personalities make for great content, and I couldn't be happier kicking off my production venture at your doorstep!'

'My first suggestion would be to go for a less tacky movie title,' muttered Prachand, mostly to himself. Nothing missing, no one dead, no thief at large, no property dispute, no cheating spouse. Essentially, no problem to solve. Prachand felt completely at sea, not knowing what to say. What on earth would he contribute on a movie set, he wondered.

The news had the opposite effect on his wife who squealed like a happy schoolgirl. 'A movie? Thank you, thank you, and thank you God!'

'Vidya, can you just ...'

'Prachand, you will not shoot this down without giving it due consideration. Promise me.'

'Vidya ...'

'I know how your mind works, Mr Tripathi. As someone who is an integral part of this agency, and who has played a key role in every case, you owe it to me. Now promise me!'

'Shouldn't we first check if this is monetarily worth our effort?' Prachand lowered his voice and leaned towards his wife. 'Look at this figure. It doesn't look like much,' he said and placed the envelope in her hand.' You're the one who keeps lecturing me ...'

Vidya whispered to Prachand. 'Firstly, NEVER discuss finances in front of the client. Secondly, think of the exposure, Prachi. A film. Based on us! That's many years of our paltry marketing budgets becoming effective in one go.'

Paramveer Khattar realized that he had no role to play in the conversation. Vidya Tripathi was doing the needful. He leaned back in his chair and sipped on hot chai as the irritating cleaning lady returned to do some dusting.

CHAPTER 7

'It's been two days and your friend is still suspicious about Paramveer Khattar! Yatish, can you please explain to him that the man isn't a prospective groom but a client? I admit the money isn't great, but think about the exposure!' Vidya said.

The trio of KKPL had stepped out for a quick bite to Shiv Shankar Bhojanalaya, a two-storeyed eatery nearby.

'When have you known my instinct to be wrong, Viddu?' Prachand asked his wife.

Vidya reached out and squeezed her husband's hand. 'Almost never. It's our most valuable asset. But you are honestly overthinking this one, Prachi.'

Prachand set his glass down. 'Just hear me out, all right? There's something not quite right about this man. His grandiloquence, his manner, the way he sniffs and twitches every few seconds; I've seen it before, when Chandu from my hostel got hooked on to cough syrups. Such people aren't reliable. When he was speaking of us being hosted by royalty in Rajasthan, he kept pulling at his earlobes and fidgeting with his fingers. These are clear physical signs of stress induced by lying. What does he have to hide from us?'

Yatish laughed. 'Bhaiyya, since when is having cough syrups or a runny nose a crime?'

'Yatish, don't trivialize the matter. Are we supposed to place our trust in a stranger who is offering us a movie deal in Rajasthan without as much as a thorough background check? I am usually the gullible one.'

Yatish raised his arms in surrender. 'All right, Bhaiyya. While you look at the script and the papers he has left with you, will it help if I dig up some more information? There isn't much online beyond political news, so I'll use some of my on-ground sources. Does that work?'

Prachand nodded. 'Thanks, Yatish. That will help a great deal. It might not hurt to find out about the shoot venue as well.'

Vidya, meanwhile, had ordered a royal *falooda* to round up the meal and was slurping for the *sabja beej* that usually collected at the bottom of the tall strawberry-coloured milk. 'This is all so exciting! Prachi, do you know who will be the most excited on hearing about this project?'

'Viddu, I haven't promised ...'

'Oh ho! I get it. Now let me think happy thoughts. Chachu will surely break into a dance, but the one person sure to shoot through the roof with joy is Ma. You just wait!'

'How can they unceremoniously chop me out of the script? Am I some unwanted vegetable peel?'

'Ma, please don't take this to heart.' Vidya tried to assuage her irate mother-in-law.

'Really, Vidya? How can I not take offence? Am I unimportant? Didn't I help you in that Pamela Kapoor case? Even then you didn't take me to *Bambai*.'

'But, Ma, this movie is not based on that case. It's a fresh story featuring me and Viddu. And we didn't go to Mumbai on a happy sojourn, we were running from the police!'

Chachu Tripathi settled next to his sister-in-law, looking even more doleful. 'You seem to have forgotten that the other person found unworthy of being in this film is the only one who has lived his entire life trying to act in one.'

Prachand looked at Vidya for help, already wary of the emotional upheaval that this problematic film was causing.

'Ma, Chachu, from what I can tell, they want the story to be taut. It should convey the flavour adequately with minimal characters. Especially because it is set in another city,' she tried to explain.

When his mother only grunted in response, Prachand looked exasperated. 'I didn't write the script, did I?'

Rachna Tripathi got up in a huff. 'Now where are you going?' Vidya inquired.

'I need to make achar.' Everyone knew that when Rachna Tripathi was upset, she made achar after achar till there was a sea of it, or till she had cooled off, whichever came first. It was time to bring in stronger ammunition.

'Ma,' Vidya said, drawing her mother-in-law back to her seat. 'Do you know that the royal family is hosting us?'

Rachna Tripathi did not respond. 'Are you trying to make things better or worse?' muttered Prachand who was sitting nearby.

'Ma,' Vidya continued, unfazed. 'Did you know that the invitation extended to other members of our family as well?'

Rachna Tripathi set down the empty glass *barnis* and looked at Vidya, her interest piqued. 'If you do plan to visit us at some point, I'm sure you would be treated like royalty. Imagine the pictures you could share with your Gilehris. You'll become an even bigger sensation,' Vidya added.

'I haven't taken a vacation in a long, long while.'

'Exactly!' Vidya said.

'And Chachu, I might be overstepping here, but perhaps we can request them to consider the Tripathi gem with the acting chops for a small role? Come with us.'

Chachu Tripathi, who was sitting in a corner playing with the end of his dhoti, suddenly perked up. 'Really? You'd do that for me?'

Prachand picked up a steel box filled with his favourite savoury snack, *ajwain-tinged mathris,* and settled into the charpoy that was usually occupied by Ammaji. He wanted to watch his beautiful and intelligent wife in action. She had once again, gently taken the reins into her hands, saved two hearts from being broken and a hundred achar barnis from being needlessly filled.

CHAPTER 8

'There's no dearth of information if you know where to look,' Yatish announced with a swagger. 'My cousin stays in Bhatinda. Between the *lassi dukaan*, the barber and the old men smoking hookahs and talking about the "good old days", he had all the information we need.'

The digging had revealed that Paramveer Khattar had a penchant for trouble—drugs, skirmishes, money scams that his father would cover up, he finally landed in jail. After his father threatened to disown him, he checked in to a rehab centre and cleaned up his act. At this point, the family moved bag and baggage to Jaisalmer. The movie project was his way of proving his worth to his father so that he can secure his place in the party.

'It turns out that there is a production unit making inquiries about equipment and labour in and around Jaisalmer. But ... ummm ... the locals say that this production is cursed,' Yatish said.

'Did you just say ... cursed?' Vidya said.

Yatish dropped his voice. 'About eighteen kilometres from the city, the shoot location is a haveli in Kuldhara village. Legend has it that centuries ago all the inhabitants of this village abandoned their homes overnight and disappeared. Ever since, it has been considered a terrifying and inauspicious place.'

Vidya stroked her arm inadvertently to discover goosebumps on her skin. She looked at Prachand and knew that his mind was churning as fast as her stomach.

'I think we should go,' Prachand announced.

'Exactly, Prachi ... curses ... maybe ghosts ... how can we ... what? Did you just say we should go?'

'Of course, Viddu. Haven't you been trying to convince me all along? You're right.'

Vidya looked nonplussed. 'I'm right, huh? Just when Yatish announced that we are to travel to a cursed village?'

'That's the very reason I want to go, Viddu!'

'What are you talking about?' Yatish asked.

Prachand turned his placid gaze on the inquisitive Yatish. 'Can't you see it? All this while, I was reluctant as I didn't know of a problem. Whatever would I do on a film set? But now I've found a mystery to solve. It's the curse of Kuldhara!'

CHAPTER 9

It entailed a mammoth effort from the senior beta and bahu of the Tripathi clan to convince the jittery family about the project they were to undertake, but they soon realized that even getting to Jaisalmer would turn out to be the next big debate.

'Why don't they just send us on a bullock cart?' Vidya complained.

'Viddu, *they* don't have a problem with us flying down. The air and rail connections are circuitous and time-consuming. That's all.'

'Let's be gracious and save them the trouble of hiring a broken-down vehicle. Let's walk there.'

Prachand was amused at his wife's frustration. 'It will be a fun two-day drive. We can break our journey in Jaipur.'

'Jaipur!' Vidya squealed, her dark mood dissipating. 'I've only been there once, that too as a child. Now I am excited! I hardly have any time to go to the tailor. There's so much packing to do.'

Prachand was unsure about whether she was complaining or celebrating, but she sounded happy and that's what mattered. Perhaps this break would do everyone some good, he thought.

However, things weren't progressing so smoothly on the sets of Adhunik Ramlila Sangathan. Chachu Tripathi had gently broken the news of his departure to Bhushan, who had promptly blown his top, accusing him of sabotaging the credibility he had taken years to build. Though Chachu Tripathi was very unclear about the said credibility and how exactly it had been built, he wisely chose to keep silent.

'I am truly appreciative of this opportunity, Bhushan. But I couldn't live with myself if I didn't even try to get a part in this movie. It remains my only minuscule chance at the big screen. You'll be able to find a replacement with ease. The hairy suit and make-up will take care of the rest.'

'You're punishing me for the small role I assigned to you, aren't you?' Bhushan asked, narrowing his eyes.

His uncle smiled affectionately. The militant expression was all too familiar. '*Bachche,* don't get me wrong. I was being honest. It is a good role, but anyone can do it. And how will an oldie like me kick and swivel like a lithe mountain goat? I don't even understand what's going on half the time.'

Bhushan looked crestfallen. 'Be honest with me, Chachu. Have I made a complete joke of myself?'

Chachu looked his nephew in the eye. 'Bhushan, you've always had a penchant for unusual destinations, but you cover the distance with all your heart. You have a vision, and Srivastava ji believes in it. That's all that matters. You are my *sher bachcha*. Buck up!'

Bhushan gave his uncle a watery smile. 'You're right. Why should I get intimidated? I know that Bhalla Uncle deliberately misplaces his tail whenever we have the Lanka dehen scene. And Dayal Uncle, playing Kumbhakaran, doesn't wake up on purpose even when I say cut. They think they can badger and corner me into hanging up my boots? No way! I'm Bhushan Tripathi, the visionary, and I won't give up!'

'That's my boy!' Chachu Tripathi patted his reed thin nephew lightly on the back lest he keels over.

'When are you all leaving, Chachu? Between this production and college, I've hardly spent any time at home.'

'Next week. I am so sorry that we will be missing the play, Bhushan.' He then bade farewell to the intrepid young director, thoughtfully wiping out a hurtful message written in chalk outside the premises—*Keval paagal pravesh karein*.

He enjoyed walking and often left his noisy two-wheeler parked at home during rehearsals. As he made his way back, taking a few shortcuts through narrow lanes, his heart felt lighter. He was glad he had chatted with Bhushan.

When in Kanpur, the devil often comes dipped in *kadais* of ghee or coated in jalebi or samosa batter. And Dinanath Tripathi wasn't one to resist. As the aroma of fresh jalebis perfumed his nostrils, he joined the queue at Tiwari Mishthan Bhandaar, waiting to get some crispy little devils packed for everyone at home. He decided to throw in a few for Hirwa as well. She was known to moan theatrically through the night when left out of family treats.

As his eyes scanned the street, he noticed a man. The street lights had come on and the man, who looked like some kind of sadhu, stood directly under one such lamp post, almost aglow. Chachu Tripathi would have thought nothing more of it till he noticed that the man was heading straight towards him, his gaze unwavering.

When he was very close and Dinanath Tripathi had decided to stand his ground rather than take flight without his jalebis, the man spoke in a portentous manner. 'Don't go there. You are all in danger. Everything will end. Don't go. Don't go!'

And with these words, he turned on his heel and walked away, leaving a slack-jawed Dinanath Tripathi holding two packets of crispy, hot jalebis.

CHAPTER 10

Packing for a trip was a community activity in Gwaltoli. The length of the trip was inconsequential. The *kirana* store would receive a list of supplies that bore the tell-tale signs of a journey and before long, the news would be broadcast to every home within a five-kilometre radius.

The neighbours started flocking to Awadh Niwas, offering their two cents on the state of the roads, on Rajasthan, on movies, on shoots and offered a list of distant relatives who could be contacted in case of emergencies.

In conjunction with these unavoidable social calls came the most peculiar addition to the to-do list, thanks to the mention of a cursed village. A *Panchmukhi hanuman kavach puja,* the ultimate protection and nostrum for all travel-related issues. This decision was expedited when an unusually large crow was found sunning itself on the roof of Awadh Niwas. The final nail in the coffin was an owl casually stationing itself on Ammaji's head, both incidents considered ultimate *apshaguns* that drove Rachna Tripathi to the point of hysteria. The day before the travel, a panditji arrived officiously with a few assistants trailing behind him like a presidential detail. They set up the puja in the middle of the aangan, with more than a few family friends in attendance.

During the panditji's twentieth washroom break, Prachand revisited his conundrum. 'You know, I went through the broad storyline. Isn't it odd that there is no ending? I mean, aren't stories meant to have some kind of conclusion before you base an entire film on them?'

'I noticed that as well, Prachi. Perhaps that is some creative idiosyncrasy of the scriptwriter?' Vidya proffered.

'I still think it's strange.'

Vidya altered her position to face Prachand. 'I'm still sensing resistance. I gave my consent only after being thoroughly convinced that it's the best thing to happen to us since dhaniya ke aloo.'

Prachand smiled at the reference to one of their favourite snacks, but then he rebutted, 'And what about the curse? You'll be the one getting anxious once we reach.'

'You let me deal with that,' Vidya said reassuringly and then gestured for her husband to focus on the instructions. The panditji had returned and announced that he would need buttermilk was mentioned before to ease his delicate stomach.

Chachu Tripathi, who was sitting nearby, sensed the ongoing debate and joined in. 'I'm telling you, Prachand, desperate as I am for this opportunity, that man I saw yesterday had me quivering. It felt as if his eyes were searing a hole through me. When a man of God warns you about something, it's akin to being on destiny's hit list!'

'Chachu,' Prachand dropped his voice as the panditji shot a disapproving look in his direction. 'Our mind can be our kindest friend and most distracting foe. Now, tell me, what made you think that he was a man of God? His clothes? His long beard?'

Dinanath Tripathi nodded and Prachand continued. 'Well, I can tell you I've seen him very often in that area. He is addled on most days and lives off the generosity of the vendors. But because it was getting dark, your mind added up the kurta and dhoti, the scraggly beard and the discussions over the last few days to gallop ahead and give credence to his drivel.' He winked at his uncle and added, 'He was possibly asking you not to go to the counter so he could have more jalebis.'

'*Koi maryaada nahin hai!* Dinbandhu Tripathi's baritone voice admonished them from behind. 'This puja has been organized for your well-being. Is it so hard to sit still for an hour?'

All furtive discussions and exchanges were abandoned.

It was late evening by the time the puja was wrapped up, the Brahmins were fed, the *dakshina* was given and Hirwa was bathed and fed and made to feel like a goddess. Rachna Tripathi had been in low spirits all day. She had been distracting herself by preparing food for the journey. Prachand came and sat next to her as she pulled out some steel boxes.

'I want my boxes back, Prachand,' she said, 'No lids or spoons should go missing. I have no idea why people can't be considerate and return what has been borrowed. Just the other day I remembered that Kamla from down the street had taken some *kofta curry* in my Tupperware box and never returned it. It's been ...'

Prachand squeezed her hand and smiled. 'Ma, it's a question of a month. And we'll be in touch on the phone. Don't be sad.'

Rachna Tripathi's eyes welled up. 'Don't do your *jasoosgiri* on me, okay? I'm your mother. Go analyse someone else.'

Prachand drew her into a hug. 'But I don't want to! You're my favourite. What I do want to understand though, is why you're packing so much ration, as if we are heading into a siege. It's a two-day drive with several stops along the way, Ma.'

'When you have kids of your own, you'll know.' Then she shook her head and said, 'But at the rate at which you two are going, I'll have to bribe the neighbour's grandchild to call me dadi.'

'All in good time, Ma! Now cheer up. When the time is right, I'll ask Bhushan to bring you and Ammaji for a visit. I promise!' As Prachand got up, he turned once more to his mother and asked, 'Do you think Pitaji will come?'

Rachna Tripathi shrugged. 'You know him as well as I do. He is as temperamental and unpredictable as the forecasts from the weather bureau. Given his irritation about Bhushan's play and Chachu's absence for this coming month, I wouldn't want to rile him up any more.' She then ruffled her son's hair, noticing the wrinkled forehead. 'Don't worry, Mr Detective, I'll keep him stuffed and in good humour. Let the Diwali preparations begin a bit early!'

Prachand decided to drop in to the office for some last-minute work. When he returned a couple of hours later, he found the house unusually silent. Everyone, Hirwa included, seemed to have retired early. He walked towards the only room where the lights were still on.

Vidya sat crouched at the edge of their queen-sized bed, scribbling in her notebook. The bed creaked as Prachand sat next to her. 'What are you writing? You really should sleep.'

'This is important, Prachi. I'm preparing a notebook for all the expenses we incur on this trip. Between your philanthropy and my excitement, we might end up losing track and paying out of our pockets. I'd like Mr Khattar to do all the spending!' Vidya said and placed the notebook carefully in her purse. She turned to see that her husband was looking at her with a hint of a smile on his face. She raised her eyebrows.

'What would I do without you, Viddu?'

'Clearly, nothing!' she laughed. 'Now let's sleep. The car will be here in a few hours.'

That night, Prachand dreamt of camels, palaces and restless spirits eating jalebis at Tiwari Misthan Bhandaar.

CHAPTER 11

Prachand twisted the gold Hanuman locket flecked with small diamonds, tracing the familiar outline of the much-revered god. Ammaji had slipped it into his hands as they were leaving. Through the curtain of saliva and paan, Prachand had guessed that she was worried. 'It will protect all of you,' she had said stroking his head. '*Doosran ke phate mein taang mat daalna*,' knowing only too well her grandson's penchant for getting snared in problems not his own.

'Prachi, I want to use the bathroom, please,' Vidya announced.

Yatish, who was sitting in the front with the driver of the grey Innova, exchanged a look with Prachand. This would be their sixth stop since leaving Kanpur. Yatish had known the couple snoozing on and off in the back seat for years, but a few hours into this journey he had become freshly acquainted with his Bhabhi's bladder that was like a newborn's.

'At this rate we will reach Jaisalmer after a week,' muttered the driver to Yatish.

'If you don't want to get beaten up, zip it,' Yatish cautioned the driver.

'Are we stopping again?' inquired Dinanath Tripathi who was dozing right next to Vidya. 'Good, I'll get to stretch my legs.'

Dotted with intermittent stops, they finally reached Agra for a late lunch. While they did manage to feast on local favourites like *bedhai*, which is a lot like a kachori, served with a spicy potato gravy and *petha*, the chewy and syrupy sweetmeat made from pumpkins, a sighting of the marbled wonder of the world eluded them, much to Vidya's chagrin.

As they drove on, Yatish tried to make small talk with the driver whose brow was forever creased. 'Chintan Bhaiyya, why are you always looking so *chintit*?' he said and chortled at his joke. Detecting no reciprocity from the man behind the wheel, he cleared his throat and continued. 'When do you think we will reach Jaipur?'

'With these many stops, late at night.'

'Do you have instructions for our Jaipur accommodation?'

'Yes, Sir. I am to take you to Lal Haveli guest house.'

On the highway, time seemed to blur as they drove endlessly, barring the intermittent jams caused by cows, goats, school-children and an infinite number of tempos ferrying fruits and vegetables. Prachand and Yatish took turns to sit in the front seat and keep the driver alert. While they couldn't stifle their own yawns, it seemed as if he was made of stainless steel. He would keep drinking tea from his thermos and chew paan constantly. They made sure to have the windows up every time he leaned in to spit, lest they reach their destination looking 'lal' themselves.

'I marvel at that bladder of his,' muttered Vidya reverentially at one point.

After what seemed like ages, from the arms of the Aravalli hills and under the blanket of the star-studded sky, rose the twinkling lights of the pink city. Though the hills weren't really visible in the dark, they seemed to be like sentries on vigil, incandescent in a way, radiating the heat trapped through the day under the treacherous sun.

The excitement on the four faces was evident as they rolled into the outskirts of Jaipur, which looked more orange than pink in the glow of the street lights. After driving some more distance dotted with homes and other commercial buildings, they reached the heart of the city. While it still looked colourful despite the late hour, a lot of shutters had been downed. Vidya's eyes shone at the endless displays of shoes, clothes, bags, trinkets, local sweetmeats and glistening street food. As they drove past the famous Hawa Mahal in the Vaastu-compliant palace quarters of the city, Prachand had to physically restrain Vidya from launching herself through the window for a closer look at the breathtaking 'Palace of Winds.'

Soon, they pulled into the driveway of a quaint and charming guesthouse. It was a three-storeyed building with the trunk of the structure branching out on both sides. Facing the entrance was a dancing water fountain where some folk artists were gathered, singing in the Maand style that dates back to the time when royal courts were in session. It seemed as if they were wrapping up for the day, but seeing the guests they settled back down.

It was an invigorating welcome for the tired passengers. While they stretched and interacted with the performers,

Chintan handed their luggage to the hotel staff and announced curtly, 'A man by the name of Arjun Prajapati will meet you here and take care of anything you need. We need to leave by 8 a.m., so please be ready on time. I'll see you in the morning.' He bowed slightly, turned on his heel and walked back to the car, leaving his guests standing at the entrance. Dinanath Tripathi, who was dancing enthusiastically to the beats, had to be coaxed inside the guest house where a smiling face greeted them.

'*Ghani-ghani khamma! Atthe padhaaro sa!*' boomed a jovial voice, welcoming them with true Rajasthani warmth.

CHAPTER 12

Prachand appraised the man standing in front of them. He wore a smart brown *bandh gala* with a colourful traditional turban. His most prominent feature was his substantial handlebar, flecked with graceful strands of silver, under which was stationed the most disarming smile.

Vidya elbowed Prachand. 'I told you to get a suit. See how smart he looks?'

'This isn't an interview. Relax. Plus, my Bata sandals are my good luck charm! You know that,' Prachand replied. Vidya made a quick mental note to burn her husband's extremely worn-out footwear as soon as they returned to Kanpur.

The man cleared his throat and Prachand smiled, folding his hands in greeting. 'Pranam. Myself Prachand Tripathi.'

'Welcome to Rajasthan! My name is Arjun Prajapati and I serve His Royalness Ramnarayan Rathod, your host in Kuldhara and a very dear friend of Mr Paramveer Khattar. I shall be at your beck and call and will happily escort you to where the film is being shot. Can I please usher you to your rooms for now? The kitchens are closed at this late hour, but I took the liberty of ordering some food for you in advance.'

Dinanath Tripathi's stomach gurgled audibly. 'Let me guess. *Dal baati* with *churma* and *malpua*?'

Arjun Prajapati chuckled. 'Mamoji, that's special food. Our daily fare consists of staples like dal, chawal, sabzi and roti. You're going to be in Rajasthan for a while. If you start eating heavy food everyday, your stomachs might stage a mutiny!'

Vidya and Prachand had a double room while Dinanath Tripathi and Yatish were to share another. At the behest of his tired guests, Arjun Prajapati decided to negotiate with the driver for a later departure. 'I'll see you at breakfast,' he said and walked away after giving them a slight bow.

A few hours later, Prachand awoke with a start. A noise had drawn him out of his exhausted slumber. He blinked in the dark and was relieved to see Vidya sleeping next to him. A large window at one end of the room channelled the diffused light from the garden lamps outside, creating a luminous pathway to the bathroom. Prachand carefully walked over and pressed his ear to the door. Nothing.

He then walked to the entrance of the room, easing himself out noiselessly.

The corridor lights had been dimmed. He could hear the gurgling of the fountain in the distance. Wondering if the sound was merely his imagination, he turned to go back in. And that's when he heard voices. He walked in the direction of the noise, tiptoeing on the carpeted floor.

At the end of the passage, he turned right, towards a section of the guest house that didn't seem familiar. The passage opened into a central courtyard filled with trees and flowering plants. Wrought-iron benches dotted its length and breadth. Barring the insomniac owls and crickets, the night seemed to have devoured every other sound.

He heard footsteps and jumped behind a bench. Peering above the backrest, he could decipher the outline of a heavy-set man, who looked very much like Chintan, walking past the courtyard. He seemed to be on the phone. He hovered near one of the doors and then walked up to the bench Prachand was crouching behind.

'Sorry, Saab. Haanji. I have the box. Don't worry. They won't suspect anything.' He spoke haltingly, all the while keeping an eye on his surroundings. He hung up, looked around furtively and then disappeared around the other end of the courtyard.

An owl flew down to the bench, looking curiously at Prachand. 'What was that all about?' he whispered as the night bird cooed softly.

The next day at breakfast, he updated Vidya and Yatish about his late-night walk and the driver's odd behaviour. Yatish's face rose from behind the stack of parathas like the early morning sun, white butter and crumbs smeared on his face. This distracted Prachand from his story as he regarded his friend's face with much amusement.

'It has always amazed me how such a tiny frame can pack in the amount you do, my friend.'

'You forget that I am half Bengali. Where your imagination ends, my appetite begins!' Yatish said proudly, licking his fingers.

Prachand laughed and glanced sideways towards the buffet where his uncle was precariously balancing two plates of food. 'I'm in a way thankful that we're leaving today. This hotel isn't adequately rationed for the significant appetites of the Tripathis and their friends!'

Vidya tugged at his sleeve. 'What do you think Chintan was doing? Who was he speaking to?'

Yatish burped. 'This is what happens when you run a detective agency. Both you and Bhabhi are the same. Leave the poor guy alone.'

'*Suprabhat!*' A cheery voice greeted them.

'Why don't you join us, Arjunji?' Dinanath Tripathi invited their host as he finally made it back to the table with his plates, employing the dexterous precision of a juggler.

'No, thank you, Mamoji. I've already eaten,' Arjun Prajapati said and bowed respectfully. 'You're too kind. But I will sit down for a cup of tea.'

'Arjunji, will it be possible to visit some of the shops we passed last night?' Vidya asked.

Arjun Prajapati looked unsure. 'You see, Madam, they are expecting you at Jaisalmer. We have another 500 km to go and are already running late.'

Vidya made a sad face and it worked. 'Let me see what I can do,' Arjun Prajapati said and left the table. A few minutes later, from where they sat, the four of them saw the driver animatedly move his hands as Arjun Prajapati spoke to him with a furrowed brow.

'This driver seems to wield some authority,' Prachand observed. 'Look at his body language. He is objecting and has no qualms displaying his reaction.'

'Prachand Da, train your eyes on the *ras malai* on your plate,' Yatish said, tapping his friend's hand.

Arjun Prajapati returned in a few minutes. 'Vidya Madam, it would be my pleasure to take you around the city. Even Prachand and Yatish Da, if they are interested.'

'I hope Chintan is not too upset about the change in plans?' Vidya inquired cautiously.

'Don't you worry about him, Madam. He is a bail buddhi, focused on the task at hand and refuses to pressurize his brain to think beyond. Now, are you ready for some delightful shopping with a Rajasthani *tadka*?'

'Oh yes!' Vidya replied, the excitement dripping off her face.

'My only request is that we check out, load our luggage and target heading out straight from the market. Is that fine?'

'Absolutely, Arjunji,' Prachand assured the man. 'An hour or two at the most and we will be back on the road. Right, Vidya?'

CHAPTER 13

When revered Rajput ruler Jai Singh II went about visualizing one of the earliest planned cities with designer Vidyadhar Bhattacharya, little did they know that their architectural armament for the beauteous city of Jaipur was missing a key ingredient. It was the one *Kanpuriya* factor that could have helped them negotiate and erect this historical marvel at a fraction of the cost. Vidya Tripathi, possessing bargaining and haggling prowess that could put seasoned negotiators to shame, was unfortunately born a few centuries too late, but she was determined to leave her mark on the city.

Largely pragmatic, Vidya Tripathi had forgotten all reason somewhere in the colourful by-lanes between Johari Bazaar and Tripolia Bazaar. She went on a rampage, oohing and aahing at every mojri, shawl, jewellery or home decor item. Then came the shortlisting and formidable haggling. Her years spent scouring for deals on the streets of Delhi's Chandni Chowk had trained her well but spelt doom for the local economy.

Prachand knew his wife well. After the initial cajoling to hurry things up, he capitulated, deciding to walk around while Yatish and his uncle took turns in trying to draw her out from every shop. The driver glowered in a sullen silence. Arjun Prajapati approached Prachand with his head bowed.

'Prachand Sa ... we will ...'

Prachand interrupted him with a resigned look. 'I know, Arjunji. We are running terribly late. Please give me half an hour and I'll carry her to the car if I have to.'

Nine bathroom stops and a whole day later than scheduled, which warranted an extra night at Ajmer, the dust-laden Innova rattled its way in the dark towards Jaisalmer. The inordinate delays and jams along the way didn't help. Every hour or so, Vidya apologized profusely to each and every person, especially to Prachand. She knew how abhorrent the prospect of inconveniencing others was to him.

'Don't worry about it. You're allowed to go berserk once in a while,' he said and winked as she blushed, squeezing his hand under her dupatta.

'What must Chachaji be thinking of me?' she mumbled.

'That you weren't ever allowed to shop as a child on the streets of Delhi.'

Vidya smacked Prachand's arm as a beautiful melody wafted to them from the front of the vehicle.

Hiwade su door mat,
Jaay lag jawe tawadiyo.
Hiwade su door mat,
Jaay lag jawe tawadiyo.

'What a lovely tune, Arjunji,' Vidya leaned forward and said with a smile.

Arjun Prajapati chuckled. 'Oh! I didn't realize I was audible. My tunelessness is quite legendary. I must apologize!'

'Wah! You sang pretty well.' Chachu Tripathi, the self-proclaimed arts and music afficionado, added magnanimously, turning in his seat.

'It's a popular folk song,' Arjun Prajapati explained. 'Many of our songs are about the eccentricities of the heart or a beloved.'

'Do you hail from Jaisalmer, Arjunji?' Prachand asked, curious about their interim host.

'Born and brought up here, Prachand Sa. I belong to the proud community of the Kumhars, from the pottery trade. My baap-dadas used to earn a living as potters, but some of my ancestors also served in royal courts. A few family members remain in Jaisalmer, but most of the ambitious young crop prefers to migrate to the larger cities in search of better opportunities,' Arjun Prajapati spoke wistfully. 'My own son is in Mumbai. I tried convincing him to stay back, to help me serve His Royalness Ramnarayan Rathod and his family, but the ripples of young capricious hearts are rarely sustained in serene waters. He is working as a cook in some Chinese restaurant called Big Chow. Wah, *chora*, wah!'

Prachand sympathized with the poor man, but then he steered the conversation to His Royalness Ramnarayan Rathod. 'So, about Rathodji. You refer to him as His Royalness. I haven't heard that term before. He belongs to the royal family I presume?'

Arjun Prajapati remained quiet.

Wondering if he had perhaps not been audible enough, Prachand repeated his question. The response was evasive.

'He is a proud Rajput, and very royal in manner,' Arjun Prajapati said. 'And ... well ... he is connected to the royal family, Prachand Sa.'

Prachand wondered how a person could attain royalness by virtue of behaviour. He decided not to pursue the matter noticing Arjun Prajapati's reluctance.

'Arjunji,' Yatish piped up. 'Is what they say about Kuldhara being haunted true?'

Even in the very dim light, Arjun Prajapati's face was visibly suffused with fear. His body stiffened.

'We must not speak of damned places.' This surprising statement came from the otherwise quiet driver. 'We awaken them by remembering.'

Yatish chuckled. 'How can we not speak of it if that is where we are going? What should we rechristen it? Kamlapur? Kareenadhaam?' he guffawed at his suggestions.

Just then they were hurtled forward in their seats as the car came to a screeching halt. Looking ahead, the reason for the sudden braking became visible to all of them.

An old man with a long white beard, wearing a shapeless tunic, stood in the middle of the road. He was holding a wooden stick and there was a fire and determination in his bulbous eyes that belied the wrinkles on his scraggy face.

Vidya clawed into Prachand's leg. 'Beta, that's my pyjama and the nada is loose. Please let go.'

Red-faced, she relinquished Chachu Tripathi's garment. 'Who is that, Arjunji?' she whispered, her voice hoarse.

Arjun Prajapati bowed his head low. As did the driver. The old man continued glaring at them.

'What does he want from us, Arjunji?' Prachand asked in an even tone even though his heart was racing.

'That is Bhutaari Baba. I've known him for years. He is a great tantric, very well respected in these parts.'

'All right. But what is he doing in front of the car?' Yatish said impatiently.

As if on some telepathic cue, the old man raised his stick and pointed it at the car, his lips moving, mumbling something.

'Sri Ram jai Ram, jai jai Ram!' chanted Yatish, quivering in the back of the car.

And just as suddenly as he had appeared, the old man disappeared. Arjun Prajapati cleared his throat and announced with a forced lightness, 'Welcome to Jaisalmer!'

CHAPTER 14

In today's times, when you speak of male royalty, one conjures images of imposing forts and fortresses bound by ageless traditions, ably helmed by an erudite descendant who becomes a bridge between the old and the new—a handsome, polo-playing, world-traveling polyglot who is a picture of grace, poise and beauty.

In startling contrast, the man who greeted the Tripathis and Yatish could at best be described as the seed that remains after all the juice and pulp has been sucked out of a mango. Loyalty compromises objectivity, and demonstrating this very norm Arjun Prajapati announced the arrival of His Royalness Ramnarayan Rathod with much pride and ostentation, as if he were a proud grandparent introducing his ward to society.

'He doesn't look very royal,' Yatish whispered to Prachand who placed a hand over his friend's to silence him.

His Royalness Ramnarayan Rathod walked into the lobby of Aatithya Hotel where they had alighted upon reaching Jaisalmer. He was a wiry little man with a fair complexion and one of those impossibly thin, pointy moustaches that seemed like it had been sketched on with a colouring pencil. There was a distinct swagger to his gait, like a showstopper modelling the latest fall collection.

'*Zindagi jhand hai, phir bhi humein ghamand hai!* Wah!' tittered Yatish as Prachand quelled his exuberance yet again.

Ramnarayan Rathod was flanked by the rakishly handsome Paramveer Khattar, in his usual crisp white shirt, shouting at someone on the phone.

'These bloody fools can't follow simple instructions!' he spluttered, cutting the call.

Prachand wiped the spit from his face and politely folded his hands in a greeting. 'Happy to meet you again, Mr Khattar. You know my wife, Vidya, and my friend Yatish. This is my chachaji, Dinanath Tripathi.'

Paramveer Khattar's expression changed as he greeted his guests and an ingratiating smile appeared. 'Of course! The famous family is at our doorstep. We couldn't be happier. Let me have the pleasure of introducing you to the one and only, the regal, the suave, the pride of Jaisalmer and my very best friend, His Royalness Ramnarayan Rathod. He is an extremely busy man, so I was thrilled when he offered to stay on in Jaisalmer only to grant his guests a personal audience,' he said and slapped Rathod's back, causing the little man to almost buckle over. 'This web film will be a trail blazer, Param. And a super-duper hit!' Rathod said magnanimously.

'Web film?' Vidya couldn't hide her surprise. 'What does a web have to do with a film?'

'He meant a digital film. The ones that are released on the internet,' Paramveer Khattar clarified.

'I thought it was going to be in a cinema,' Chachu Tripathi pouted.

Paramveer Khattar waved his hand dismissively. 'It's all the same. Trust me. The online space is where the money is these days. Even the biggest of films and the most high profile stars have online premieres. This film will make your agency a household name.'

Since most of this explanation floated right above Vidya's radius of comprehension, she focused on the next exciting topic. 'Talking about stars, where are the Bollywood celebrities of this production? I'm dying to see the actors who are playing us! Any movies of theirs we might have seen recently?'

Paramveer Khattar cleared his throat. 'Sure. Vikas Kishen is our male lead. He has worked in several acclaimed box-office hits such as *Dheere Chalo Sayyaan, Gajab Hoi Gava*.' Taking in the blank faces, he continued, 'You must surely have heard of *Hindustani Hunk*?'

'Aren't these Bhojpuri films? He's a Bhojpuri star?' Dinanath Tripathi inquired suspiciously.

'*Ji haan!*' said a cheery voice. It was Vikas Kishen in the flesh, bounding towards them like a battery-charged fox terrier. With a pleasant, chubby face and floppy hair, he seemed like a likeable enough fellow. 'I am famous. Search for me online. I have 4,082 followers on social media.'

Since Prachand was rather obtuse about the online world, he nodded politely.

Dinanath Tripathi looked at Paramveer Khattar. 'Let me guess, your female lead is also from the Bhojpuri film industry?'

'Of course!' Paramveer Khattar said. 'There needs to be an organic chemistry on-screen. We decided to focus on home-grown, earthy, relatable characters …'

Vidya whispered into Prachand's ear. 'I thought our fee was indication enough, but this is worse than I imagined! Car travel, "earthy" cast, a home shoot; I know where this is headed. Their budgets must be even more minuscule than we had imagined.'

Either by sheer coincidence, or perhaps having caught a whiff of Vidya's hushed strictures, His Royalness raised a puny hand. 'My money is also invested in this project. My keen eye is on every penny and you shall get what's been promised to you. Yes, things are a bit tight, but I will keep everything under control. Nothing escapes these eyes that have hunted tigers,' he remarked with a certain air, almost jabbing his own eyes to make a point.

'So, Sheikh Chilli here is responsible for the thinning tiger population?' Yatish tittered, nudging Chachu Tripathi. He received a disapproving look from Arjun Prajapati who was within earshot.

'Moving on,' Paramveer Khattar said, 'our female lead is Ranjana Jha. Another well-known Bhojpuri face. You can meet the other cast and crew on the set.' He then smacked his head. 'How can I forget our main man! Aaloo, our young and supremely talented director.'

'That's it! Now they'll tell us they could only afford to hire a vegetable for screenplay and direction. I wouldn't put it past them,' Vidya muttered.

Prachand squeezed her hand. 'Relax. Let's give them a fair chance. As long as we do our job and get our money, this can only be fun! You're still going to be on a movie set!' Vidya's set lips betrayed a small smile.

'Ah, there he is,' Paramveer Khattar beamed. 'Aalok Bhatnagar. Our shining gem, scriptwriter, director and award-winning talent from Mumbai! Aaloo, come here.'

A young, giant of a man emerged from the restaurant. His hair was unkempt, large red glasses framed his round face and his white shirt looked as if it had last met any washing powder a few months ago. Despite a decorous introduction, his eyes remained downcast.

Chachu Tripathi eased his way to the front, his mind firmly set on the role he was promised. 'Beta Aaloo, I am Dinanath Tripathi, an actor. You have to find me some role. I am willing to do anything.'

Aalok Bhatnagar shot Paramveer Khattar a grim look. 'Aalok is f ... fine.'

In an effort to break the ice, Prachand asked, 'So, Aalok, tell us, what are the wonderful awards you've been showered with? Some national critics award, or maybe some Filmfare or Stardust award?'

'I ... I won ... D... d ... d ... Dombivili Films Club award and Pydhonie Movie Maniacs awards.'

'Oh!' Vidya said looking resigned.

CHAPTER 15

The Innova now part of a larger convoy, snaked its way through the outskirts of Jaisalmer down roads that were intractable in several patches and flanked by equitably spaced, two or single-storeyed houses. There were hardly any tall buildings in sight, making the neighbourhood look like one homogenous mass. Some stray porches hosted a cow or buffalo as the locals sat about for an evening chat, the women moving about doing their chores wearing the traditional and colourful kanchli ghagras, shooting curious glances at the moving vehicles with eager faces pasted in the windows.

Dinbandhu Tripathi smiled. 'I wonder what that naughty Hirwa is up to.' As the sun set in a horizon, which was streaked crimson and dotted with birds, the convoy of cars made its way towards Kuldhara that was another eighteen kilometres away.

'There is something magical about a city in the middle of a desert, na?' Vidya nudged Prachand, her eyes twinkling. 'Have you seen how the mood and lighting just change when dusk falls?' Yellow lights dotted the landscape as far as the eyes could see, and beyond that lay the darkening expanse of the mighty Thar Desert. As they left the city behind, fewer cars were visible and they saw more kuccha houses with tin roofs popping up around them.

Prachand decided this was a good time to dig out information about their royal host. 'So, Arjunji, how is Ramnarayan Rathod really connected to the royal family?'

Arjun Prajapati, who had just switched spots with Yatish to sit in the front seat, took his time to respond. 'You see, Prachand Sa. He is a distant cousin of the family.'

'How distant?'

'Umm. Quite, I believe. He is the fourth cousin on the maternal side.'

'You mean he shares a great-great grandparent with the royal family?' Vidya asked incredulously.

The loyal Arjun Prajapati seemed to bristle on behalf of his employer. 'The connect cannot be denied. That is why he uses a title.'

'A manufactured title,' Yatish muttered from the backseat.

Arjun Prajapati continued. 'It's just that ... well, they treat him with disdain, finding his life choices, his business and his associates to be unsuitable to their pedigree. He made money in mining, and before that in the lavatory business.'

'What exactly was that about?' Prachand inquired.

'He manufactured commodes. In fact, he was once called the Commode King in these parts,' Arjun Prajapati announced with a flourish.

'At least he is a king of something, even if it has to do with flushing,' Vidya chuckled audibly enough.

'And the palace?' Chachu Tripathi asked, looking up from his phone, hopeful for a confirmation on this front.

'It has been in his family for many years.'

'What is with the network here?' Chachu Tripathi abruptly changed the topic, whacking his phone against his palm.

This time, a response came from the driver in a deadpan voice. 'Hardly any phone works near Kuldhara. No matter how many towers are set up, it's as if this part of the world wants to be left alone,' he said and briefly turned around to look at his passengers in the eye, before continuing to drive in silence.

Soon enough, the passengers were treated to the magnificence of the desert taking shape around them. The golden city was fading into plumes of dust in the rear-view mirror. They kept driving on a long stretch of road that didn't seem to be a part of any city planning. Even though minimal lighting remained, the sand dunes loomed in the distance like gentle shifting giants watching time morphing and migrating. It was like finding a passage to another world. The vegetation was sparse and nothing visible for miles, barring the few mud huts that appeared from time to time.

Arjun Prajapati turned in his seat. 'You must be wondering how anyone survives in the desert. We are accustomed to survive and thrive! Yes, water is scarce and the landscape is intimidating, but we have our small-scale industries. Some people till the land where possible, like the Seervis, a local farmer tribe. Our people believe that it doesn't matter if you're surrounded by parched land or the sea, happiness comes from within,' he said sagaciously as the passengers listened in silence.

After another half an hour of driving, they took a sharp turn to the right and drove on a barely discernible dirt road that tossed around the car's occupants like popcorn.

'My head might just separate from the rest of my body by the time we reach,' said Dinanath Tripathi in a high-pitched falsetto.

'Roll up the windows,' Yatish demanded.

'I can't,' Dinanath Tripathi shot back, holding a handkerchief to his mouth. 'I need air or I'll throw up.'

'Chachu, this isn't air. It's dust!'

An animal wailing in the distance cut their conversation short. 'I wish we would get there already,' Vidya whispered, inching closer to Prachand.

Minutes later, the car, filled with a homogenous mass of dusty brown, pulled into an unpaved driveway that led to a grotty and dilapidated haveli. Prachand's eyes scanned the remnants of what he assumed could have been a citadel of grandeur in its heyday. The external facade was dotted with intricate *jharokhas* harbouring neither shy women nor spies, nor mantris. The archways, pillars, *chabootaras,* every crevice and corner seemed to have become the uninhibited kingdom of pigeons and decay. The dim bulbs and fleeting shadows made it look even more uninviting. The cars stopped and the passengers alighted.

'Welcome to Naveli Haveli!' Arjun Prajapati beamed like a proud father.

'If this haveli is "naveli", then I'm two years old,' Vidya quipped. 'It looks like the set where *Vikram Vetal* was shot.'

'I bet an old kaka will open the door holding a creaking lantern,' chuckled Yatish.

Prachand watched these reactions with amused equanimity. Expectations usually paved the way to disappointments, and considering he had no high expectations from this venture, he took in everything dispassionately.

All the passengers trooped into the house while he walked around, taking in the vanity vans parked outside and all the lights and equipment strewn around. It was something he always did, with the intention of getting a lay of the land. He smiled to himself, admitting that it would be exciting being on a film set, even if it was a cash-strapped one.

He walked towards the back of the house and his sight instantly fixed on the ruins of the ghost town in the distance. He was a man of faith, but too much of a realist to believe in curses and ghosts. However, the conviction with which the locals spoke of the curse piqued his interest. Deciding to pay a visit soon, he retreated.

That's when he saw two figures to his left, partially concealed by the large shrubs that were planted along the periphery of the property. Prachand hid behind a vanity van, observing the odd, furtive body language. And then he knew. It was the driver and Paramveer Khattar.

They seemed to be having an argument. Eventually, a box was handed over to Paramveer Khattar. He checked it, wagged his finger at Chintan and then turned on his heel, stomping off towards his car.

What on earth was going on between these two, Prachand wondered. What was in the box? Was Paramveer the one the driver was talking to at the Jaipur hotel? Prachand's thoughts were interrupted when Yatish came looking for him. He made a mental note to get to the bottom of this odd relationship, his instinct warning him that something suspicious was underway.

CHAPTER 16

The lady of the house, Padmini Rathod, had been the first one to greet them at the door. Resplendent in her Rajasthani poshak, she bowed respectfully before her husband who sauntered past without acknowledging her. Paramveer Khattar was greeted with a perfunctory nod.

Vidya's eyes took in the petite woman who fussed over her dandy of a husband. He was curt with her, responding testily to everything she said. She had a small frame, but she was carrying off the layers of carefully embellished and embroidered clothes with grace. She seemed energetic and peppy and was possibly in her early thirties, Vidya surmised.

'*Pati hai ya pardada*?' Vidya whispered to Prachand. 'Why is she behaving in such a servile manner?'

'Aren't you being a bit judgemental, Viddu? We haven't been here more than five minutes. Every place has its own traditions.'

'Five minutes is all it took to size up this relationship.'

'Jo hukum, *Jassoosni* Sa,' Prachand guffawed, mimicking Arjun Prajapati.

Padmini bustled towards them next, drawing a surprised Vidya into a warm embrace.

'*Thai bahut phutri laag riya ho!*' she said. Vidya assumed her dishevelled appearance was being complimented as Padmini pointed at her and gave her a thumbs up.

Vidya laughed. 'You look stunning! And it's kind of you to be polite, but I am certain I look like what's left after a camel stampede!'

Padmini laughed heartily and bowed with folded hands to greet Prachand, Yatish and Dinanath Tripathi. 'This attire,' she said, pointing at herself, 'is usually reserved for special occasions, and your arrival is no less important for me,' she added sweetly.

After everyone had washed up and changed, it was time for dinner. Beyond the central courtyard, which was a typical feature of havelis in these parts, there was a circular living room branching off into corridors and multiple rooms. Prachand and Vidya had been given one of these rooms on the ground floor. Dinanath Tripathi and Yatish were assigned a smaller room nearby. The first floor hosted the rooms of the owners and the cast and crew while the remaining property had been offered up for the shoot.

Vidya fell in love with their sparsely furnished but tastefully done room with its big windows and Kota stone flooring. She walked around while Prachand unpacked each item, placing the contents in the cupboard in a particular order, just the way he liked it. A framed Bholenath photo had been lovingly transferred to the study table. He was dusting it when Vidya chided Prachand. 'Can we please turn down the OCD, at least when we are travelling?'

Prachand smiled. 'A little bit of order is comforting, wouldn't you agree?'

Vidya shrugged. 'Let's just say I don't want to get too familiar. There's something strange about this place. Can't you feel it?'

Padmini Rathod's delicate sensibilities steeped in local culture were the redeeming factor that made the not-so-Naveli Haveli mildly liveable. They were evident in the decor: spilling forth through the colourful tapestries and wall hangings, lending some much-needed warmth to the interiors that had seen a lot of callous patchwork over the years. Her best efforts couldn't rid the mansion of the cobweb of cracks spreading their talons into all corners, or the musty heaviness that came with age and neglect. The walls of the capacious dining area were peppered with stuffed heads from the animal kingdom. Dinanath Tripathi was observing one such deer head with much distaste, when Ramnarayan Rathod cleared his throat audibly.

'The handiwork of my ancestors, before hunting was banned. What a waste!'

Dinanath Tripathi reserved his comments, imagining that the odd man wouldn't make a very appealing taxidermy exhibit in his next birth if karma had its way.

Cutting a rather debonair figure, Paramveer Khattar sat by the fireplace in a white kurta-pyjama teamed with a Nehru jacket. His hair was damp and fell over his eyes as he concentrated on filling his pipe. Without looking up, he addressed Prachand and Vidya who had just stepped into the main hall with Yatish in tow. 'We do hope your accommodations are comfortable?' The guests nodded politely as Padmini ushered everyone to the dining table.

Aaloo, the director, was tired and had turned in early after having a shower, but they were joined by the lead actor, Vikas Kishen, a man with a very curly head of hair named Venky, who was the DOP (director of photography), and a rotund sour-faced woman who introduced herself as the 'heroine ki mumma.'

'Ranjana will not be joining us tonight. She has a headache,' she announced.

'One tantrum each day,' muttered Padmini under her breath. Prachand was probably the only one who heard the comment and found it unusual given her otherwise cheerful demeanour. He dismissed it, distracted by the array of delectable local dishes on the table. From the famous dal baati and churma to the *gatte* and *guar ki sabzi* to sweetmeats like *imarti, gulgule and laddoos,* it was an irresistible fare.

Vidya, a veritable gourmand in an average-sized body, looked entranced by the spread. 'You shouldn't have taken so much trouble, Padminiji. This is a feast!'

'It's nothing really,' gushed Padmini. 'I have two great cooks. Please take some more.' She ladled a spoonful of mixed vegetables in Yatish's already overflowing plate before he could block her hand. After belching, he covered his mouth apologetically.

'Chachu,' he elbowed Dinanath Tripathi. 'I hope you're carrying churan. This Bengali warrior is on his knees. *Aar parchi na baba!*' This time, he was successful in refusing another serving of dal from Arjun Prajapati, who was hovering around the table, keeping an eye on the guests.

'So, where does the rest of the cast and crew stay?' Prachand asked.

'Besides the actors and their staff, Venky, Aalok and you all, everyone else is in guest houses closer to Jaisalmer,' Paramveer Khattar explained.

'They return to Jaisalmer every night? Isn't that cumbersome?' Yatish inquired.

'Well ...' Paramveer Khattar seemed to be choosing his words. 'All for superstitions really. It is indeed an avoidable expense if you ask me.'

'No one wants to stay here after sunset.' Vikas Kishen had lowered his voice to a hoarse whisper. 'Kuldhara is cursed. Restless spirits roam the land. Weary travellers and locals lurking around at night have been known to disappear.'

Vidya had stopped eating and was listening intently. Prachand noticed her reaction and decided to intervene. 'Surely this is an old wives' tale, am I correct? Have there been missing persons reports? The police must have a record.'

'This is a land where reason and faith are in constant battle,' Padmini said, her brows creased. 'There are times when all is peaceful. But over the last few days, the winds have changed and strange things have been happening again. I've seen this before.'

'What do you mean?' Dinanath Tripathi leaned in. Now everyone, as per the norm of social conformity, was speaking in a hoarse whisper.

'There are noises you can never explain, like screams, moans, disembodied voices, flickering lights and objects moving around. Sometimes you see nothing but there's a feeling of dread that takes over, making you feel sick to the stomach, an inexplicable feeling. Soon you start doubting what's real and what's not.'

Yatish gulped audibly and a faint murmur of the Hanuman Chalisa wafted in from where Venky and Vikas Kishen sat. It looked as if they were holding hands in solidarity.

'Now, now, Rani Sa,' Ramnarayan Rathod said with a wave of the discoloured sleeve that he had moments ago dipped into hot potato curry. 'Stop scaring our guests on their first night. I am a God-fearing man, but I don't believe in this hogwash! My superior intelligence forbids it!'

It was doubtful whether anyone around the table agreed with this self-assessment, but the gravity of the topic under discussion left everyone distracted. With an intention to lighten the atmosphere, Padmini brought out a dessert plate laden with gulab jamun, jalebi and *ghewar*. 'I'm going to go back with two of me at this rate,' Vidya complained with a crammed mouth.

As the dinner time chatter came to an end and the clatter of cutlery, furniture and ablutions reduced, an almost-deafening silence came to claim the night. All the guests were tucked in bed under thick blankets, sheathing themselves from the cold draft in the haveli despite the warmer temperature outside. Prachand had shut the windows tight and was walking back to bed when the only light in the bathroom started flickering.

'Prachi,' Vidya called out into the dimly lit room. 'What's going on? Is it true then ...?'

Prachand sat on the edge of the bed, observing the light as it continued flickering. 'I have no idea, Viddu. Not yet.'

CHAPTER 17

'Lights, camera, ac ... ac ... tion!' The otherwise quiet and tepid Aaloo was a transformed person on set, calling the shots and yelling at people.

Prachand and Vidya had spent a good part of the morning with him, discussing the script and characters. Taking method acting a little too far, Vikas Kishen had been tailing Prachand, much to the latter's discomfort. He would stand at a distance and emulate Prachand.

'At least he is invested in the role,' Vidya quipped. 'The actress behaves as if she is doing me a favour by acknowledging my presence. God forbid if people assume I am anything like her in real life!'

The lady in question was preening herself in one corner of the hall while her stylist Preeti was reprimanded by her mother for not carrying the right clothes for her 'baby'. 'What are these nonsensical salwar-kameezes?'

Ranjana Jha complained as well. 'So plain and dowdy! She is playing the wife of a small-town detective, not a homeless woman.'

Vidya gritted her teeth. 'Relax, Bhabhi,' Yatish cooed, but his eyes were fixed on the starlet. 'She's a star. It comes with the territory.'

He felt a hand on his shoulder and turned to see Chachu Tripathi grinning at him. 'I'm familiar with that expression on your face, bachchu. This isn't Kanpur matrimonial. Forget about her.'

Yatish looked cross. 'Kya, Chachu! Why must you puncture my flight of fantasy?'

Unbeknownst to Yatish, Dinanath Tripathi's entire attention was focused on Aaloo, the man who had agreed to cast him as one of the bad guys the hero would tackle in the film. It was a small role, but Dinanath was convinced that with his dedication and acting chops, he would gently persuade the director to expand it. Filled to the brim with ideas and suggestions, he tried engaging the director many a times, but Aalok had eyes only for Prachand and Vidya, who he would seek out intermittently.

As he settled between them in a rickety chair, he updated them on some outdoor sequences that had already been shot to save time.

'You see, unlike other d ... d ... d ... irectors, all I need is a rough story to shoot my sss ... sss ... sequences.' Aalok produced a thick file that had frames sketched and sequenced like a comic book. 'I'm trying to shoot this story in a te ... telenovela ss ... ss ... style.' He paused and cleared his throat.

'What on earth is a telenovela?' Vidya inquired.

'It's a kind of limited series, never done before in India. A slightly d....d....dramatic mix of a soap opera and a novel,' Aalok explained.

'Then this is really everything but a movie set,' Vidya sighed.

'D ... d ... don't worry,' Aalok reassured her, 'It will feel like a film, but a condensed one. You'll love it in the end.'

'Talking about the end,' Vidya pressed on, 'your script stopped midway. That's odd!'

'Aah, that.' Aalok betrayed a small smile for the first time. 'While the story is clear in my head, I like k ... keeping things fluid and adding frames as we go.'

The day wore on as successive scenes were shot. Considering they had to call it a day at 5 p.m., there was no time to waste.

Around five-thirty in the evening, with the house emptier, the lady of the manor emerged with some snacks and tea, eager to be updated about the day's events. She had taken a special liking to Vidya. As she walked up, Vidya inhaled sharply. 'That's a lovely perfume, Padminiji,' she said, smiling at their hostess who nodded politely. She nudged her husband.

'Prachand, shouldn't Padminiji be joining us during the shoot? It isn't as if we are busy the whole time. From what I can tell, our "job" entails consultations and keeping an eye on things. That leaves ample time for some chit chat,' Vidya said.

Prachand nodded. 'Of course. You must, Padminiji.'

'Oh no!' Padmini Rathod shook her head. 'I wouldn't want to get in the way. While Rajaji is away at work, I oversee some NGO-related work. I work with a talented group of women who create handmade products like lac bangles, puppets, tie-and-dye clothes and block print diyas. It makes them economically independent and gives me happiness.

Between that and managing the house, there's not much time left.'

'You're such a talented and compassionate woman. Don't you feel suffo ...' Vidya bit her tongue before the word could escape her mouth.

Padmini Rathod looked at her. 'I believe in making every moment count instead of blaming my circumstances. After all, I live in a haveli. Who can complain!' She laughed and then caught Arjun Prajapati's eyes. 'It's time,' she said.

As the guests had tea, Arjun Prajapati, aided by two other men, moved from window to door, shutting and bolting each one.

Aalok Kumar protested. 'I need to head out for my stroll. P ... please wait.'

Paramveer Khattar shook his head. 'Why must you wander alone when we live in a cursed neighbourhood? You'll trip in the dark and they'll blame a poor witch for it.'

'Don't speak lightly of those we cannot see,' Padmini snapped at Paramveer Khattar. 'You'll offend them.'

'I'll b ... bb ... be back shortly.' Aalok hurried out. It was dark already.

'Scoff at my beliefs all you want, but I am going to light some diyas as I always do. For protection and my own peace of mind,' Padmini said and left.

'I'm glad Ramnarayan isn't here, otherwise he ...' Paramveer Khattar's pipe hung on his lips, much like his words, as every single light in the house started flickering.

On cue, Dinanath Tripathi started reciting the Hanuman Chalisa. '*Bhoot pisaach nikat nahi aave, Mahaveer jab naam sunave* ...' The remaining cast and the DOP fled from the hall towards their rooms, while Ranjana Jha and her mother came running out of theirs.

'It's happening again! And we heard noises. What's going on?' the actress asked, looking around.

Vidya turned to Prachand, but he was nowhere to be seen. Her heart went cold as she called out to her husband.

CHAPTER 18

After a few minutes of utter chaos and brouhaha, the lights stopped flickering. Padmini Rathod was the first to recover her wits and notice that Prachand was walking into the hall through the kitchen area. 'Vidyaji, he is back!' she said, trying to catch her breath.

Vidya was by Prachand's side within seconds. 'Where on earth did you go?' she asked, her voice tremulous with concern.

'To catch the ghost who has taken a fancy to the lights here!' Prachand replied.

'You saw something?' Vikas Kishen inquired in a shaky voice from behind the sofa where he was hiding.

Prachand raised his arm as a murmur of queries filled the air. 'Everyone, calm down,' he said.

Right that minute, the front door opened and Ramnarayan Rathod walked in followed by Chintan, the chauffeur. 'Why is everyone collected here?' He looked genuinely surprised.

Prachand volunteered. 'I had to get to the bottom of the mysterious flickering of the lights. There are things in this world that are beyond our comprehension, but some mysteries are easier to unravel if we are willing to truly open our eyes. You see, one obvious explanation for the lights is the fluctuating voltage, which might be very common in these parts.'

'We haven't really had any such problem since the last elections,' Ramnarayan Rathod shrugged, beaming at his friend. 'Param has been a godsend. His father pulled a few strings at his behest.'

'All right, that's acceptable,' Prachand nodded. 'I went to the fuse box, which I knew is located right outside the kitchen. The lights and generators are also connected there to draw power for the shoot. By the time I got there, the lights were back on.'

'Ghosts are wily and quick that way,' Arjun Prajapati blurted and then looked embarrassed at having spoken out of turn.

'Only that this ghost left behind some footprints,' said Prachand.

'What!' Paramveer Khattar looked foxed.

'Yes, indeed. You see, whoever was fiddling with the mains would have been caught had I not banged into a stool in the kitchen and warned them. There were people moving around the house, shutting doors and windows, so the footprints have to belong to someone who was near the meter as the lights were flashing. Only, this someone was obviously in a hurry and didn't realize that the meter room's floor was damp. Has there been a recent leakage?'

'Yes,' Arjun Prajapati said. 'The small tap has been leaking since this evening.'

'If I hadn't chanced upon the footprints when I did, they would have dried up soon enough on the stone floor. Hard to say more, but what I can tell you is that they establish the presence of a human.'

Shock and disbelief were writ large on every face.

'Even if we assume that it is a person, it would mean that this same person has been responsible for previous episodes as well,' said Padmini Rathod.

Prachand turned around to see her standing some distance away. 'Why would anyone in their right mind do this?' she asked incredulously.

'I'm not sure at this point,' Prachand confessed. 'Let's just keep our eyes and ears open.'

Vidya excused herself, the excitement proving to be too much for her bladder. Walking to their room, she wondered what mess she had dragged all of them into. A haunted village nearby, and now some sort of meter-savvy ghost? Her mother-in-law would happily have her rump for dinner if she found out what was going on in this strange little village.

She opened the door to the room and froze. It looked like a hurricane had selectively chosen one room to wreak havoc on. Their luggage had been turned inside out, chairs and tables were lying legs up, papers from Prachand's bag were strewn all over the floor. She shouted out for Prachand. He came, but with an entourage behind him.

'What on ...' the loquacious Ramnarayan Rathod had nothing to say for once.

Prachand walked around the room, his brow furrowed. He paused by the window, looked under the bed, checked his papers and then went into the bathroom. He turned to

Vidya who was shuffling through their things. 'Anything missing?' he asked.

'Not that I can see,' she said, grabbing the saucy underwear purchased from Dream Girl Hosiery back home and stuffing it under the mattress.

'I am so sorry about this,' said Padmini Rathod, looking as if she would burst into tears.

Vidya patted her arm reassuringly. 'How is this your fault? Perhaps someone has a bad sense of humour.'

'Or what we heard is true and the spirits are offended. They're trying to tell us something,' Arjun Prajapati mumbled.

'Shut up, Arjun!' bellowed Paramveer Khattar.

'This is very stressful!' announced Ranjana Jha dramatically. 'I can't handle it!'

Before her rotund mother, dressed in a ridiculously frilly nightgown, could assuage her fears, Yatish moved in, cooing sympathetically. 'It's completely understandable,' he clucked. 'You need your beauty sleep. Shall I escort you back to your room if you feel too scared to go alone?'

The mother whacked his extended hand and declined his offer on her daughter's behalf.

Aalok Kumar walked into the room just then. 'Wwww ... what's all this? A b ... b ... burglary?' His eyes widened.

'No,' said Prachand, who was squatting by the bed, shaking his head.

'All right!' Paramveer Khattar walked to the door decisively. 'Show's over. Everyone, please file out and give them some space. We will figure this out. There is no need to panic. Just go to your rooms for now. We shall call you back when dinner is ready.' He barked some more instructions to the home staff standing around looking startled.

When they were finally alone, Vidya walked over to Prachand and held his arm. 'I know you're more devastated at the way this room looks right now,' she said, allowing herself a smile, as did Prachand. And then it struck her. 'Prachi, do you think this could be a ruse, a distraction?'

Prachand stood up and smiled affectionately at his wife. 'Well done my darling! That's exactly what I was thinking.'

CHAPTER 19

'I need a clump of goat hair, cow urine, a crow's feather, a lizard's tail and the milk of a local cow that has just delivered its first calf.'

Arjun Prajapati, pen and a writing pad in hand, was standing with Keshav, a production assistant, noting down this odd list of ingredients dictated by Bhutaari Baba. With the events of the last few days, the hosts considered it prudent to invoke other-worldly protection for the home and the ongoing shoot, especially to appease the local crew. Now commissioned, the ferocious-looking man with bulbous eyes stroked his white beard, commanding everyone, knowing fully well that he would not be denied.

Keshav scratched his unkempt beard. 'I have local suppliers, but I've never really needed to track down a goat or lizard.'

Chachu Tripathi, always in the vicinity of action, was rehearsing his lines. He made a magnanimous offer. 'I can lend you some gau mutra. We have a brand of our own you see,' he announced proudly. 'My dear brother never lets us leave home without it.'

Arjun Prajapati reviewed the list again. 'That's great. Thank you. But what about this calf business? It's not as if we have bovine census data to figure out first or second calves.

Vidya overheard the comment and smiled indulgently at Arjun Prajapati. 'Arjunji, these are dire circumstances! There's no harm in getting some help,' she joked.

His chest puckered up like a belligerent turkey. 'Help? Did you know that we can clean utensils without a drop of water, just by using sand? They shine and glisten like a twinkling oasis when scrubbed. The desert heals and provides with zero intervention. The answers to all our problems lie in the dunes, the sun and the warm winds, not in lizard tails, crow feathers or cows!' he complained.

The diatribe was met with scorn. 'You want all the fruits, Arjun Sa, but no one is willing to do the hard work. That's what ails the world today. Shortcuts!' Bhutaari Baba snorted. 'Now keep aside your pride and bring me what I ask. Do not inundate me with your problems.'

So, while hapless lizards and crows were being chased down in and around Naveli Haveli, other troubles were brewing in front of the camera. Due to his recent year-long stint with a Ramlila troupe in between movies, Vikas Kishen was finding it hard to relinquish some habits from his time on stage.

The assistant director was ready to pull his hair out. 'Vikas Sir, why are you shouting?'

Ranjana Jha, who was dressed demurely for the scene in a cotton salwar-kameez, blew at her freshly painted nails. 'My ears are hurting and he is spitting in my face. Please make him stop.'

Vikas Kishen looked contrite. 'Sorry. Old habits die hard!'

Aalok, who was watching the footage on the shoot monitor, added his feedback. 'P ... p ... p ... please go easy on the expressions as well. You d ... d ... don't need to h ... ham.'

'But I'm not singing at all, Aalok. I promise!'

'Ham, not hum. Like over-act ... ting.'

Prachand and Vidya were suitably entertained. When Yatish joined them, it provided an opportunity to discuss the events of the previous night.

'Prachi, how can you be so certain that what you saw were footprints? Isn't it possible that your eyes played tricks on you in the dim light?'

'Do you have another explanation, Viddu? That a mischievous ghost is on the loose?'

'What worries me more is that someone was in our room,' Vidya said 'Do you think this was some kind of a message for us?'

'I know what message it might be. Stop playing detective all the time!' Yatish said.

'And since when do you believe in ghosts, Yatish?' Vidya retorted.

'I'm no scaredy cat, but there are things in this world that we can't understand, Bhabhi. Like when I was eight years old, I remember waking up in the middle of the night, feeling a great pressure on my chest. I opened my eyes and couldn't breathe. Sitting on my chest was a *bhootni,* with white hair and long claws. She tried to strangle me. Luckily, I started chanting a prayer. After some time, she floated up and disappeared through the window. Can you explain what that was?'

'A nightmare,' Prachand suggested.

'But it felt so real!'

'Our subconscious is a great magician, capable of conjuring the realities we want to see,' Prachand said

'Sure. As if that woman was some aunt of mine who I invited home for a meal.'

'Can we get back to the matter on hand now?' Prachand interrupted, wanting to end the banter. 'I was working out the timing. Aalok went for a walk and returned just after the lights flickered. Even Ramnarayan Rathod walked in just after the incident. But there is a gaping hole in terms of purpose. There is nothing for either of them to gain by disrupting the shoot or trying to scare us. Everyone else, including the servants, is accounted for.'

'And how do you explain the ransacked room with the doors and windows shut?' Vidya asked.

'I don't know yet, but I'll explore every other angle before giving credence to the neighbourhood ghost theory. Which reminds me,' he looked at Yatish. 'I think you should keep an eye on Aalok.' Yatish nodded.

'That Ramnarayan Rathod seems like a strange fellow, you know,' Vidya said. 'Nothing remotely straightforward about him.'

'Is that opinion perhaps a little tainted given how he treats his wife?' Yatish suggested.

Vidya bristled. 'My objectivity remains intact, Yatish. He is mean-minded. I heard the servants mumbling about how he ill-treats and punishes them by holding back their salaries.'

'Still doesn't make him complicit,' Prachand shrugged. 'We must keep vigil and stay alert.'

'You do realize this is not one of our cases, Prachand Da?'

'That doesn't matter, Yatish. There are strange things happening here. We must get to the bottom of it so that the shoot progresses unimpeded. Think of it this way. It'll help get us home quicker.' He then studied Yatish's face and added. 'That is, if you wish to return early. You seem to have grown roots in and around Ranjana Jha.'

'Kya, Prachand Da! Nothing of the sort,' said Yatish, his face betraying his words with a blush.

'Great. Then it is imperative to keep an eye on Rathod and Aalok for the next few days. Report back to me please.'

Yatish's blush was replaced by a frown.

Paramveer Khattar walked up to them just then with a mug in his hand. 'Chotu, tea for everyone,' he hollered in his usual style and took a seat.

'What is this khoofiya exchange now?' he smirked, taking a sip from his mug.

'Nothing at all,' smiled Prachand. 'We were just discussing your new sorcerer friend on the set. We've seen him before. In Jaisalmer.'

'Oh, Bhutaari Baba?' Paramveer Khattar slurped. 'Yes, he gets around. Doesn't stay in one place for too long. I hear he is effective in these matters.'

'Well, the locals certainly seem happier having him around,' Prachand said, looking around at the spot boys and crew members milling around. 'A few of them seem to be quite young. Are they underage?'

Paramveer Khattar's upper lip curled into a sneer. 'Beggars can't be choosers, Mr Prachand. The educated ones flee their hometowns. The smaller home-owned businesses have fallen on hard times as well. In fact, I'm doing them a favour by creating employment,' he said with grandiloquence.

'Exploitation can be given any fancy name,' said Vidya with a stern gaze. 'But it is what it is.'

Paramveer Khattar laughed. 'Look, no offense, but I don't care for emotional bulldozing. I am a businessman and a politician. I am a driven man, goal-oriented, and nothing gets in my way. This production is tight and we needed to hire locally because it is cheaper and more conducive to shoot here. Whatever helps me get to my goal quicker is all that matters,' he said with a casual shrug.

Prachand squeezed Vidya's hand to stem any further parleys. He did, however, make a mental note that Paramveer Khattar, for all his charm and wit, was an ambitious man with no scruples. In his experience, that was the dangerous kind, the ones you needed to watch out for.

Aalok's voice reverberated through the haveli, announcing the next shot, 'And ... action!' he barked.

'Praise the lord! Siyavar Ram Chandra ki jaiiiiiii!' hollered Vikas Kishen with vigour, as the assistant director came charging at him again.

CHAPTER 20

The next couple of days went by without incident. The lack of any more ghostly activities was attributed to the presence of Bhutaari Baba, who felt emboldened and wrote up even more bizarre demands that left the production team baffled.

That morning, an outdoor sequence was to be shot in a small patch of woods on the property, something that had thoroughly confused Dinanath Tripathi. 'I've been shivering at night, and now I hear of a jungle. Seems like I know nothing about deserts!'

One of the production assistants handed him a cup of piping hot ginger-infused sweet chai, which was very popular among the locals. 'Everything here is an anomaly, Mamoji, a deviation, just like this cluster of trees. No one knows how they survive and what hidden underground water reserve quenches their thirst. We do get some showers during this time but look at the weather today. It's an aberration as well,' he said.

Due to the overcast sky, the crew had to create artificial sunlight. This got Dinanath Tripathi very excited. The main reason was that after a long wait, and after being tossed around amidst Aalok's confused storyboard sketches, it was his day. He had two scenes to be shot and was kicked about the fact that the crew had decided to play God and create sunlight, undertaking something so revolutionary on his special day. Venky informed him that using Einstein lights on set was a pretty common feature, but Dinanath Tripathi was undeterred in his celebration. 'The miracle of making sunshine on a cloudy day, on my day!' he exclaimed.

Meanwhile, not very far away, an altercation was in progress at Naveli Haveli. It was a known fact that Ranjana Jha was impertinent and testy, but her most frequent entanglements had been with Paramveer Khattar, the man who controlled the purse strings on the sets.

'This is inhuman! To be fed this oily and abominable food every single day.' She stamped her foot like a petulant child and stood with her back to Paramveer Khattar, arms crossed defensively over her chest.

'My poor baby ...' the mother bristled, her voluminous double chin quivering with indignation.

Paramveer Khattar raised an arm in a dismissive gesture and turned his attention back to Ranjana. 'Miss Jha, I must tell you that we didn't sign up for this. From your wardrobe to the weather to the food to the script to the accommodation, you have a problem with everything. Yesterday you had a meltdown because you saw a lizard. Have you even considered that this movie is a fantastic opportunity for you?'

'Yes, I do, but does that mean I need to lie prostrate and give my thanks every day? Don't I have feelings? Can't I have a say?' she protested.

Predicting even more conflict, Paramveer Khattar deflected the approaching storm by saving his rebuttal for another time. Thankfully, the shot was ready and the assistant director called out to the actors. Ranjana vented her frustration on her stylist, Preeti, and headed for her shot, while Dinanath Tripathi prepared himself to play the role of Vidya's kidnapper.

'And ... a ... ccction!' shouted Aalok.

'*Chhod do mujhe!*' Ranjana Jha moaned.

Dinanath Tripathi, who had her by the arm, let go immediately. '*Theek hai, Beta.*'

'Cut!' Aalok stood up looking perplexed. 'What was that?'

It took about ten takes for Dinanath Tripathi to relinquish his avuncular gene and get into his character.

Arjun Prajapati was sitting in the director's enclosure, behind Prachand, watching these proceedings in utter fascination. Since he was otherwise always running errands, Prachand decided to wrest some information from him.

'Arjunji, how long have you been with Rathodji?'

Arjun Prajapati tore his gaze away from the shot of Dinanath Tripathi giving chase to Vidya as his thick, stick-on beard fell to the ground. 'More than ten years. I used to work in a potters' market that Rajaji would frequent because of a popular ghewar shop in the area. I impressed him and he hired me as his personal staff. That's where he met Rani Sa as well,' he said, smiling indulgently. 'Her family used to own the shop but fell on bad times. It had to be shut down eventually. That's when they got married.'

'Oh, so it's a love marriage,' Prachand concurred, sounding surprised. 'And why did he choose to settle down in Kuldhara of all places?'

'Well, this haveli was actually used as a summer lodge by the royal family many years ago. Rajaji told me that he was very fond of this place even as a child. When he finally had the money, he bought it and tried to fix it as much as possible. He joked once that in order to stay here, he would even make his peace with the devil!' Arjun Prajapati looked around wistfully. 'This was a beautiful patch of green alongside the desert. Now most of the trees are gone thanks to endless mining and road projects. The remaining trees owe their lives to Kuldhara and the folklore associated with it. The work was abandoned because people are too scared to come here. That's why the public amenities are lacking.'

'Can you please tell us what happened here in Kuldhara?' Vidya asked him in a saccharine voice, sensing that he would be unwilling to have this conversation. 'We only know what we have gleaned from snatches of conversations, or what we read on the internet. No one seems to want to talk about it.'

'That's because talking about the past unsettles the present.'

Padmini Rathod was standing behind them. Arjun Prajapati leapt to his feet and dragged a chair for her. 'Apologies, *Rani Sa*. I was just ...'

'It's okay, Arjunji,' she gestured for him to sit down. 'Go ahead, tell them. They have a right to know.'

Arjun Prajapati sat cross-legged on the ground with an air of mystery, rocking back and forth as if professionally trained to tell tales around bonfires. 'Legend has it that about two hundred years ago this used to be a thriving province. Kuldhara in particular was inhabited by the Paliwal Brahmins, a devout and proud lot who believed in living simply and peacefully. Our ancestors are correct in saying that too much of a good thing attracts the evil eye. The same misfortune befell the poor Paliwal Brahmins. Their troubles came in the form of an evil diwan who laid his unchaste eyes on the daughter of the village chief. They begged and pleaded with him to let her be. However, he unleashed his vengeance on them by pressurizing them financially and giving them an ultimatum to hand her over. As it was a matter of honour, they chose to abandon the village overnight.'

'Even the children?'

'Yes.'

'The elderly?'

'Yes.'

'The goats, cows and chicken?'

Prachand gave his wife a look for her ill-timed curiosity.

'I'm just trying to get the practical details, Prachi,' Vidya said. 'It sounds like a mammoth task, the movement of so many people, all in one night. Imagine trying to move that militant Hirwa against her will. I also think history and folklore travel through people. Which essentially means that there can be many versions and interpretations. What proof is there that all of this really happened? Anyway, my apologies, Arjunji, I'm just thinking out loud. Please continue.'

'They cursed the village before they left, so that no one would ever inhabit it,' Padmini Rathod continued in his stead. 'And to this day, the abandoned homes and streets of Kuldhara echo their angst, their helplessness and their grief. Many passers-by and travellers who have dared to trespass at night have disappeared, never to be found again.'

'A compelling reason could be the terrible food available in these parts!' tittered a grating voice. It was Ranjana Jha, sauntering up to them with a teacup in hand.

'The suffering of these spirits is no matter for levity. They don't like it,' Padmini Rathod implored her. 'You are asking for trouble.'

'And I bet they've hired you as the sole PR lady and mouthpiece?' Ranjana Jha sneered.

'She is right!' thundered another voice from behind them. Bhutaari Baba, too, had decided to join the conversation that had transformed into a free-for-all. He pointed his long stick at Ranjana Jha who raised her thin eyebrows in defiance. 'You mock the land and its legends! The ones who do so perish!'

'Oye, you fraud, did you just threaten me?' Ranjana Jha gasped.

Paramveer Khattar decided to mediate before the situation deteriorated. 'Come now ... he did nothing of the sort. Bhutaari Baba, let's go. I need to have a chat with you.'

As he was being led away, Bhutaari Baba paused to look at the retreating figure of Ranjana Jha. '*Tu dekh*,' he hissed.

Prachand looked at the baba walking away with concern, wondering if those parting words were a threat.

CHAPTER 21

The next morning, in connivance with the desultory weather, the sun decided to play truant and sent the rain instead. The lodge woke up to inclement weather. Thunder and lightning ripped through the firmament, low and rumbling, as if threatening to set the trees ablaze and make the sand dunes tremble. It didn't rain a lot, but it was enough to impact the shoot. There was another outdoor sequence planned, further into the woods and closer to the ruins, a plan that had the local crew vastly agitated.

'See? This thunder and lightning? This weather is a sign, the desert's way of preventing us from shooting near the ruins,' piped up Sattu, the spot boy, complaining to the production manager who nodded sympathetically. 'My nani told me about a nostrum for turbulent times. Praying to Moonch-wala Balaji! And if the problem is too severe, there's always Current-wala Balaji who grants wishes faster than electric current.'

'Wow!' Prachand's interest was piqued. 'Who is this accomplished gentleman?'

'Arey!' the production manager gave the Kanpuriya a what-an-imbecile look. 'Hanumanji, of course!'

'Any levitating rotis then? Or did the bhindi on your plate reorganize to look like Yamraj?' Paramveer Khattar snarled. His comment had the desired effect, putting a temporary lid on the chatter.

The rest of the day was a veritable washout. Since the rain had picked up, even the crew was sent back. Everyone remained indoors, congregating again for dinner. They sat around the table laden with kofta, a variety of gravy dishes, bajre ki rotis smeared with ghee and stuffed parathas served with a specially prepared haldi ki sabzi that was considered a nostrum for all aches and ailments during the cooler months in Rajasthan. Dinanath Tripathi, who had shot a few of his scenes over the last few days and gained some confidence as an actor, tucked into the fare in good spirits. Cramming a large piece of a paratha in his mouth, he said, 'Delicious food, good company and even better dessert. What more can one ask for!'

Ramnarayan Rathod felt the need to disagree. 'But the danger still lurks. I'm honestly quite surprised that the famous detective Prachand Tripathi has not apprehended our friendly neighbourhood daakan yet!'

His wife, who was walking around the table serving everyone, shot him a look of censure. 'Must you speak with such disrespect?'

He raised his arm to silence her, raising Vidya's hackles. 'Prachand, we should try this kind of non-verbal communication at home, don't you think? You raise your arm and I bring you food. You raise your leg and I bring you dessert. It makes talking unnecessary. How refreshing!'

Padmini flashed Vidya a grateful smile before heading to the kitchen, while Yatish stifled a laugh.

'Your wife certainly has a mind of her own, Mr Prachand,' remarked Paramveer Khattar, his eyes fixed on Vidya. 'I like outspoken, independent women.'

Vidya responded with a militant expression, while Prachand chose to change the topic, not entirely comfortable with the manner in which his wife was being analyzed.

'Mr Khattar, do you wrestle? Or did you wrestle at some point?' Prachand asked casually.

Paramveer Khattar watched Prachand with some interest. 'I might have. How do you know this?'

Prachand took a banana from the tray and peeled it. 'Well, your muscular body type and approximate height-weight ratio are suggestive of the body of a wrestler. I've also noticed that on some days you look like you've done maalish before breakfast. My father was a wrestler too, when he was young. He would tell me that an early morning maalish helps rid one of the aches and pains of training. The biggest clue, however, were the langots I've seen drying in the backyard whenever you return from Jailsalmer. I deduced they were yours, and I doubt that a man of the world like you would wear one unless it's for the traditional wrestling sessions, as is the custom. That, or you are generally a langot lover like my father.'

Paramveer Khattar smiled. 'Nothing escapes you, does it? Even my langot! Well, yes, wrestling is something my father frowns upon and terms a distraction. But I still manage to get a few sessions in every week at an akhara in Jaisalmer. I need to wake up at 4 a.m. on those days, but I look forward to it.'

'Interesting,' Prachand nodded. An audible sigh drew his attention to his uncle who seemed to be chasing a jalebi around his plate. 'All okay, Chachu?'

Dinanath Tripathi looked up. 'Haan, Beta. Just that this jalebi and, well, the mention of a langot made me feel homesick and think of Bade Bhaisaab.'

Yatish gave him a sideways hug. 'Another couple of weeks and we will be back home, Chachu. Don't worry!' He then put together another plate of food. When Vidya raised an eyebrow, he smiled.' Ranjanaji will need her strength for when we resume shooting. Poor thing hardly eats anyway.'

On his way, he paused by Prachand and whispered conspiratorially. 'That Aaloo is crazy, Prachand Da! You were right in having me follow him. Last evening, during his evening walk, he looked supremely nervous in the woods. In the end, I found him ... looking into a well and speaking to someone!'

'So,' said Prachand murmered back. 'Let me get this right. Flickering lights, the ransacking of our room and now our director is talking to someone invisible. I thought we had a film shoot here, but it's sure starting to feel like I'm back in my chair at Kanpur Khoofiya Pvt Ltd.'

As Yatish shrugged and left with the plates, Paramveer Khattar returned to his rant. 'She's a spoilt brat if you ask me.'

'Sorry?' Prachand asked.

'Ranjana Jha. It's always her way or the highway. Which actress behaves this unprofessionally at the start of her career?' His cheeks were flushed.

'Do you know her personally?'

Paramveer Khattar shot Prachand an irritated look. 'No. Why?'

'Just a fleeting impression given the way you speak about her.'

'Well, this is my first project with her. Let's just say that I arrive at conclusions about people quickly, and I am largely accurate!' he boasted. Prachand had a rebuttal in mind but chose to nod and end the topic.

As the table was being cleared, a commotion on the first floor got everyone's attention.

'Is that noise coming from the actress's room?' Ramnarayan Rathod spoke up.

They all made their way up the stairs to her room to find Ranjana wagging a finger in Vikas Kishen's face. The mother sat on the bed holding her head. 'I have heart palpitations. Someone hand me my medicine!'

'I swear on the almighty, I haven't done anything. Why will I want to intimidate you? For what reason?' Vikas Kishen spluttered.

'I don't know! But I returned from the washroom and I saw it right there on the window.'

'Ranjana, I swear I came to your room so we could discuss some scenes. I hadn't even looked at the window till you pointed it out.'

Prachand stepped in and raised an arm to separate the two from shouting at each other. 'Can we help? What's going on?'

Ranjana Jha scowled, pointing a finger at the window. A disorienting clap of thunder echoed through the walls. When it passed, Prachand narrowed his eyes to decipher what he was looking at. Water droplets coursed vertically down the glass pane in small rivulets, but they seemed to navigate around a particular spot in the centre of the window. 'Is ... is that a handprint?'

A shriek emanated from behind them where Padmini Rathod stood, looking as white as a ghost, half-hidden by a curtain. 'She's been cursed!'

CHAPTER 22

'In Kuldhara, you're more likely to find people harvesting curses than crops!' Vidya lamented, holding her head. 'If Ma finds out, she will kill me and empty an entire barni of achar on my head.'

'Which achar?' Yatish, ever the pedant, sensed a conversation about food. Vidya glared at him. 'Don't worry, Bhabhi. There's hardly any network here. You are safe from her calls,' he said.

'Both of you, quiet,' Prachand admonished them and turned his attention to the window. He leaned in and examined the two bloody palm prints.

'They're quite small. Perhaps they belong to a child.'

'That's what I thought,' Ranjana Jha acceded. 'But this man here says it's some kind of curse. And that I'm in danger.'

Vikas Kishen bristled. 'It's not as if I pulled out a story from my personal Ramsay Brothers collection. One of the local boys from the crew told me this. I informed you out of concern.'

Ranjana Jha did not look convinced or pleased. Prachand reached out to touch the spot but was startled when Padmini shrieked again. 'Don't touch it!'

'Please behave yourself!' Ramnarayan Rathod hissed through gritted teeth.

'It's true,' said Padmini Rathod who seemed impervious to any admonishment. Her eyes were fixed on the window, as if she were in a trance. The fear of what she believed was to be their fate was writ large on her face. 'There was a woman named Mahua who used to live with her child in a village nearby. She was a widow and made her living by doing odd jobs. She lived the life of a daily wager. One day, while fetching water, she strayed too far into the desert and lost her way, accidentally landing up in the ruins of Kuldhara. Her child, who would always accompany her, was by her side as they stumbled into the ruins at night. They must have wandered far and somehow made their way to this property. No one knows what really happened, but their screams were heard in the dead of the night. When a search party went out the next morning, they were found dead in a well not very far from here.'

'A well?' Yatish's throat went dry. 'Nearby?'

'Yes. In a clearing in the woods, near the abandoned village. Ever since that night many, many years ago, the woman and her child have been seen roaming the ruins and the woods, ready to take anyone they can find to the well. To join them.'

'Bholenath!' exclaimed Dinanath Tripathi. 'And they're still there!'

'No, Chachu,' Prachand rubbed his uncle's arms, hoping he had taken his blood pressure medication. 'I think what she meant was ... their spirits.'

'Yes, their spirits. And whenever a child's handprints are seen, death follows,' Padmini concluded, almost whispering now.

There was pin-drop silence in the room, the only noise penetrating the thickness of dread was the faint sound of the rain and receding thunder.

Ranjana Jha broke the silence with her laughter. 'You're seriously falling for this mumbo-jumbo? Can't you see? It's such a typical narrative. Stick a *chudail* in the midst whenever convenient. And what irritates me is why these ghosts and ghouls are always women? Men directly go to heaven or hell, but women are left to roam the earth as bhootnis, conveniently giving the film industry and folklore fodder. It's the men vilifying us, controlling us, using us, trampling on us as they deem fit and then labelling us witches,' she said, her eyes smouldering.

'Is this the time for your *naari morcha*, Ms Jha?' Paramveer Khattar asked with a hint of asperity in his voice. Ranjana Jha silenced him with another look.

Vidya, who was watching Ranjana, felt a fleeting wave of respect for the actress. Her mother on the other hand bleated away. 'Our end is near. I can feel it.'

'What she possibly feels is the cholesterol building up inside her heart. Every single time I bring food for Ranjana, she is the one who gobbles it up!' Yatish whispered to Vidya, not feeling charitable towards the meddling mother any longer.

'Call that baba. Only he can save us now. He will have some idea. Call him!' she shrieked hysterically. But it had the opposite effect on her daughter who threw her head back and laughed.

'Of course! Why didn't I think of this before? It's that fraud baba who is behind this.'

Paramveer Khattar shook his head. 'Really? How the hell did you reach that conclusion?'

'It's simple. I'm the only one who didn't fall for his tricks and tales the other day. So, he resorted to this new drama. Plan B!'

Prachand scratched his temple. 'As much as I would like to find an "earthlier" explanation, he hasn't returned since last night. These marks seem to have been made from the outside, if you look closely enough. So, unless he owns an invisibility cloak and has been hovering around surreptitiously outside the house all this while, it doesn't look like he is behind this.'

Ranjana Jha's mother had tuned out of the conversation. 'I better eat one more hearty meal before it's my time. Then I need to speak with my lawyer,' she sniffled melodramatically. 'Ranju, will you please charge my phone? One last time?'

'Just stop! I don't believe in this crap, and neither should you. Fabricated stories are all they are.'

Paramveer Khattar clapped his hands. 'All right. Can everyone please go back down and wrap up dinner?'

The room was soon empty, except Prachand and Vidya who stood by the window. They stared at the hand impressions in silence.

Vidya nudged Prachand. 'What's going on here? How on earth do you explain this?' she said and shivered involuntarily.

Prachand put an arm around her shoulder, drawing her close. 'I really don't know, Viddu. These seem like disconnected incidents, but something tells me they are all little pieces of a much larger picture. I need some time to think, to observe, to make sense of it all.'

'There is indeed one explanation if the locals are to be believed. I ... I never thought I would be saying this, but maybe we have bitten off more than we can chew, Prachand. This mystery seems way beyond the capabilities of Kanpur Khoofiya Pvt Ltd. I have a feeling that we're heading from the frying pan into the fire. In my opinion, we've helped as much as we could and should now prioritize ourselves, Yatish and Chachu. Let's just pack up and go home.' She looked at Prachand searchingly.

'Viddu, have you seen the height at which these palm impressions have appeared?'

'Huh? What are you talking about Prachand?'

'Just look. They are pretty high up.'

Vidya looked at the window and then back at Prachand. 'So what? Ghosts don't need ladders and stools. They can fly, you know.'

'Oh, come on, Viddu. Aren't you even curious? I mean, haven't you wondered whether its paint, why it hasn't been washed off by the rain yet, or whether it could have just been made from the inside by opening a window? If I can just go outside and ...'

'Prachand!' Vidya stood with her hands on her hips. 'Did you register anything I said? I'm talking about leaving and you want to perform a fingerprint analysis while hovering outside a first-floor window! Sometimes there is wisdom in acknowledging that we don't know what we are dealing with. You are not stepping outside, you incorrigible man!'

Before Prachand could respond, Vidya stalked out of the room. On her heels, a cold draft found its way into the room despite the windows being shut, making Prachand shiver. Remembering his cherished Bholenath, he rubbed his hands for some warmth. His rational mind was rejecting the possibility, but he couldn't help but wonder if there was any truth to the stories. He took one last look at the small handprints, which now seemed to be dissolving in the rain, and hurried out of the room.

CHAPTER 23

Aalok Kumar scrutinized his sketch. The last few days had not been easy. Paramveer Khattar's constant interference and Ranjana Jha's grating remarks had made him nervous. But today looked like a good day. The sunshine continued to be timid, but the rain was held in abeyance. He was excited about the scene to be shot, a chase through the woods that he wanted to nail. The world would see his genius one day. Then his diffidence and disability would fade into oblivion and a new, improved version of him would emerge.

He blew some eraser dust from the surface of the paper and stuck it on to the shoot board like a proud father. 'V ... Venky,' he called out to the DOP who was sitting nearby, sipping on his chai. 'We are g ... good to go. L ... let me brief you all and we roll in h ... half an hour.' Venky gave him a thumbs up.

As history has proved many times, all mavericks face stiff resistance when it comes to the execution of their revolutionary ideas. Aalok Kumar was no different. Letting his script evolve and asking the actors to improvise on the set with their dialogues were path-breaking ideas that led to much confusion. While Ranjana Jha was more pliable, at least in front of the camera, he had to work very hard on Vikas Kishen, trying to convince him that his female lead was not Goddess Sita and that her honour would remain unblemished even if he held her by the waist.

Having finished their discussion with the director, Vidya chatted with Padmini Rathod while Chachu Tripathi shared a cup of chai with the other junior actors, who he now referred to as people from 'his industry'. Sauntering about, Prachand bumped into Yatish who seemed to be in a hurry. He had a small white box in his hand.

'What's this?' he asked Yatish out of curiosity.

'Who knows, Prachand Da.'

Prachand took the box from Yatish and turned it around in his hands. It was unmarked, but Prachand had a feeling that he had seen it before.

'Ice cream?' Yatish shrugged. 'I got it from the fridge. You know, she doesn't look too well today. And her mother, who is still alive, is driving her up the wall. Poor thing. She asked me to fetch this from the refrigerator in her room, so I'm taking it to her. Whatever it is, I hope it makes her feel better.'

Prachand smiled at his friend, taking in his small yet determined frame and gleaming eyes. He looked like a man who had found a new purpose in life. 'You've developed quite the fondness for Ms Ranjana Jha in a short period of time, haven't you?'

Yatish smiled bashfully. 'Nothing of the sort, Prachand Da. I'm just helping her. *Kahaan Raja Bhoj, kahaan Gangu Teli*!' he said, patting his friend on the arm as he highlighted the contrast between the two of them. He then headed towards Ranjana Jha's vanity van.

Prachand caught a glimpse of Aalok Kumar's storyboard. He froze. There was something macabre and discomfiting about the one frame that caught his eye. It bore a lifelike resemblance to Ranjana Jha. She was sketched lying on the ground, legs splayed in an awkward manner, mouth agape and eyes like lifeless beads. Her hands clutched at something invisible, making his skin crawl. As Ranjana Jha, in the flesh, walked past him with a curt nod and a flustered Preeti in tow, he collected himself and walked out after her.

The day wore on, the sky turned grey and there was a rumble of thunder in the distance.

Bhutaari Baba was on the set again. He had been informed that the shoot was to take place in the dreaded part of the woods, in the clearing close to the well. '*Ghor anarth hai yeh*!' he announced as the crew cowered in anticipation. Then he looked westwards and pointed to the lighting in the sky. 'A storm is coming.'

'I must say that's a bit obvious,' Vidya muttered and scratched her arm. Seated near the director's monitor, they were being feasted on by mosquitoes and other insects lurking around. The shot in progress was one where Ranjana Jha was having an argument with Vikas Kishen.

Vidya couldn't deny the fact that the woman was striking. Her long and luscious black mane moved theatrically. Vidya's eyes lingered for a little longer on the actress's ample bosom before glancing at her own ruefully.

And then, in the middle of the shot, Ranjana Jha turned pale and gestured for some water. 'C ... cut!' shouted Aalok Kumar and announced a break.

As if on cue, the skies roared their acquiescence. With a crackle of deafening thunder, the clouds gave way. As the rain picked up, the entire unit ran helter-skelter, trying to save papers, equipment, wires and everything else they could.

'I have never seen such a storm in Kuldhara!' Arjun Prajapati huffed, holding an umbrella over Vidya.

'Global warming!' quipped Paramveer Khattar.

Chachu Tripathi offered a scientific explanation. 'First the sun and now the heavy rain can mean only one thing. A witch somewhere is getting married with great pomp and show!'

In about half an hour, the entire unit found itself back in the haveli. Eventually the rain subsided and the sky cleared up, as if to compensate for its aggression. However, with the ground still wet and the crew eager to get to their accommodations lest they get caught in another downpour, the remaining schedule for the day was cancelled, leaving Producer Paramveer Khattar scowling.

Exhausted from the day's events, most people turned in early, but not Prachand. He was restive and lay in the dark, his eyes wide open and his ears picking up every sound—a moving utensil, a closing door or the supressed murmurs that drifted into the room.

Oscillating between disturbed sleep and wakefulness, at some point he thought he heard raised voices. He ignored them thinking they were part of a dream.

Sometime later, his ears perked up to a sound that woke him up completely. He walked to the window and squinted into the dark. A figure was hotfooting it towards the gate to the right of the haveli. A flash of striking white as the figure turned made its identity patently clear. It was Bhutaari Baba. With no clue as to why the man was sneaking about in the dead of the night, Prachand pressed his head, realizing that a headache was settling in. It was exhausting and troublesome to think of the list of people he needed to keep an eye on. He decided to rest his weary head on the pillow, eventually drifting off to sleep, oblivious to the fact that everything was about to change.

CHAPTER 24

The banging on the door wouldn't stop. After the fitful sleep he had had, Prachand didn't budge. Vidya stumbled to the door, her heart racing and her mouth shooting sleepy invectives at whoever was behind the racket. She reached for the light switch, but there was no electricity. Her mobile phone told her it was five in the morning.

Dinanath Tripathi stood at the door with an ashen-faced Yatish next to him. Someone was shouting instructions further down the corridor.

'What's going on, Chachu? Has the electricity gone?' Vidya asked, fiddling with the switchboard next to the door.

Dinanath Tripathi nodded slowly. 'Yes. And so has Ranjana Jha.'

Vidya moved her hand away from the switchboard and stared at him. 'Huh?'

'She has disappeared,' Yatish said in a broken voice.

Prachand, who was wide awake by now, rushed to the door. 'Ranjana Jha is missing?'

'Yes. Her mother was tired so she went to bed early. When she woke up to go to the washroom, she realized that Ranjana wasn't in the room and raised an alarm.'

Prachand's brows were knitted, trying to remember when he had last seen the actress. It had to be at the shoot. But where could she have gone in the dark? His eyes darted to his poor friend who bore the signs of someone who had suffered a personal tragedy. 'Are you all right, Yatish? When did you see her last?'

'At the shoot. Then the scramble in the rain distracted me. I thought she was in her room and would eat upstairs like she usually does,' he said and bit his lip. 'I should have stayed with her.'

Dinanath Tripathi regarded the young man with dismay. 'I see that a few days in her company have already turned you into a love sick puppy. Stop this melodrama and invest your energy in helping Prachand locate her.'

Chastised, Yatish smacked his forehead. 'I forgot why we came here. Paramveer Khattar is requesting for you to come down.'

The mood in the sitting room was sombre, with candlelights and shadows playing hopscotch on the walls and the furniture. Paramveer Khattar was pacing up and down, smoking his pipe. Ramnarayan Rathod's expression was inscrutable as he sat in his favourite fauteuil-styled chair, almost consumed by it.

Vidya went and sat beside Ranjana Jha's mother who was whimpering on the diwan. 'Auntie, don't worry. We will find her.'

The moaning only grew louder. 'It's my fault. She wasn't feeling well all day. I should have kept an eye on her.' Her voice was heavy with regret.

On seeing Prachand, Paramveer Khattar placed his pipe on the table and covered the distance between them in a few long strides. Prachand noticed that his boots were muddy. Paramveer Khattar ran a hand through his hair, which had gone limp just like the general mood. He was clearly shaken by the turn of events. 'I know this is asking for much more than you promised, but could you please help us in this search? I've sent for a few more men. We can break out in batches to look for Ranjana.' It was odd hearing him use a first-person reference instead of the caustic 'Ms Jha' he usually reserved for her. 'We could really use your … skills in this situation.'

'Of course, I'll help. Has the haveli been searched properly?'

'Every nook and cranny. That's what we've been doing since the last half an hour. When her mother came to me, I wanted to be sure before raising an alarm.'

'And you've tried calling her?'

Paramveer Khattar nodded. 'Several times. Her phone is switched off. But that just might be the network. You know how it is.'

'Are there any homes, rest houses, or any other such place where she could have sought shelter at night, in case she stepped out for a walk and lost her way?' Prachand's mind was whirring with possibilities, but he was determined to keep his thinking methodical and structured.

'Nothing for five to six miles, except a hut nearby. No one would want to walk that far. In the other direction are the woods and the ruins. Why on earth would she step out in the dark?'

'That's the thing. Maybe she wasn't thinking clearly,' Prachand explained and then turned to her whimpering mother. 'You said she wasn't feeling well?'

The mother blew her nose noisily. 'She was looking a bit pale since lunch. Perhaps she should have eaten something more substantial before ...' she stopped talking and looked a bit red in the face.

'Auntie,' Vidya prodded her. 'You can speak freely. It will only help your daughter.' But the lady refused to say more.

Ramnarayan Rathod thundered from his chair. 'Speak up! I command you to. I don't want anyone harmed under my roof.'

Paramveer Khattar reached out and placed a firm hand on his friend's shoulder. 'Don't worry. We will find her. We have Prachand Tripathi with us.'

Prachand squirmed and turned his attention to the distraught mother. 'Mataji, please talk to me,' he pleaded.

'My Ranju is severely diabetic. She needs insulin shots. It's something she wanted to keep a secret because this industry is full of vultures who are always ready to use any sign of weakness against women. She was refused many opportunities in the past as no one wanted a liability on their hands. She then decided to keep this information to herself,' she said and threw an accusatory glance in Paramveer Khattar's direction. 'That's why she wanted to avoid the greasy, unhealthy meals on set.' Sniffling again, she added, 'My brave bachcha. You must find her!' she implored Prachand. He patted her hand reassuringly.

'Mr Khattar, there is no time to waste. She might be unwell and unable to contact us. Let's hurry,' Prachand said and turned around. And then he remembered. 'One quick question. Did anyone hear an argument late last night?'

Prachand noticed the furtive glance Ramnarayan Rathod darted his way but there were other urgent matters to attend to.

Two teams were formed. Padmini Rathod offered to stay with Ranjana's mother. Ramnarayan Rathod objected when Vidya started to wear her shoes. 'She can stay with the women,' he said.

Before Vidya could launch herself at the puny man, Prachand intervened. 'She is extremely proficient in these matters. Trust me. We need her.' Ramnarayan Rathod did not look very convinced but nodded. Vidya grinned at Prachand and he winked back.

The earth felt mushy under their feet. Phones and torches punctuated the dark like restless fireflies in pursuit of something unknown. The air was rent with Ranjana's name being called out repeatedly. Prachand and Arjun Prajapati decided to head into the forest.

Arjun Prajapati hung on to Prachand's arm like his prom date. He looked around with trepidation and jumped at every sound. An owl hooted its displeasure as the flashlight hit the branch where it sat surveying the forest. 'Prachand Sa, please don't let go.'

'I couldn't if I tried, Arjunji,' muttered Prachand as he felt the other man's nails dig into his skin. 'Can you please just walk ahead while I check this path? If we are glued to each other, we won't cover much ground,' Prachand tried to reason.

It had only been a few minutes of separation when he heard a screech. He would have passed it off as an angry owl when he heard another scream, calling out to him. Prachand ran towards the sound as fast as his legs could carry him down the slippery path.

'Here, here! She's here!' the voice called out. This could only mean that Ranjana Jha had been found. Feeling a big weight lift off his chest, Prachand reached a clearing amid the trees where he could see Arjun Prajapati standing still, torchlight in hand.

He stood catching his breath for a few seconds, remembering how Vidya would berate him for eating unhealthy food and never exercising. 'Where is she?' he inquired, looking in the direction of Arjun Prajapati's raised arm.

A few feet away, a motionless figure lay sprawled on the ground. He walked ahead even as every instinct in his body told him to run in the other direction. All Prachand could hear was the deafening sound of his own heart. Finally, he stopped and peered into the lifeless face of Ranjana Jha, her mouth open and her eyes staring into the night.

CHAPTER 25

Naveli Haveli, in its dilapidated state, was unlike the other better-preserved vestiges of Rajasthan's history, but it shared a common feature with them—its walls. They were a medley of brick, sandstone, marble, wood, plaster and granite that insulated the interiors from the onslaught of the winds both during the summer and the winter. However, on a quiet and grey morning, after the discovery of Ranjana Jha's body, it seemed like the early winter chill had penetrated into this defence and eviscerated the natural warmth within, freezing every heart with cold foreboding.

A light fog had moved in from the direction of the ruins. Piercing through this curtain came a police jeep, making its way through the muddy driveway with some difficulty. Ramnarayan Rathod was the one who had made the call to the police, to a special contact who had recently been transferred out but had promised to inform the new officer in-charge immediately.

Five officers emerged from the dirt-streaked car. Two khakhi-clad men, one broad and burly and the other with a bit of a pot belly, made their way to the main entrance where Prachand, Vidya and Paramveer Khattar stood in a neat row, like schoolchildren awaiting a nail inspection. Prachand glanced at Paramveer Khattar. His hands, crossed behind his back, were twitching, his pampered hair was plastered against his sweaty forehead and his demeanour was reminiscent of a cornered wild animal. Prachand found this peculiar.

As the officers climbed the few steps to the main entrance, Ramnarayan Rathod joined the line-up with his usual aura of insolence, head cocked like he was sniffing something unpleasant. 'Which one of you is Senior Inspector Gupta?' he demanded.

'That would be me.' The men stepped aside and gave way to a young lady dressed in a khakhi uniform. She had a petite frame, but there was something in her manner and the set expression on her face that made her look competent and reliable. She nodded at Ramnarayan Rathod and Paramveer Khattar. Both of them looked at her with distaste and disbelief evident on their faces. Prachand noticed the three stars on her shoulder.

She took off her cap and stuck it under her arm, revealing tightly slicked back hair ending in a curly bun. Removing the cap had let loose spring-like tendrils of hair that framed her face like a desi Medusa. She smoothed them down while taking note of Prachand and Vidya standing nearby. Her eyes lingered for a little longer on Prachand but then moved back to Ramnarayan Rathod.

'I am Maya Gupta, the investigating officer, and I request your full cooperation,' she said.

Ramnarayan Rathod gave her a once-over, his eyes lingering on her breasts, and snorted. 'I didn't ask for ladies. Go and get your superior. I want the best person in Jaisalmer on this case.'

Prachand studied her face for any obvious signs of anger or distress. He detected none. Either she was thick-skinned and extremely professional or the newest find for Bollywood's Next Top Actress would come from the police cadre in Rajasthan. Her eyes scanned the area as she replied, courteous but firm. 'I'm all you get at the moment, Sir. I am the officer in-charge here. Don't bother wasting your time by calling my superiors. No one wants to come here. Trust me.'

Vidya looked at the young lady in awe. She couldn't be very old, but the steel in her voice and her body language made it pretty clear that she was not to be toyed with. Ramnarayan Rathod seemed to understand this and gave her a perfunctory nod. He introduced everyone, and then Prachand, right at the end.

She seemed to bristle imperceptibly as Prachand greeted her with folded hands. 'Oh! So, you're him. The famous Mr Prachand Tripathi.' Something told Prachand that this statement wasn't intended entirely as a compliment. He nodded politely. The way her husband was being scrutinied made Vidya want to protectively hold his hand, but the officer seemed to be done for the time being. She turned to address Paramveer Khattar, the man she had been told was in charge.

'Who was the first person to see the body?'

'Arjun Prajapati,' replied Paramveer Khattar. 'I'm the executive producer of the film she was acting in. Arjun has been with this family for many years. He is His Royalness's personal assistant.'

Inspector Gupta nodded and greeted him back. 'Who is he and where is he?'

'Arjun Prajapati?'

'No. His Royal ... what was that?'

Ramnarayan Rathod cleared his throat and spoke haughtily. 'That would be me. I'm the descendant of the ...'

'Ah, okay,' she said dismissively. 'And the other chap?'

'He must be inside helping Padminiji,' said Vidya, pointing towards the door. 'I'm Prachand's wife and a partner at Kanpur Khoofiya Pvt Ltd,' she added with an air of importance in response to the inspector's eyebrow raised in inquiry.

'Thank you,' said Inspector Gupta and then turned to the other officers. 'Sarthy, take Ramsingh and Hiren and secure the crime scene while I get some details here. Brijesh, where is the medical examiner and photographer?'

Brijesh looked amused. 'Madamji, what medical examiner? Here we catch hold of doctors on duty at the government hospitals and get them to help if a case demands it.'

Inspector Gupta wasn't impressed. 'And what about the crime scene photographer?'

Brijesh shrugged. 'We don't have one specifically for the department, but there is a part-timer we outsource sometimes. I called him, but he refused to come at this hour. When I threatened him, he said he had to drop his daughter to school and then pick up some groceries before heading to work. All because his wife is visiting her parents. Poor fellow,' he said, shaking his head empathetically as someone who had experienced a similar predicament.

'I don't remember asking for his horoscope or his family chart.' Her eyes flashed with irritation. 'Get him here quickly. And I need to talk to this ... Arjun Prajapati and whoever else has seen the body till now.'

'I have.' Prachand raised his hand like a schoolboy.

Inspector Gupta smoothed her hair down and put her cap back on. 'I'm not surprised,' she quipped.

Prachand had no idea why she was being hostile towards him. He could see the agitation on Vidya's face as well. Without waiting for her to say something unsavoury, he rubbed her arm. 'Don't react, Viddu. It's okay. It's a tense situation,' he said to his wife and then turned to the inspector. 'I'm happy to talk.'

'Wait. You can come with me to the crime scene,' she said. Then she asked Vidya, 'Can you first take me to Arjun Prajapati?'

Later, as three policemen headed into the forest, guided by a very reluctant watchman, Prachand stood at the door watching everyone. He felt numb despite the involuntary shudder that coursed through his body. Try as he might, he couldn't forget the lifeless form of Ranjana Jha and how it reminded him of Aalok Kumar's almost prescient storyboard sketch. Or, for that matter, the inconsolable and wretched sobs from her mother. It made him very sad and remember his own mother and her ageing, animated face, longing to be back in the warmth of her embrace and his home. What he had to contend with for now was the chill seeping into his bones, a body lying nearby and a restless owl hooting into the morning, something that he had been told as a child was a bad omen.

CHAPTER 26

Maya Gupta had not lived an easy life. Being the eldest of three daughters in a conservative Bania family had ensured that everything came rationed, be it clothes, textbooks, food and even love. Her father, who was the personal assistant of a local politician, had married off his two younger daughters but could not prevail upon his stubborn oldest daughter who had barely made the cut for the state-level police entrance exams. Had it not been for the calming influence of her uncle, who was a well-respected local doctor and her idol, she would have ended up a bigger rebel. She didn't know the meaning of giving up and it was this stubbornness that had helped her navigate discrimination, jibes, ridicule and bigoted social conventions. She had made her peace with the fact that her recent transfer was a punishment posting for taking up the cudgels against a rogue politician, but she planned to make the most of it. She would be damned if she let a century-old curse and some oily haired detective take the credit for solving what was a rare crime in these parts.

She stood at the crime scene with a notepad and pen, scribbling furiously. She had been trained to trust her instinct while following due process and noting each detail. Every few seconds she would find Prachand inching closer to the body and reprimand him. He was inspecting the dead woman's arm when she decided she had had enough. 'You step away from that body right now,' she said sternly.

Prachand apologized and complied. Inspector Gupta turned her attention to her colleague. 'Brijesh, did you check the area? Any eyewitnesses? Someone who heard something, saw something?'

Her colleague, who was smoking nearby, stubbed out his cigarette and came running to her. 'No, Madamji. Everyone keeps away from this area. You know that. There are only a few *kacha* houses a little distance away.'

'Well, I still want you to go to each and every house.' Her eyes flickered back to see if Prachand was following her orders. They moved back to Brijesh. 'Why is the photographer still not here? Is this a bloody joke? I'm not inviting him for lunch. A woman has been murdered,' she said.

'Madamji, you know how things work here. Plus, the rain last night didn't help,' he said with a shrug.

'Well, keep trying!' she said. Tucking her unruly curls back under her cap, Inspector Gupta squatted next to the body. 'No signs of a struggle. No scratches or bruises,' she noted, craning her neck to get a closer look at Ranjana Jha's face but lost her balance staring into her eyes.

Prachand rushed forward. 'Are you okay?'

Inspector Gupta was up in an instant. 'Yes. I'm fine. I've seen my share of bodies, but the eyes always get to me. It feels as if they are gazing into your very soul.' She realized that she was getting chatty and turned her attention back to the body. 'No defensive wounds,' she said and inspected the fingernails on both hands with the end of her pen. 'Her artificial nails are still intact.'

Her colleague nodded, looking mighty impressed.

'And it seems she has some sort of injury on the back of her head, possibly from falling. There's dried blood if I'm not mistaken,' she continued and then straightened herself, scribbling the whole time. Walking over to the other side, she said, 'See the ground here? It's still wet. The only footprint I can see looks like a woman's. Has to be hers. But let's check the entire area. It's private property, so there can't be many people traipsing through, though there is an open passage from the direction of the ruins.' She pointed to the ground. 'Can you lift this impression, Brijesh?'

Brijesh came forward heroically and tried to scrape the mud below the footprint.

She lunged forward and whacked his hand. 'Are you crazy, Brijesh? Have you ever been on a crime scene? I didn't ask you to claw at it like free halwa but to get an impression taken.'

'Sorry, Madamji. I thought I'll transfer the entire patch on to a thick sheet of paper or cardboard.'

'No. If it dries and crumbles, we will have nothing. Place some box over it for now and get someone to come and make a mould of it.' Taking in Brijesh's expression, she added, 'Now don't tell me you have no one for that job. Figure it out. Be innovative, but don't destroy it.'

Prachand, meanwhile, had walked over to the well. It was the kind that didn't protrude above the ground. A low circumference of discoloured, broken bricks girdled the earth. A gnarly banyan tree stood protectively over it, regarding Prachand with suspicion. He peeped into the well. 'This has to be one of the largest and deepest ones I've ever seen,' he said. His comment did not elicit a response from the inspector. 'Jai ... jai ... jai ... Bhole ... Bhole ...' his voice echoed, ricocheting within the confines of the well. The juvenile smile that appeared fleetingly on his face disappeared the instant he noticed Inspector Gupta's expression.

Staring at the ground, he noticed something. 'There is one clear shoe print here.' This got her attention.

Inspector Gupta carefully walked around to where he stood and frowned. 'Stop walking all over the place. This could even be your print.

'No, it isn't,' he said, raising one of his Bata sandals up. 'This is from some tapered, formal shoe. Like someone wore the wrong footwear in the wrong place. Besides, the entire crew was beyond the trees over there. People are fearful of this spot, so no one comes this far. Also, this print looks fresh. Someone must have stood here for a few minutes for this deep an impression. I bet ghosts don't care much for fashion or footwear.'

Inspector Gupta looked at him with a curious expression, assessing him. There was no spark of triumph or one-upmanship. Warm, earnest brown eyes stared back at her.

'Yes, I've heard about the mother and child. I had a hard time forcing my own unit to show up here. They're walking on eggshells.' She looked sideways at one of the constables who had a rudraksh mala twisted around his fingers for protection and was glancing around nervously. She instructed Brijesh to get the shoeprint collected.

Prachand nodded. 'I know what you mean. May I add something?' Since her expression was a little less militant than before, he continued without waiting for a response. 'Ranjana Jha did not plan to be out here.'

'What does that mean? She couldn't have floated here.'

'What I mean is that she may have walked here, but she didn't intend to go for a walk. No walking shoes, a flimsy T-shirt and pyjamas, no warm jacket despite the cool weather, and no rain gear. I don't like speaking ill of the dead, but she did seem a bit high-maintenance. She wouldn't just leave for a walk without being mindful of her attire. She might have come here in a hurry, or at someone's behest? Perhaps she wanted to get away from something, or someone, in the house?'

'Hmm. Food for thought.'

Prachand raised a finger like an obedient pupil. Inspector Gupta nodded for him to continue.

'The way a body falls is very telling. I remember how my Gunni Chachi doubled over when she ate something poisonous and fainted. You see, if your body is racked with pain, you assume the foetal position.' He bent over to make his point. 'Ranjanaji's body doesn't look contorted. It's almost as if she just dropped to the ground. What we ... I mean you, need to figure out is why?'

Inspector Gupta looked at Prachand with some grudging respect and then leaned in, ensuring none of her officers were within earshot. 'Look, let me be very clear. I don't care what hotshot detective you are or what connections you might have. This is my case and I won't take any meddling.'

Prachand tried to protest, but she silenced him with her hand.

'However, you seem like you might be able to help me, and I will need it given the resources and team at my disposal,' she said rolling her eyes. 'So, will you help me without being a nuisance?'

Prachand responded with a wide grin. 'Absolutely, Guptaji. Nothing would make me happier.'

Their conversation was interrupted by a commotion and voices floating in from the direction of the haveli. They sped out of the clearing through the passage of trees to witness a peculiar sight. A little distance away stood a short man with a bag hung over his shoulder. He seemed to be in an argument with one of the constables while the rest of the men were trying to control the large camel that stood by, moving unsteadily on the wet earth.

'Is that a ...' Prachand couldn't hold back the gleam of childlike excitement in his eyes that were only used to the sight of dogs, cows and monkeys.

'Camel.' Inspector Gupta's face was impassive, belonging to someone who had braved much absurdity in life and was now beyond it. 'Yes, that is a camel standing on my crime scene,' she said and walked up to one of the officers. 'Sarthy, what is going on?'

'Madamji, this is Ginni,' he said stroking the camel.

'I can see that. What are Ginni and her companion doing here?'

'He is Natwar, the photographer.'

Natwar bowed low. 'Khammagani!'

'Is there any reason why this camel has joined the investigation, or is this part of some local tradition?'

'Madamji, my brother-in-law runs a tourist camp in the desert. My scooter broke down. Since it was an emergency, he lent me Ginni. I took a shortcut through the desert to get here.' Natwar looked proud of his quick thinking.

Inspector Gupta sighed and glanced at Prachand. 'I'll be taking some statements after this ... this circus is done with. Let's connect later.'

'Sure.' Prachand nodded. 'You might also want to talk to Bhutaari Baba, the tantric. He hangs around for good luck on the set. I saw him creeping out of the gate late last night. He was the one who told Ranjana that she was in danger a few days ago.'

'Tantric, huh? And I thought I had seen enough bizarre things during my last posting in Jabalpur.' She shook her head and added, 'I'll check up on this baba.' She turned and walked back towards the forest with the photographer and her team as Ginni chewed on something invisible, giving Prachand a doleful look. Prachand's thoughts went back to Hirwa and he felt another pang of homesickness.

Walking back to the haveli, he realized that he was shivering underneath his thin cotton kurta when someone roughly pulled him to one side. The man's hand jerked up instinctively as he peered at Aalok Kumar. His placid face had given way to a tormented one with chewed-up red lips, puffy eyes and dishelleved hair.

'What is it, Aalok? Are you okay?'

'You ... you ... h ... have to help me. P ... please. I think I murdered Ranjana Jha.'

CHAPTER 27

Confessions were Prachand's bane. And they came from all quarters. Even his second-grade teacher had confessed to him about stealing from the school canteen. To this day, he was unclear about what prompted people to spill the beans before him. From insidious crimes to lonely warbles, he was a magnet for all those who felt repentant. While he was happy to help, sometimes he hoped that these people would go to their grandmothers, local priests or barbers.

This was one of those days. There was a police team on the premises, and his own crew and colleagues, yet Aalok Kumar chose to sniff out the reticent detective from Gwaltoli to confess to his alleged crime. Prachand regarded him warily as they stood chatting discreetly behind the haveli. The director was pacing around like a caged animal, narrating his apprehensions to Prachand.

'Were you upset with how she treated you on the set?' Prachand inquired, watching Aalok intently. According to Prachand, facial expressions were an inbuilt lie detector.

Twitches, tremors and the eyes could tell a tale that a person might be unwilling to divulge in words. But other than the fact that he was extremely agitated and nervous, Prachand's instinct, something he relied on heavily, told him that the man before him was either no murderer, despite what he believed or that he was as proficient an actor as a director.

Aalok narrated the sequence of events with a haunted look in his eyes. 'It was getting d ... dark when I started walking into the forest.'

'What time was this? Prachand asked.

'I can't b ... be sure, but it was later than my usual time. I think it was ap ... pproximately seven thirty in the evening.'

'So, you left at seven thirty, went past the clearing where the well is and heard a noise, correct?'

'Yes. I ... I've had a feeling for these last few days that I'm being followed when I head out for walks. You know that f ... f ... eeling? Of being watched?'

Prachand nodded, hoping the guilty crimson rising to his cheeks would pass unnoticed. The stalker in question would have to be Yatish.

'Just when I passed the clearing, I heard a s ... s ... sound.'

'Like a scream?'

'No.' Aalok tapped his head as if trying to spill a sharper memory. 'I can't really tell. Just a loud indecipherable sound. I felt that I was in danger, so I picked up a large rock, hurled it in the direction of the sound and bolted without looking back.' Here, his eyes became bulbous, like an owl hunting for some juicy bugs.

Prachand backed away a couple of steps. 'And?'

'And that's how I k ... k ... killed her.'

'That's your assumption, Aalok? That your rock killed her? Did you hear a scream or the sound of the rock hitting something?'

'Well, she was found dead right there. I haven't seen the body, but there are rumours that there is a head wound. Am I right?'

Prachand nodded cautiously. 'There might be,' he said, unwilling to divulge any details of an ongoing police investigation.

'There you have it! I'm going to jail. No m ... movies, no career, just a criminal record. My parents will come to jail, celebrate their final victory and say "we told you so"! Who will feed Meow? My f ... f ... friend is looking after her for now, but once he hears that I'm a criminal he will throw her out on the street,' Aalok Kumar moaned and squatted on the ground.

Prachand placed a hand on his shoulder. 'I can understand that you are concerned about Meow, but I think you should bother about your future first. Let's go over a few things.'

Aalok Kumar straightened up and wiped his runny nose on his sleeve like a flu-ridden toddler.

'Pick up a rock that resembles the one you threw into the clearing.'

Aalok Kumar looked around and retrieved a broken brick lying nearby. 'I would say s ... s ... something like this in weight. But it was a rock, not a brick.'

'Now throw it the way you did yesterday. Try and match the angle and swing of your arm.' Prachand walked some steps in the opposite direction, halted and then turned around. 'This is the approximate distance between where you say you stood and where she was found. Now throw it.'

Aalok awkwardly moved the brick from one hand to the other before hurling it in Prachand's direction. It fell right next to Prachand's foot. He looked at Aalok curiously. 'It could have reached her all right, but I have my doubts if it killed her.'

For the first time since they started speaking, Aalok Kumar didn't look as despondent. 'You think I have a ch … ch … chance? That I might not really have k … killed her?'

Prachand had no ready answers. Could this man be pretending to confess, only to confuse him? 'Can you please tell me why you go into the woods every evening? Is it really to get some air, or …'

Aalok Kumar's double chin became more pronounced as he lowered his head and stared at his shuffling feet. 'I … it's personal. But … I pr … promise it has nothing to do with anyone else. Or Ranjana Jha.'

'Surely she was a difficult person to work with?'

'My m … mother is the most difficult person to live with. D … does that mean I'll get rid of her? Though I must say that the thought has crossed my mind.'

Prachand noticed how strange he looked during this contemplation. And then his facial features crumpled again. 'Will you help me figure out if I k … killed the actress? Do your detective thingey, you know.'

'The inspector in charge, Maya Gupta, seems like a competent and reasonable woman. I can speak with her on your behalf.'

'No, no, no! You don't understand. If there is a slight chance of my being innocent, I can have my life b … back. If the police get involved, my n ... name and reputation will be besmirched irrevocably.'

Prachand found this line of reasoning to be a bit extreme, but he let the director's paranoia slide.

'Aalok, I can keep an eye out for you, but the police will question you eventually. I suggest that you tell them everything without claiming that you're the murderer, of course. Let them investigate.'

As a distraught Aalok walked away after thanking him, Prachand felt uneasy, as he always did with concealed information. At least he had a human stepping in as a suspect instead of an invisible foe. Was he in some way helping shield a potential murderer? What about the sketch on Aalok's storyboard? Diabetes, ghosts and now a nervous young man were in the suspicion pool. As Prachand tossed around these odd possibilities in his mind, he had an intense urge to see his wife and confidante who was always brimming with sage advice.

CHAPTER 28

'I think we should be transparent with our family about what's going on, Prachi. Ma has been insisting on a video call with the actors for days now. I can't keep avoiding her.'

'That's the worst advice you've ever given, Viddu!' The thought of his mother's stagy and emotionally charged response and his father's bellicose attitude over the most minor of infractions left Prachand more horrified than the ghost stories that pickled every single conversation in Kuldhara.

'Prachi, they have a right to know if we are in trouble.'

'We are not in trouble. We are only going to help with ...'

'I knew it! You're going to poke your long nose into this investigation, aren't you? I've also noticed you prattling on with that lady officer and the way she looks at you.'

'Viddu, we don't chat about camel rides. There is a murder to solve. It's always good to have the police on your side. She trusts my point of view, so I've agreed to be involved only in an advisory capacity. The quicker this is resolved, the faster we can go home.'

Vidya didn't look impressed. 'Helping is one thing, but we are not being paid a dime for it. Now you've gone ahead and become privy to the confession of a possible suspect. He wasn't confessing about having stolen some money from his mother's *aate ka dabba* but about killing a woman. Guilty or not, you have no business getting involved, Prachi. *Baura gaye ho kya*!'

Their conversation was cut short by Inspector Gupta striding out of the room on the ground floor that was being used for interrogation. A tense Vikas Kishen followed her, gulping a glass of water. While Maya Gupta scanned some sort of list in her hand, he walked unsteadily to where Prachand and Vidya sat.

'I swear to God, I felt like fabricating something just to give her any useful information. She's scary!'

Dinanath Tripathi and Yatish joined them, too, holding transparent tumblers of tea. 'You bet!' Yatish expostulated, his eyes red and puffy. 'She made it sound like I had a love child with Ranjanaji. How will I not stutter when she takes my genuine affection and moulds it into some sordid love affair gone sour! I mean, Ranjanaji wouldn't let me near her anyway!'

The others were confused about whether Yatish was lamenting the police interrogation or the disinterest from his amour.

Dinbandhu Tripathi was despondent. His mind had other peas to shell. 'This was my one chance. To escape that smell of leather, to escape the shop and even Bhaisaab's barbs about my acting chops. Death had to sink its icy talons into my dreams.'

'Seems as if you're more bothered about this movie than the fact that a young woman has lost her life,' said Inspector Gupta, suddenly appeared behind him.

Dinanath Tripathi aged about ten years in an instant and abandoned his tea on a side table. 'I did not kill that poor child, Madamji. In fact, I was one of the few people who liked her. She had her airs, but her acting was decent. I've watched some of her films and she was ... is ... I mean, was ... quite talented.'

The inspector looked amused at the ramblings of the old man. 'I'm sure,' she said and went back to her list. 'I need to speak with Paramveer Khattar next.'

Paramveer Khattar's customary whites looked like they had missed an ironing appointment. He looked jittery.

'Are you all right?' Inspector Gupta asked him without a trace of concern in her voice. If anything, she was observing him.

'Yes, Inspector.' He nodded, and forced a smile. 'Thank you for accepting my request to conduct the interviews here rather than at the police station. We don't really need the negative press.'

'I represent the dead and not production houses, so my loyalties only lie with the people who can't be present to tell their side of the story. But you needn't worry too much. Your father is doing his bit by pulling strings remotely. Short of taping people's mouths shut, plenty has been done to keep this under wraps,' she said, her voice laced with contempt.

Paramveer Khattar remained composed but hurriedly changed the topic. 'Is it really necessary to conduct such an intensive investigation when it is obvious that the poor girl died because she had a diabetes problem? Perhaps she fainted and hit her head.'

Inspector Gupta's gaze was piercing enough to burn a hole through his kurta. 'Wow! You seem updated. How did you know about the head wound?'

Paramveer Khattar's mouth opened and shut like a breathless fish, trying to formulate a response. 'Word gets around, Madam. I have a lot of people here under my employ.'

She regarded him for a moment. 'I am not at liberty to share my assumptions about the cause of death at the moment. The body has been sent for an autopsy, which is always the case in medico-legal deaths, where a person has died without the presence of any witnesses and where a medical officer has not been present to determine the cause of death. So, we cannot assume anything at this point.'

She then turned to everyone gathered in the sitting room, including Ramnarayan Rathod and Padmini who had just entered. 'Since most of the crew was already in their guest houses when the deceased was alive, they are out of the perimeter of our investigation. But they will still be questioned. However, I request each and every person present in and around the haveli since day before night to remain here till the initial investigation is complete. To leave the property, you must take my permission. I hope everyone will abide by these rules.'

Ramnarayan Rathod arched an eyebrow and banged the stick he always carried as a fashion statement. 'This is ridiculous! I refuse to let me, my wife or my guests be subjected to this shoddy criminal-like treatment. Do your job and stop bothering us.'

Inspector Gupta spoke in a clipped voice. 'This isn't your durbar that you can order me around, Sir. I am the investigating officer and it will serve you well to abide by my instructions. I have already been informed that this case is "sensitive," and if you feel like kicking up dust and media attention, I'm more than happy to oblige.'

The puny man and his curly haired adversary stared each other down. Inspector Gupta continued with her charge. 'Do you have an alibi for the night of the murder?'

Ramnarayan Rathod looked like he was controlling himself with much effort. 'Yes, Madam Inspector! I was with my wife. Why don't you just check with her? What else do you want to know? The colour of my underwear?'

Padmini stepped in. 'Yes, Inspector Sahiba. We were together,' she said and then placed a hand on her husband's shoulder. 'Rajaji, the sooner she finishes her job the sooner we can get on with our lives. Aren't you the one always telling me not to let emotions impede our thinking?' She smiled at him ingratiatingly, diffusing the tension as he nodded and tweaked his moustache with pride.

'Yes, you're right.' He flicked his hand and smiled at the inspector. 'This might actually be fun. I've never had any woman question me. About anything. Please find me when you're ready with your twenty questions.' He chuckled and walked away as Inspector Gupta nodded at Padmini Rathod.

'After Paramveer Khattar and Ramnarayan Rathod, I'll be speaking with Venky and Ranjana Jha's mother. Then Mrs Padmini Rathod,' Inspector Gupta announced.

'Poor Mrs Jha. She hasn't left her room and is inconsolable, blaming the curse and Mahua and her child for her daughter's death. I'll try and prepare her for your conversation,' Vidya offered.

Inspector Gupta thanked her and then asked after a pause. 'Mahua?'

'Yes. The mother who accidentally fell into the well with her child. They both perished there. A few days ago, a child's bloody handprint appeared in the window of their room. It's supposed to signify death. Bhutaari Baba had cautioned her as well.'

'Now how on earth do I summon a ghost for interrogation!' Inspector Gupta mumbled. 'Sarthy!' she hollered. Did you find this Bhutaari Baba?'

'No, Madamji. I have checked everywhere. No one seems to have seen him.'

'Well, keep looking.'

Before heading into the room, she paused and gestured for Prachand to join her. 'I'm heading for the autopsy tomorrow morning. Would you like to come?'

Prachand nodded with enthusiasm. 'Absolutely. Thank you!'

His smile disappeared the instant he noticed his wife hovering near the staircase, shooting him a murderous look.

CHAPTER 29

From the police jeep, Prachand watched in fascination as the undulating, sandy ocean stretched as far as his eyes could see. The infinite expanse was dotted by low and barren hills, locally referred to as *bhakars*. It was the first time he had seen the desert at such close range. It seemed to radiate a life of its own, a harsh habitat that the locals had carved their lives around like an accommodating river around a resolute landform. Every few miles, a cluster of mud and brick houses would emerge, with old men puffing away at their *chillums*. When they stopped at a shop to get a bottle of water, Prachand savoured the distinct smell of frying onions and charred bajre ki rotis wafting out from a window nearby. It was too early in the day to be thinking of food, but his stomach grumbled. He was craving a fresh roti with ghee and gur, just like the ones he ate back home.

He had been riding with the police driver in the front till Inspector Gupta decided to drive. She was unlike any police officer he had interacted with; with an air of confidence and unflappable calm about her.

Inspector Gupta caught him staring and raised an eyebrow. He smiled. 'I hope I didn't offend you. I tend to stare when I'm thinking.'

Inspector Gupta kept her eyes on the road. 'What are you thinking?'

'I'm trying to read you,' Prachand said with a shrug.

'I've heard that about you. Come on. Let me see how well you can figure me out.'

Prachand resisted, but relented when she kept insisting. 'You pay great attention to detail and you're authoritative,' he said. 'These are skills acquired through observation and influence, not just through police training. This could have come from someone you admired very much at home. I sense a male influence. Possibly your father or uncle. But you don't smile much. This could mean you had strict parents.'

He glanced at her impassive profile and continued. 'You detest people who use clout and influence, which could mean that you've been at the receiving end of unfair decisions. You don't trust easily and you're a micromanager, which means you've seen a fair number of hardships at a young age and have had to fight for everything you have, be it at home or at work. You were either married or engaged at some point, but it didn't materialize,' Prachand said with a glance at Inspector Gupta's ring finger on the steering wheel.

She instinctively rubbed her middle finger against her empty one, something she did often. 'And you hate your hair,' Prachand concluded.

Inspector Gupta betrayed a smile. 'Fine. You're not bad. But what makes you think I hate my hair?'

'You're very rough with it and keep it hidden. You wear your police cap more than any other officer I've ever seen.

Women, in general, tend to hate headgear as it messes with their hair.'

'You're right. I hate it. It's a liability and I hate anything that entails a fuss. Given a chance, I'd go bald. I was fortunate enough to train under an officer who taught me much of what I know. He also cautioned me against letting physical attributes affect me. Only then could I keep my focus. Plus, my uncle, who was a big influence in my life, was a pathologist who dabbled in autopsies. I heard so much about dead bodies as a child that I grew up with a macabre and colourless outlook, not bothering with girly inclinations and indulgences. Those were the influencers you made guesses about. As for my father, the less said the better.'

Prachand sensed her reluctance to volunteer more and changed the topic. 'You know, Guptaji, Viddu, I mean Vidya, my wife, also believes in being as natural as possible. She is smart, intelligent and empathetic, the perfect woman really. And she's so beautiful that she doesn't ...' his voice trailed off as he realized that he was being excessively chatty.

Inspector Gupta continued staring at the road. 'It's refreshing to meet a man who is besotted with his wife and respects her. Not something I've seen a lot.' The last line was spoken softly, more to herself than the man sitting next to her. 'Something else that's amused me throughout my career is how the worst of people are venerated as angels once they die. No one seems to remember one negative thing about the dead. But it's unfortunate that this girl, Ranjana Jha, is an exception to this rule.'

She lapsed into a moody silence for some time and then steered the conversation back to business. 'I want to make one thing clear. You are not officially a part of this case as it isn't standard protocol to include visiting detectives. I'm happy to consult with you, but if I see you overstepping or crossing me, I will throw you out of this investigation immediately. Clear?'

'Like the Ganga in Bithoor,' Prachand nodded earnestly.

'Now, have you ever seen a body up close?'

Prachand nodded. 'Of course!'

Half an hour later, in the dingy corridor of Kasturba Gandhi Government Hospital, Prachand stood leaning against a stained wall. His threshold for blood and death had deserted him and hurtled out with the water and tea as soon he stepped near the medical examiner's table.

The first thing he had noticed as they took the stairs to the morgue was the lack of light, natural or otherwise, as if the walls and corridors were keen on remaining sequestered and tight-lipped. The air was redolent with the strong smell of finality and phenyl. Prachand instinctively held up his handkerchief to his nose following Inspector Gupta and the medical examiner. He had seen bodies before, but the sight of Ranjana Jha's colourless face made him balk. Taking in the V-shaped incision that disappeared under the thin white sheet placed over her dissolved his last strand of resolve and made him run for a dustbin. When he found hair, nail clippings and bloodied gloves staring back at him, he made a beeline for the bathroom that stank with a fetid intensity. Light-headed and embarrassed, yet determined, he washed his face and went back in.

A man, possibly in his late fifties, with a pale complexion and slouching back stood peering at a paper over his thin-rimmed glasses. Inspector Gupta stood next to him. As Prachand entered, the man looked in his direction and said, 'At least we don't have a fainter on our hands. They are tiresome. As if I don't have enough dead weight to carry around.' He snorted at his own joke and then turned to Inspector Gupta without waiting for Prachand's reaction.

'As per my estimate ... she died ... mmm ... anywhere between eight and nine the previous night.'

Prachand looked at him with interest. 'That's quite a specific window. Can one be that accurate?'

The man looked annoyed. '"One" can't, but I, Behraam Wadia, can, given that I've only been fraternizing with dead bodies for the last fifteen years. As a student, I harboured thoughts of saving people and here I am, cutting them up and playing detective.'

The crudeness of his comment made Prachand queasy again, but he kept his mouth shut.

'You must already know this,' the doctor continued. 'From the time of death, the body keeps changing. Markers like decomposition, state of cooling and rigor mortis are considered. Other factors such as pre-existing conditions, ambient temperature at the time of death, etc., also matter,' he rattled off. 'Now, if you need any more information, go see a YouTube video.'

'Is there any way of determining if a pre-existing condition is the cause of death?' Prachand asked.

Inspector Gupta looked at Prachand. 'Are you referring to her being diabetic?'

Behraam Wadia shrugged. 'Not really. Only if she had taken too large a dose of insulin and not eaten anything at all, it could cause a dangerous reaction in the body, even leading to hypoglycaemic shock.'

'Then she didn't die of diabetes?'

'Like I said, it's not a masked murderer that stabs you in the head. But it does weaken the body.' As the medical examiner paired this sentence with a matching action, Prachand wondered when the poor man had had anyone living for company. 'She might have died of a cardiac arrest,' he added. 'For the living, cardiac activity can be easily checked with a cardiac enzyme test, but it's a trickier matter when it comes to the dearly departed. At that stage, it is more of what the eyes can see and checking valves, vessels and heart muscles for irregularities.'

'But she had no cardiac history as per the mother. Other than the diabetes she was in pretty good shape,' Prachand contested.

'Heart attacks are also known to occur in people without any acute cardiac problems. It can happen because of a severe shock to a frail constitution, sometimes a pre-existing unknown blockage or a traumatic posture or movement that impedes blood or air flow.'

Inspector Gupta toyed with her tendrils. 'Well, whatever the trigger, a heart attack seems to be a natural cause of death. I suppose the body can be handed back to the mother, and I can get on with the police panchnama. She is pretty distraught and wants the body returned for a cremation back home,' she said and then looked at Prachand. 'I'll need your signature as one of the five witnesses.'

Behraam Wadia cleared his throat and then fidgeted with his gloves, humming and looking at his guests with shifty eyes.

Inspector Gupta stared at him. 'Is there something else you'd like to share with us?'

The doctor sighed and complained. 'This is how I get myself into trouble. I could have easily made an excuse and sat at home, avoiding this autopsy altogether, but no. First, I have to perform it and then I have to divulge all possible details like someone's torturing me. I had a feeling this case would be trouble. And I've heard there's some politician involved.'

Prachand stepped forward and placed a hand on the old man's shoulder. 'You can tell us anything. This inspector is very capable and won't let anything happen to you. What do you want to tell us?'

After some more dithering and stalling, Behraam Wadia spoke with a look of resignation. 'The wound at the back of her head?'

Inspector Gupta nodded. 'Yes, I've seen it. The one she got after falling backwards.'

'It seems to be a post-mortem wound, not a perimortem one.

'Can you please explain that in simpler terms?' Prachand requested.

'It means that the wound appeared on her head around the time she dropped dead. Is that clearer?'

Prachand shuddered. A familiar, prickly sensation was building in the pit of his stomach. 'Are you saying ... Ranjana Jha was murdered?'

CHAPTER 30

Behraam Wadia walked to a table and pulled out something from his bag. It was a vape stick, which he took a long drag from. 'My nephew got it for me from Bombay. Helps me cut down on my smoking, not that the dead were complaining,' he sniggered. His audience of two was watching him patiently, knowing this man had some answers they needed.

'Mr Wadia, if we could please discuss your theory about Ranjana Jha,' Inspector Gupta interrupted, polite but firm. The old man nodded.

'Let me dumb it down as much as I can,' he said rather indelicately. 'And then I'll tell you why I'm confused,' he added and took another drag of his vape, pausing for dramatic effect.

Clearly enjoying the attention, he continued, 'You see, death normally occurs due to brain, respiratory or cardiac distress. We can only assume that the hypoglycaemic shock triggered arrythmia and then a cardiac arrest, but please note that every episode doesn't necessarily end in one. There could have been an external trigger as well.'

'Like stress due to something she saw or something that happened to her?' Prachand offered.

He nodded. 'Coming to the contusion on the back of the head. It might be on the back of her head, but it's unlikely that it occurred due to her falling. According to the initial details I've received, if she hit her head on something, the stone or rock would be found close to the body with bloodstains, head tissue or her hair on it.'

'There was nothing near her head,' Inspector Gupta confirmed.

'Exactly. Also, my second reason to believe that she didn't die of the wound is its position. The back of the head has some of the toughest bones. Now if this injury was, say, in the temporal bones, here,' he said pointing to the area behind his ears, 'smash, whack, gone. From the tissue and the staining in the area, I am pretty sure the impact couldn't have been hard enough to kill her.'

'I don't get it. So, she might have died of a heart attack, yet someone whacked her on the head after she was dead??' Inspector Gupta inquired, walking around the autopsy table.

'Yes.' the doctor said.

Prachand had spent a fair share of his years being a problem-solver; he was good at it. But wedged in this unfamiliar and morbid world of contusions, temporal bones and cardiac problems, he felt much like he did in the presence of technology—nauseated and clueless. He was desperately trying to keep track of Behraam Wadia's multiple theories.

Wadia chuckled. He seemed to be enjoying throwing googlies at both of them.

Prachand walked up to Inspector Gupta. 'This is all a bit convoluted. If this poor woman was indeed murdered, then we owe it to her to at least figure out what really happened.'

Inspector Gupta's jaw clenched. 'I don't need a sermon, Prachand. You have no idea what muck I've had to wade through to get where I am. I'm new here and under a lot of pressure to "clean this mess" as soon as possible. If the official cause of death remains unknown, this matter will stretch on inordinately. I might even have to call in my bosses.'

'Now, now, children. Don't fight. I might have an idea,' Behraam Wadia chided them in an avuncular manner.

'Let's not jump the gun here. Why think of calling Optimus Prime when you can make do with the brilliant local Shaktimaan,' he winked and pointed at himself. 'Here's what I can do. Since there is no certain cause of death, just to be sure, I can send the viscera for further analysis. It's perfectly normal to do that. If that report doesn't throw up something more conclusive then we will come back to the table and discuss the final conclusions.

'Viscera?' Prachand sounded puzzled.

'The internal organs,' Inspector Gupta explained.

Prachand imagined a medley of the liver, spleen, stomach and intestines floating around and had to clamp a hand on his mouth.

Inspector Gupta stood up. 'So that fixes it then. If you could please send the viscera for further analysis, I'll manage the pressure.'

Prachand gave the lady an appreciative nod and a warm smile. He was glad they were on the same page, wanting to get some real answers about the poor girl's death.

Behraam Wadia, meanwhile, plucked out a sandwich from his bag. He walked to the small attached room, plonked himself on a stool and without courtesy or ceremony began eating it.

Inspector Gupta's face broke into a deep frown. 'Isn't that … unhygienic and against hospital rules?'

The old man didn't look bothered. 'Wah, *Dikri*! I'm bending the rules for you and now, when I'm hungry, you throw them at me. Look here, these bodies are like my family. I know their secrets and they know mine. We look after each other. What's the harm in eating with them? You just make sure that I don't get into any trouble because of you!'

Inspector Gupta and Prachand had no inclination to hear more from the coroner or his dead-weight family, so they sped out.

On the ride back home, they discussed the queer old man. 'He might sound eccentric, but he is extremely sharp and gifted,' Inspector Gupta explained. 'He is quite legendary in these parts. Most others are only too happy to do the bare minimum, but this guy can go out on a limb if he likes you.'

'I can't tell whether he liked me or you, but I'm glad he is helping,' Prachand said with a smile and then lapsed into silence. When he finally spoke, his voice was heavy. 'Can we hand over the body? Her mother wants to return home with it.'

Inspector Gupta nodded. 'Yes I'll get that arranged. You keep your ears and eyes open and report back to me.'

Prachand could detect some concern in her voice when she spoke next. 'Be careful. There might be a murderer on the loose.'

CHAPTER 31

'Had fun on your date? Now fill me in!' Vidya settled down next to Prachand with a paratha and a cup of tea. She received a disapproving look in response but ignored it.

'Us as well!' Chachu Tripathi and Yatish joined in with their plates, forming a cluster around Prachand.

'This house feels like a prison now. And we have no clue what's happening,' Yatish complained.

Prachand filled them in, cautioning them against divulging the details to anyone.

Dinanath Tripathi moaned. 'Beta, Bhabhi is bound to sniff out something sooner or later. I keep making up stories about the shoot and how much fun we are having. Then I have to rinse my mouth with *gangajal* for lying to her. I'm sure I'm going to hell for this. How long can we keep up this pretence?'

'Chachu, I don't really know. Even if Inspector Gupta uses her influence to expedite the reports, everything takes time. Yatish, has Inspector Gupta spoken with Aalok Kumar yet?'

Yatish didn't respond. He was staring intently at the chutney on his plate. 'Yatish,' Prachand called out again.

'Sorry, Prachand Da,' he looked up. 'I just can't stop thinking about Ranjanaji. Who could have done such a thing?'

Prachand felt a pang of sadness at his piteous expression. 'I don't know, Yatish. We will have to wait for the reports. Perhaps it was an accident after all,' he lied, knowing fully well that this was highly improbable.

'In our times, dying was so simple,' Chachu Tripathi rued. 'People would die of pneumonia, high fever, small pox or accidents. Once in a while, an irate bull would spear someone in the backside. But nowadays it seems as if you have to do a PhD to understand death.'

Prachand gently drew everyone's attention back from his uncle's ruminations and his friend's moping. 'Yatish, has Aalok Kumar spoken with the police yet? You've kept track of who all Guptaji has questioned so far?'

Yatish nodded listlessly. 'Yes. But I think Guptaji will speak to him again. He was feeling unwell, so she let him go and called in Padminiji.'

Prachand drummed his fingers on the table. 'I think she suspects something as well. Did you tell her anything about following him into the woods?'

'No. I had no reason to. I mean, I still have no idea who the hell he was talking to in the woods, but he could just be a little cuckoo,' he said, tapping his temple. 'Doesn't make him a murderer.'

'That's true,' Vidya said. 'I mean, someone has to be off their rocker to confess that they killed someone by mistake, without any solid evidence.'

'He isn't mad. Just troubled,' Prachand said. 'From the conversation at the hospital, it seems unlikely that the rock killed her, because the wound occurred after she died. But then we don't know all the facts. I'll try and convince him to be straightforward with Guptaji but without any unwarranted confessions.' Prachand ended the discussion as Paramveer Khattar walked up to them. He still had that haggard look about him, but had thankfully decided to bathe. He sat down heavily.

'The autopsy is done?' he inquired. Prachand nodded.

Paramveer Khattar rubbed his hands, staring at them. 'Since the body is being handed over to the family soon, I presume we can think about restoring some normality around here.'

Vidya's expression reflected her thoughts.

'Look, you possibly think I'm heartless, but businesses do not run on love and fresh air; you need money. And I'm losing money every single day. The entire crew is contracted, the equipment is booked and advances are paid. I have money locked in here and neither my family name nor my connections are going to bail me out this time. It's now or never for me. If I fail, Papa will ...' He banged the table hard, making the plates jump. Recomposing himself, he went back to staring at his hands. 'I feel so sorry for that girl. I really do. But ... I have no option.'

'He has a valid point, you know,' Dinanath Tripathi said, but zipped up as Vidya's menacing gaze settled on him.

'The police are still conducting investigations,' Prachand said. 'I don't think they'll let you resume the shoot.'

'Well then, I'll wait a couple of days, but no more. I'll speak with the inspector to wrap this up quickly. She seems reasonable.'

'And I bet if she acts "unreasonable", you'll find a way to make her amenable,' Vidya challenged him.

Paramveer Khattar stared at Vidya for a few seconds, taking his time to respond. 'I think we might have got off on the wrong foot here. Whatever you think of me, I'm not a heartless boor, just someone under a lot of pressure.'

The conversation was interrupted by Prachand's phone ringing.

It was Inspector Maya Gupta. 'We found Bhutaari Baba,' she said.

CHAPTER 32

The tantric's bulbous eyes were fixed on a wall. He had refused to speak to any of the policemen, threatening to smear the potent ash he carried in a small pouch and send them to their doom. Not one officer, constable or staff volunteered to take on the man with the dreadlocks. He had ordered endless cups of tea and was eating a plate of pakoras when Inspector Maya Gupta walked into the room.

'I was waiting for you,' he said, licking his fingers and wiping his hand on his dhoti.

'I hope my department treated you well,' she responded, casting a look of censure at the officers standing nearby who had lowered their gaze. 'Let's have a chat,' she said and gestured to one of the officers to bring the tantric into the interrogation room.

Bhutaari Baba settled in a metal chair across from Inspector Gupta.

'I want my phone back,' the old man said. 'I have an online appointment and other clients to inform.'

On receiving a scathing look from the inspector, he shrugged. 'You don't assume people from these parts can be digitally savvy? In fact, I am the founder of BhutaariIsBae.com. An international client helped me set it up,' he beamed with pride.

'How lovely,' Inspector Gupta said tartly. 'Your clients will have to wait for much longer if you don't tell me what you were doing sneaking out of the haveli on the night of the murder.'

He kept his gaze level. 'That's easily explained. I was with my friend, Arjun Prajapati.'

Inspector Gupta raised an eyebrow. 'Your *friend* hasn't mentioned anything to us.'

Bhutaari Baba clenched his jaw and leaned in towards the officer. She could smell tobacco on his sour breath. 'That's because he is scared. Everyone is scared. You don't know what you're dealing with. There are forces at play here that are beyond your comprehension. I had predicted this a long time ago. I felt it in my bones.'

'Probably arthritis,' Inspector Gupta quipped.

'Sneer all you'd like, my child, but these parts have a history of suffering and pain. It's in the sand, in the water, in every shrub, in every khejri and in every kelu tree. A residue of lives cut short, their helplessness from centuries ago howls with the desert winds at night, looking for someone who will listen, who will feel, who will understand their grief.'

'You're telling me that these spirits turned up looking for Ranjana Jha and whisked her away? And you had no motive, I suppose. Silencing someone who was challenging you, calling your work mumbo-jumbo and puncturing your credibility? She accused you publicly, right?'

He snorted. 'It doesn't bother me what non-believers say, but I caution you now. Those we cannot see play a part in everything that happens here. This is their land; we are mere puppets.' Bhutaari Baba lit a beedi with deliberate movements.

Inspector Gupta could conceal her irritation no further. 'Don't think I don't know your lot. You tantrics, babas and faith healers feed on the insecurities of people. The more isolated and miserable they are, the better the prey. I hope you remember the Anti-Witchcraft Act the next time you threaten someone, like you did Ranjana Jha.'

The old man stubbed out his beedi and stared back fiercely. 'I am but a conduit. Don't kill the messenger.'

Inspector Gupta stood up and picked up her phone from the table. 'I'm done. For now. All we need is a bit of your *charan ki dhool*.'

Completely missing the sarcasm, Bhutaari Baba nodded and raised a hand by way of blessing as Inspector Gupta gestured towards an officer. 'Take an imprint of his foot and shoe.'

She then glanced at the old man's shocked face and made for the door. 'Don't leave Kuldhara. We might need assistance from your spirit world to solve this murder after all.'

Later, Inspector Maya Gupta sat before her team of two officers, two constables and one cleaner-cum-errand boy who insisted on spending all his time at the police station. The quotidian gamut of crimes they dealt with fell in the range of petty thefts of the poultry and bovine kind to misdemeanour and drunken brawls. Once in a while, the owner of an overzealous camel would need a dressing down. On the other end of the spectrum were those involved in illegal mining and the sand mafia, way beyond the league of the kotwali in Silavta Para. These were left for the larger departments in bigger cities to tackle. Despite the cloud of the curse, the mysterious murder had cleared the cobwebs of monotony for the policemen. They were more attentive now, fuelled with some inexplicable energy, and chose to forget how mercilessly they were ribbed for working under a woman.

A woman who almost always seemed to know what she was doing, except that this day was turning out to be an exception. She was pacing around like a caged lioness, reading her notes while scribbling arrows on a rickety blackboard mounted on an easel.

'This is our chance to prove to Padmakar Sir that we are capable of producing timely results. I will not allow even a single muck-up,' she said to her team of men who were listening with utmost concentration. 'Inspector Hiren, run me through your list.'

Hiren, caught unawares, fumbled with his cap perched on his knee and knocked it to the ground. He retrieved it and stood up straight, fingers locked around his cap in childlike obedience, like he was prepared to recite '*Machli jal ki rani hai*'.

'Madamji, I have spoken with all the servants, the maids and the film crew. All of them narrated the same flow of events. We have combed the homes in the vicinity, which are very few to begin with. There are no eyewitnesses either except for a small boy who lives with his mother a few metres from the gate of the property. He swears he saw a daakan with long hair running through the trees on the night of the murder. She stopped and glared at him for a few seconds but then ran away. There have been a few sightings in the past as well.'

'He saw a daakan? Running through the trees?' Inspector Gupta threw her hands up in the air. 'You know, you should have trained under Bhutaari Baba instead of the police academy.'

'Madamji, don't get angry. I'm just telling you what he said. Anyway, there are no cameras on the property or leading up to it, so we don't have much to go on.'

Inspector Brijesh raised his hand. 'Madamji, I am still checking up on the footprint. I've submitted the elimination prints from the haveli and they are looking for matches. It will take some time. And we still have to receive the call records.'

'Ask them to send a report before Diwali,' barked Inspector Gupta. She walked to the table and picked up the photographs from the crime scene. 'Never bring this photographer to the crime scene ever again! The angles are useless. I wanted close-ups. This isn't wedding or mood photography. Every single detail is important!' she said as her finger paused on a photograph of Ranjana Jha, her lifeless eyes boring into Inspector Gupta's. She felt the fine hair on the back of her neck prickle. 'What are you trying to tell me, Ranjana?'

CHAPTER 33

Finding Padmini Rathod absent from the morning bustle, Vidya inquired about her. She was told that Padminiji was unwell and resting in her room.

Vidya decided to pay Padmini Rathod a visit. Her room was located on the first floor, in a secluded part of the haveli, facing west. As Vidya reached the corridor that led to Padmini's room, her nostrils picked up a musty smell that seemed to cling to the walls. The ostentatious carvings of sandstone and latticed cornice in the balcony where the corridor ended showed signs of age and neglect. The peeling paint, the cracked marble pillars and the paintings bloated with the relentless assault of leakages were all fading vestiges of grander days. A moustached ancestor stared back at her reproachfully from one of the paintings, as if admonishing her for being so judgemental. She hurried forward, unable to let go of the feeling that those eyes were still on her.

Thankfully, she reached Padmini Rathod's room soon enough where a young woman, who was exiting the room, bowed respectfully and ushered her in.

Padmini Rathod was in one corner of the aesthetically done-up room that looked like it had received better TLC and upkeep than the rest of the haveli. She lay on an ornate diwan, facing the open window, her long hair open and trailing to the ground. Instead of her usual elaborate attire, she was dressed in a simple embroidered sharara. As Vidya's arrival was announced, she sat up with a smile. A nod of her head made the lady-in-waiting disappear.

'Please keep resting. I'll come and sit by you.' Vidya planted herself in a cushioned wooden chair. The long-stemmed fans hanging from the high ceiling were switched off, but a cool breeze floating in from the window made the air very pleasant. Padmini Rathod drew her shawl closer. 'This unpredictable weather hasn't done me any favors.'

'Are you sure your health has nothing to do with the inexplicable events unfolding around us?' Vidya asked. 'Only a little while ago, everything was fine.'

The smile on Padmini Rathod's face weakened and her eyes clouded over. 'I hope I can speak frankly with you, Vidyaji?'

'Of course.'

'I've lived here for many years now and have seen and heard many strange things. But one night, when I was taking a walk behind the haveli, I saw *her*.'

'Her?'

'The woman from the well, Mahua. Her hair was billowing in the breeze, her *odhni* hid most of her face and her terrifying eyes were fixed on me. I tried to scream, but I was paralysed.'

Vidya felt a shiver course down her spine. 'You didn't tell your husband?'

Padmini Rathod's face contorted briefly but was replaced quickly by a weak smile, making Vidya wonder if she had just imagined it. 'My rajkanwar doesn't have time for my "womanly nonsense",' she laughed without any trace of humour in her voice. Seeing the irritated look on Vidya's face, she laid a hand on hers. 'Don't worry about me. He doesn't really mean any harm. This is just the way he is. Our marriage is not about making dewy eyes and hand-holding. In this family, things remain formal between husband and wife,' she shrugged. 'Besides, I consider myself naturally conditioned for adjustments and disappointments.'

Vidya looked at her quizzically as she continued. 'You see, even my family was very conservative. Women spreading their wings was frowned upon. My aunt was training under an acclaimed *baid* at my *nanire*, something I also aspired to do. She was married off against her will. My mother was an accomplished singer, but her voice became a distant memory after she took her wedding vows. In fact, I broke a cardinal rule by choosing to marry my husband. It's a privilege reserved for the elders. I lucked out!'

'Lucked out. Hmmm. It's great if you feel that way,' Vidya mumbled. 'It's just that he doesn't seem to ...'

Padmini Rathod stood up abruptly and made her way to a small cupboard that was locked. She opened it and took out a few small bottles, taking pinches of powder from each, compiling them all in a bowl full of water and stirring them with a small spoon. 'None of that matters,' she said dismissively. 'What does concern me though is that I sense something different this time. This weather, the death, these are all signs. I can ... feel that something is not right.' She put her bowl down and took Vidya's hand. 'We are all in danger,

Vidya. I really hope that it is only my imagination ... but ...' she lapsed into silence.

Vidya's stomach gurgled audibly. It was her body's automatic stress response. She was a rational woman, but the dead walked a world she was not familiar with, governed by its own rules. For now, staring into Padmini Rathod's terrified face, she had to park aside her own fears. Padmini was someone who gave her a modicum of comfort and familiarity in this strange new world. She was strong yet vulnerable and brought out Vidya's protective instinct.

'Padminiji, you need to relax and take care of yourself. I have no explanations, but what I do know is Prachand and I are here, and we will try and fix everything. We ...' she said squeezing Padmini Rathod's hand, 'I won't let anything happen to you.'

Padmini Rathod flicked her tears away. 'I'm embarrassed. Look at me, making a fool of myself. You're my guest, my responsibility.'

Vidya smiled. 'You have already been the most wonderful host!' Her eyes swept over the tray of medicines Padmini Rathod had accidentally knocked over while reaching for her hand. She noticed a collection of vitamins and nutritional supplements, along with the bottles she had seen earlier. 'Your doctor certainly loves prescribing medicines,' she noted.

'Oh no. This is all me.' Padmini Rathod swept the contents back on to the tray and stuck them back in the cupboard, locking it up. 'I was fascinated with tinctures and potions, just like my aunt. I experiment on myself. That's how I know I'll be fine very soon!' she laughed.

'I know who to seek out next time I have a headache.' Vidya smiled and stared wistfully out of the window. 'Even when I'm happy, I feel guilty. That poor woman. What did she do to deserve this? What monster could ...'

'You mean, she was murdered?' Padmini Rathod looked pale. 'I know they were investigating all angles, but I assumed it was her diabetes or an accident.'

Vidya gulped. 'You didn't hear this from me.'

Padmini Rathod nodded. 'Of course,' she said and then wrung her hands. 'I just wish they would stop questioning my husband. It ... it makes him bitter. And then he takes it out on me. I mean, what's the big deal if he was out for a few hours that night? It's his home. It doesn't make him a mu ...' She clamped a hand on to her mouth.

Vidya stared at her. 'You lied for him? He wasn't with you?'

'P ... Please don't tell him, please don't tell anyone. He will be very upset. He ... he must have been walking, or working, I'm sure.'

Vidya nodded, looking at Padmini Rathod who was sweating profusely. 'Take a deep breath. I think you should rest now.'

As Vidya walked back through the corridor, plagued with unanswered questions and this new information, her eyes flew to the paintings. Now they all seemed to be watching her, with their unwavering gaze and grim expressions. Her heart started to race. As her pace quickened and her steps doubled, she heard a guttural sound behind her, followed by a blood-curdling scream that shook her insides.

CHAPTER 34

There is nothing particularly treacherous about aloo puri. A universal pleaser, it is a hearty and nutritious breakfast that appeases all sorts of fussy taste buds. But the manner in which Ramnarayan Rathod was peering into his plate would make one think that he was part of a bomb diffusion squad. He prodded each piece with his thin finger and sniffed at every addition that his wife, who looked on quizzically, made to the plate.

His actions didn't go unnoticed at the other end of the table. Venky, Vikas Kishen and Yatish drank from their tall glasses of buttermilk while speaking in low tones. 'See how careful he is? This is after Arjun Prajapati personally scans his food. And here we are, dispensable cattle, waiting for a murderer to strike again,' the agitated DOP muttered.

'Mr Venky, Sir,' Vikas Kishen interrupted. 'Please don't mind, but I honestly don't think anyone is interested in getting rid of you. It seems actors are on the hit list. That's why Ranjanaji was ...' he ran a finger across his neck and clicked his tongue.

'Instead of proving who is more worthy of being murdered, we should keep our ears and eyes open for any suspicious activity. You see, I am well-trained now, being part of a detective agency,' Yatish announced with an air of superiority. 'Come to think of it, this Arjun Prajapati was moving boxes late last night. Looked very suspicious. Why should he do it in the dead of night?'

Vidya walked past, picking up crumbs of this paranoid exchange. She shook her head and walked to the courtyard where Prachand was on the phone. 'Haan, Ma. Put some haldi on the skin. No ... no, on her tail. No, she won't kick you. Mishraji can come and see her in a few days if the skin still looks infected.'

Vidya raised an eyebrow enquiringly. Prachand gestured for her to sit on the swing nearby. After a few minutes, he joined her. 'Poor Hirwa has a bit of a skin problem,' he sighed. 'I don't know how long we can keep up the lies. I feel so guilty.' His voice was laced with regret.

Vidya laid a hand on his familiar fingers, tracing the small tufts of hair on his knuckles. 'No one planned this, Prachi.'

It was Prachand's turn to look at his wife. 'Something on your mind, Viddu?'

She smiled, remembering how wonderful it felt to be read so easily by someone you loved and trusted with all your heart.

'What?' Prachand prodded.

'I do have something to tell you,' Vidya said and proceeded to fill Prachand in on her discussion with Padmini Rathod.

Prachand frowned. 'This alibi business is a serious matter, Viddu. I'm afraid you seem to have contracted my disease of being a confession magnet. It's disastrous,' he said drumming his fingers on his knee. 'Why would he lie about being with his wife? What could he possibly have been up to? I can't see an obvious motive.'

'You keep telling me the usual motives are predictable and universal. Love, money, jealousy, revenge?'

'Yes, Viddu! Correct you are. Applying that logic, it doesn't seem to be money. There is no child in question, no other obvious motives. Unless ...'

'Unless what, Prachi?'

'Unless this is a matter of a spurned heart.'

'What! Are you trying to tell me he was in love with that woman?'

Prachand shrugged. 'It's possible. When it comes to capers of the heart, age doesn't matter.'

'But a face does! And she had eyes. He is such an unimpressive, supercilious idiot. Who would fall for him? Besides he has a gorgeous and loyal wife, doesn't he?'

'Viddu, your personal feelings can't drive the motives of another person. But you're right, at this point this is purely conjecture. What is more important is for Inspector Maya Gupta to have this information. She is, after all, the officer in charge.'

'Prachi, please! Padminiji will get into trouble,' Vidya importuned her usually pliable husband.

'Viddu, you know I cannot withhold this information. You yourself advised me against it when Aalok Kumar came to me. Don't worry. I'll request her to be careful and avoid creating any trouble for Padminiji.'

Vidya pouted in a resigned manner. 'There's something else. When I was leaving her room, I heard a piercing shriek. I almost fainted with fright. Do you think it was Mahua?'

Before Prachand could respond, raised voices interrupted their conversation. He looked warily at Vidya. 'Now what!'

They reached the living room to see Paramveer Khattar standing stoically in the centre of the living room, his mouth set in a grim line. Ramnarayan Rathod was positioned like second skin next to his friend, looking like he could slip into his pocket any minute.

'They remind me of those young men who walk about the streets of Gwaltoli holding hands. I can't for the life of me figure out why. *Bholenath ki kripa hai,* neither Prachand nor Bhushan have ever displayed such camaraderie.' Prachand picked up Chachu Tripathi's innocuous comment as they walked past him.

'How dare you? Have you no shame?' said Mrs Jha, who had spent most of her time confined to her room since her daughter's demise. She pointed a shaky finger at Paramveer Khattar. 'My daughter hasn't even been cremated and you want to get on with your life like she was some dispensable rag?'

'No, Mrs Jha. I only want to resume the shoot as a lot of people and their livelihoods are at stake here. We all want to finish this shoot and go home. I promise I don't mean any disrespect. She ... she was a lovely girl,' Paramveer Khattar said. Vidya was surprised to see a genuine flash of remorse on his face.

'Money is all that matters to you, isn't it?' Mrs Jha's eyes flashed with anger.

'I agree with the decision my friend is proposing. It is to everyone's benefit because ...'

'Shut up!' Mrs Jha hollered at Ramnarayan Rathod, all propriety and civility scorched in the heat of her intense emotions. 'You're no king, merely a coward! He commands and you follow him around like a dog,' she spat out as the object of her tirade stood slack-jawed.

She then blew her nose in a pink handkerchief printed with roses and tucked it back into a bag slung over her shoulder. 'I won't waste my time any more. My daughter is waiting for me.' Her voice broke as she looked fleetingly at Prachand and Vidya who were visibly moved by her emotions and obvious distress. She walked towards the main door and then looked back. 'I curse this production. *Ek maa ki baddua hai!*' The implication of these potent words was not lost on the people standing around as a collective gasp suffused the air.

Arjun Prajapati, who was following her out with a number of bags, muttered miserably as he plodded away. 'Wah! One more curse. The more the merrier!'

CHAPTER 35

The shoot resumed but the usual frenzy was subdued, as if in deference, much like a requiem for recent events. Venky barking instructions to the crew, the familiar clatter of lights and equipment being moved about and the general din of conversation infused the air with a modicum of normality. Vidya spotted Prachand weaving his way through the living room and caught up with him at the entrance.

'Where are you off to so early, Prachi?'

'Is Padminiji feeling better now?' he asked, brushing a strand of hair away from Vidya's forehead. She cocked her eyebrow.

'Yes, she is, but where are you off to?'

'Into the woods. I'll be back in a jiffy.'

'I'm coming.'

Prachand smiled and nodded, knowing better than to take on his wife when her mind was made up. 'Why don't you grab a toast on your way out?' he pointed in the direction of the kitchen.

'No, thank you. I'd rather starve to let you live a long life,' Vidya quipped, smoothing down the red and green silk salwar-kameez she was wearing with a little more jewellery than usual. 'For a detective, you're rather obtuse, Mr Tripathi.'

Prachand smacked his forehead. 'Of course, it's Karva Chauth! How stupid of me.' He looked around furtively and then ran a hand over Vidya's cheek. She blushed and her heartbeat quickened.

'Let's go,' she said, pulling at Prachand's arm.

If Vidya had any hopes that the special day meant to celebrate the living would be devoid of any conversation about the dead, she was wrong. It was all Prachand could talk about, much to her dismay. Ten minutes later, they had reached the clearing with the well.

'Somehow, the air here always feels different. Do you know what I mean?' he asked Vidya who was scowling and wiping some bird droppings from her dupatta.

'I do. But something I don't understand is how these damn birds can constantly be pooping through the day,' she muttered.

Prachand, meanwhile, had already walked towards the well. He cautiously peeped in. Having slipped into a well as a child on a family trip to Etawah, he gave them a wide berth in general, shuddering at the traumatic memory of grasping on to the wet bricks, mildew and slippery mud for dear life. Leaning in did not grant him a view of the bottom. It pained him to think of Mahua and her child who had unwittingly stumbled into this bottomless hole on a dark, dreary night.

A sound behind him made him jump. He turned to find Vidya bent over, very close to the spot where Ranjana Jha had been found.

'What are you doing?' he asked.

'I lost my earring,' she said patting the ground. Prachand joined her and drew her away to the side.

'You're standing on the spot where the body was found.'

Now, Vidya had been a track and field champion in her school days, but could never have never imagined that her best long jump would be attempted on a crime scene in Rajasthan. Vidya leapt and landed closer to Prachand with Ninja-like precision.

'Hai Ram!' she said holding her dupatta to her mouth. Prachand held her hand and bent over to look for what she had described as a small red and white jhumka. He found it and straightened up but continued staring at the ground.

'What is it?' Vidya inquired, still maintaining a distance.

Prachand pointed to the ground. Vidya had no option but to come closer to him.

'You're the best, Viddu! Your earring revealed drag marks. They end just where the body was found.'

'So?'

'So?' he threw up his hands. 'One of the theories we are working with is that she either fainted and died, after hitting her head, which seems improbable after the autopsy report. The second is that she died and then someone hit her on the head, and then there is the idea that some acute aggravation made her heart collapse. Her body being dragged gives more credence to the assault theory. Someone dragged her after hitting her and aborted the plan midway.'

'Bas? Only these many? You must add a few more!'

'We have to explore every angle.'

'Fine!' she said dismissively. 'But what about these drag marks? Why did you only notice them now?'

'I've only been here twice, and both times the light wasn't too good and the ground was still wet. These might be more visible now since the mud has dried up. I doubt Guptaji is aware,' he shrugged. 'What I need to figure out is the who and why.'

'I think you can safely eliminate one flower from your bouquet of theories. This wasn't an accidental death.'

'All the evidence points to that possibility. We were right,' Prachand said and nodded.

'We, is it? How cozy!' Vidya snorted.

Prachand gave her a wry smile. 'I'm talking about a collective opinion, Viddu.'

'Hmm.' Vidya narrowed her eyes. 'Should we head back now?'

Beyond the clump of trees, from the direction of the ruins, a strange whizzing sound responded. The wind picked up, kicking up whirlpools of sand.

'Viddu,' Prachand coughed, looking sideways at the outline of the ruins. 'Would you mind if we paid a quick visit ...' he pointed his finger, '... there?'

'Are you mad, Prachi? That is a place where people have disappeared. It's a playground for ghostbusters and tantrics, and you want to take a casual suicidal walk there on a day when I'm starving to keep you alive?'

Prachand laughed. 'Surely, the rational woman that you are, you don't believe everything you hear? Besides, I'm starving for you as well, so there's no chance either one of us is going to meet our Maker today! We are each other's protective shields!'

'Try your jokes on the ghosts. They might just indulge you,' Vidya said and sighed in a resigned manner, knowing fully well that she would not be able to rein in her husband's enthusiasm. Prachand gave her a quick peck on her cheek.

As they walked towards the formidable village, Prachand looked back at the ground. 'You know, Viddu, this might be a strange request, but if you could just lie down for a quick second and let me reconstruct the scene, I'll get a very good idea about the angle of the ...'

'Over my dead body,' said Vidya Tripathi with a demure smile and marched onwards.

CHAPTER 36

Sand has a wonderful quality. It's inclusive and accommodating—of people, of the tides of time and secrets. Prachand and Vidya gazed in awe at the brown sea and its gentle waves, licking the horizon as far as the eyes could see. And what lay between them and this horizon was a city in slumber. The cool sand beneath their feet, reassuringly alive and moving, was a stark contrast to the rows of still, derelict, yellowing brick-and-limestone houses that seemed to be waiting for some form of life.

Walking on this forgotten land felt like they were intruding in some way, stirring and disturbing some invisible routine of the nameless and faceless inhabitants. Despite the cool air, Vidya shivered and a bead of sweat rolled down her damp forehead. 'I'm not feeling too well, Prachi.'

Her husband turned to look at her, his brow furrowed with concern. 'Would you like to head back? This not eating business isn't good. We don't have to prove our loyalty and love by denying our body its due.'

Vidya smiled mischievously. 'Then why are you starving yourself and stealing my thunder?'

'That's because I promised to always match steps ... and hunger strikes with you,' he smiled back and handed Vidya some *saunf* that he always kept in a small box in his pocket. 'Here, take some of this. It can hardly be classified as food.'

Vidya took a pinch gratefully. The wave of nausea subsided as she let her flavoured saliva rinse the inside of her mouth.

Prachand and Vidya continued to walk past what seemed like the remains of a temple: a set of familiar steps snaking their way up to a wider rectangular structure topped with a triangular *shikhara*. They walked into the antechamber, paved with dust and debris, right up to the *garb griha*, or the womb chamber, where the deity was missing. Prachand was suddenly consumed by nostalgia, transported to the long and sweaty train and bus rides to Ayodhya, Vaishno Devi and Kedarnath during the summer holidays. These trips were laced with memories of tasty puri, halwa, achar, jalebi and mathris, with warm hugs and angry rebukes, and sometimes smelly toilets. He remembered sitting atop large holdalls and covering the distance holding the circuitous sweetness of an *imarti*. A small sigh escaped his lips.

Vidya interlaced her fingers in his. 'Can you imagine, Prachi, hundreds of lives, interrupted, left interred, all for the greed of one man?'

'Greed isn't selective. It claims everyone,' announced a strange voice.

Prachand and Vidya, both startled, looked at the empty spot where a deity should have been. 'Is ... is God speaking to us?' asked Vidya, her eyes wide and hands folded.

Before Prachand could respond, a man walked around the garb griha, emerging from what looked like a *parikrama*, his hands folded. He looked like some kind of priest, wearing a kurta and dhoti. A thick white beard and a clean and bald pate complimented his warm brown eyes. He had a gentle smile on his face as he turned around, bowing to the invisible idol and then turning to face the bewildered couple.

'*Pranam, Kaka.*' Prachand bowed low. Vidya did the same. 'We were told this village is uninhabited.'

The man cut Prachand off and pointed to a tree in the middle of what looked like an erstwhile town centre with roads leading in all sides. 'Come, let's sit under that neem tree.'

Once he was seated on a corroded and broken trunk, the old man looked up and gazed at various parts of the tree. 'Arishta, the reliever of all sickness and the giver of gentle breeze, that's what a neem tree stands for. Yet, it wasn't able to save these poor people,' he said shaking his head.

'Kaka,' Prachand squatted and positioned himself right in front of the weather-beaten face. 'Do you know a lot about this place?'

He nodded. 'Some days I can hear them, you know. The womenfolk, laughing and gossiping, their jewellery tinkling in the warm breeze as they walk about with their pots of water; the children, playing and squabbling on the stone-paved streets; the clip-clop of animal hooves; the men stretched out on their *charpais* after a hard day's work and the plaintive cries of peacocks gracefully gliding on to plumes of sand. All of this right before my eyes, as if it's all happening in front of me.' His outstretched arm pointed at the phantom scene only he could see.

'Are you from around here, Kaka? You seem to have heard some wonderful stories from your relatives. I've heard the story as well, about how the poor Paliwals had to flee and were never seen again.'

Moist eyes peered down into his. 'That wasn't the end of their misery. What followed was even more devastating. Drought, displacement, famine, death and disease.' When he finished speaking, he looked beyond Prachand's shoulders, eyes hardened into pebbles of stone. 'You couldn't save her. She had to go.'

Prachand's heart raced. Had he imagined that ominous timbre in the old man's voice? Was he referring to Ranjana Jha? 'But you can save her ...' his finger pointed in the direction of the haveli and the woods they had traversed to reach the ruins.

Driven by instinct, Prachand shot up from his haunches, turning to confirm what he already suspected. Vidya was nowhere to be seen. Cursing his lack of alertness, he ran as fast as his legs could carry him towards the clearing, swearing on Bholenath to exercise regularly once this crisis was behind them. A quick backwards glance revealed that the old man was no longer there.

He stumbled through the remaining distance and froze with terror at the sight that met his eyes. Vidya stood at the edge of the well. Ramrod straight, with her hands by her side.

Prachand took a deep breath and walked carefully towards the well, trying to be as quiet as possible. He knew that any sudden movement might hurtle Vidya into a free fall, the bottom of the well.

Once he was standing right behind her, he placed an arm close to her legs to prevent them from buckling and slipped his other hand into hers.

She did buckle, but his outstretched arm drew her to safety. She looked at Prachand as if she had just emerged from a leisurely swim instead of having gone through a near-death experience.

'Oh, hi, Prachi,' she chirped. 'What are you doing here? Let's go back.'

CHAPTER 37

Prachand was watching Vidya like a hawk. There had to be an explanation for what had transpired in the last few hours. More than the inexplicable sequence of events, what had turned his heart cold was the thought of losing Vidya to that treacherous well.

He tried to gauge how much Vidya remembered, but it seemed as if the episode had been somewhat bleached from her memory. She was in an animated conversation with Chachu Tripathi when he approached her again. The poor man was wistfully reminiscing the gastronomical delights that would be cooked at Awadh Niwas for Karva Chauth, salivating more than the hungry women around him. 'Ammaji makes mithi puri, kadhi chawal and malpua today. What I would give to get my hands on that food!'

'Really, Chachu? You ate a stack of puris just this morning. And if I'm not mistaken, quite a bit of ghevar as well.'

'Oh yes,' laughed Dinanath Tripathi, his cheeks turning crimson. 'I've grown quite fond of it. And if I'm not mistaken, Yatish loves it too.'

The young man, Prachand noticed, seemed to have recovered from his heartbreak with alacrity and was often seen chatting up Preeti, Ranjana's former stylist, bringing her food or running errands for her. She was rumoured to be filling in for Ranjana Jha.

The film crew was busy with a set-up on the massive terrace of the haveli. That left the rest of the palace quieter than usual, barring the kitchen. Padmini Rathod had forced Vidya to drink some cold nimbu pani that had been prepared in large *matkas* for the fasting women. 'No *nirjala vrat* for us here. We know the value of water in the desert and won't do without it, not even for our husbands,' said Padmini Rathod, laughing heartily.

After toying with the decision for a while, Prachand finally decided to tell Vidya about the events from the morning. As he narrated the episode, Vidya's eyes widened with shock. She took Prachand's hand. 'Prachi, am I possessed? Is that why I've been eating so much these last few days?'

'Umm, that might just be your increased appetite, Viddu.'

'And what about the fact that whenever your mother brings up the topic of babies, or the neighbours' reproductive adventures on the phone, it consumes me with an odd rage that I've never felt before!'

'Viddu, instead of attributing all your behaviour to demonic possession, it would help if we try to reconstruct, or in this matter, deconstruct what happened. What is the last thing you remember?'

'The old man, the neem tree ...' She was fidgeting with her fingers, her eyes blinking faster than usual, trying to conjure what had transpired. 'All I remember after that is standing next to you by the well and feeling cold.' She looked at Prachand helplessly. 'I'm sorry.'

'There is nothing for you to be sorry about, all right? This could be the stress of recent events. You blanked out for a bit. Let's not overthink this.'

Vidya nodded.

That's when Prachand's phone rang. He plucked it out of his pocket and then stole a glance at Vidya.

'Your girlfriend's calling. Take it,' she said. Prachand shook his head and took the call.

'I'm glad you called, Inspector Gupta,' Prachand said. 'I had to update you about a few things.'

'Tell me.'

Prachand then proceeded to update Inspector Gupta about Ramnarayan Rathod's movement on the night of the murder, followed by details of the discovery of drag marks near the spot where the body was found.' Prachand waited for a response. 'Are you there?'

'Yes. I was just trying to recall all the details Rathod had provided in his statement. I had a feeling he wasn't being entirely truthful. I'll need to have a word with him again.'

'Just one request, please, he might turn on his wife for this inadvertent slip-up, so could you please ...'

'I'm not here to babysit anyone, Mr Tripathi. The only thing that concerns me is this investigation.' An awkward silence later, she added, 'I'll see what I can do.'

'Thank you.'

'I should actually thank you. This is significant information. Even the drag marks. I should have combed the scene one more time.'

'There was no way for you to imagine that something would reveal itself once the mud had dried.'

'That's just an excuse. The truth often lies between chance and observation, my uncle used to say. I missed this one. Anyway, this means that someone tried to drag the body before abandoning the task.'

'Yes. It would seem that way. It's possible that this someone was startled into abandoning the task. But the question remains, why drag the body if she had already collapsed?'

'Were the drag marks moving in any particular direction?'

'I can't be sure. But possibly towards the ... well.' Prachand fell silent.

'All okay?'

'Huh? Oh, yes.' He wasn't about to share any details about his suicidal wife or a disappearing priest, lest the officer brand him a certified loon. 'I was just wondering how every fresh detail makes this case even more confusing.'

What Prachand didn't know was that he wasn't the only one withholding strange information. Inspector Maya Gupta had woken up that morning in a cold sweat and with a faint memory of a disturbing dream that she couldn't shake off. A terrifying, hollow face of a woman and child had been calling out from within a well, making her hair stand on her neck.

After hanging up the phone, she went to the washroom and splashed cold water on her face. It suddenly struck her that amidst the daily drama of this investigation, she hadn't instructed her team to verify Bhutaari Baba's alibi with his friend Arjun Prajapati. Cursing herself and making a mental note, she picked up her mobile that had been ringing for a while. She heaved a sigh of relief looking at the caller ID.

She hoped that Behraam Wadia would have some concrete information.

'Miss Gupta!' he announced cheerfully.

'Doctor, please tell me you have some answers.'

There was a loud chuckle on the line. 'How I wish life was that simple, my dear. In fact, I have news that will confound you before helping you.'

'Please just tell me, Dr Wadia. I really don't feel up to any guessing games.'

'Ah well. If you must be a killjoy.' This was followed by a dramatic sigh and the sound of someone inhaling air. She guessed he was vaping. 'Dr Wadia?'

'Oh ... I'm sorry ... oh, yes. The findings. Well, the tox report is back. Tell me, Ms Gupta, what is often considered the best way of killing someone without being present?'

CHAPTER 38

'She was poisoned?' Inspector Gupta gasped.

'Sure looks like it. There was definitely an excess of some drug in her blood. And drug toxicity can be called poisoning in a sense. An old, reliable method of killing that our forefathers heavily relied on to rid themselves of nuisance-generating friends and enemies.'

'Do we know what kind?'

'That needs some specialized testing. I've sent it to another lab in Jaipur. Just thought I'd let you know first.'

'Thank you. I really appreciate it.'

'Don't worry about it. I like you, you know, and that fainty fellow you brought with you. May be one of these days all three of us can have tea and snacks in my office.'

Not in the least bit interested in picnicking around a dead body, Inspector Gupta quickly thanked him and hung up.

Back at the police station, there was more interesting news waiting for her.

'Madamji, that tantric has disappeared again,' Inspector Brijesh announced in an officious manner.

'What do you mean he has disappeared?'

'You had asked us to keep an eye on him. When Sarthy went to his home, he wasn't there.'

'That doesn't mean he has disappeared. He might just be attending to one of his ... appointments ... yagyas ... or whatever it is that he does.'

'No, Madamji, he is on the run.'

'How can you be so sure?' A note of asperity creeped into Inspector Gupta's voice.

'Nandu was nowhere to be seen.'

'Now who the hell is Nandu?'

'His pet goat. The neighbours and whoever else we spoke with said that he treated the goat like his child. The goat disappearing is clear evidence of the fact that he has left bag and baggage, I mean, bag and goat.'

Maya Gupta sat down heavily on a chair, not taking her eyes off the officer. 'You should have been with the CBI. Police departments the world over have advanced to detecting crimes of the past, and even predicting those in the future. Yet here we are, tracking goats and camels to get to our suspects.'

'But, Madamji, you'll see that I'm right.'

'What I would have liked to see was better surveillance so that we wouldn't be in this situation. Do you even realize how much pressure I'm under? And the updates I have for my seniors are disappearing goats and sorcerers, a potful of suspects and a bucketful of circumstantial evidence. Which essentially means that I have nothing! Oh, and how can I forget the curse? Let me add an ancient curse and some restless spirits to the list. No one can deny me a promotion after that!'

Brijesh had never seen Inspector Gupta this rattled. Perhaps it had to do with lack of sleep. There were dark circles under her eyes, he noticed.

'Madamji, chai?' he asked with trepidation.

'No ... no chai.' She rubbed her head to try and ease the headache that was building up. She needed to think clearly, to talk to someone, a voice of reason who could make sense of things for her and was surprised at how swiftly her mind turned to Prachand. She quickly made the call.

'Namaste, Guptaji,' Prachand greeted her.

'You make me sound like an overweight halwai.'

'Ha ha! You couldn't look like one if you tried!' Prachand laughed and was immediately embarrassed. He changed track to a more comfortable territory. 'The shoot has resumed,' he said. 'But the general spirit on the set is very low.'

'Well, that's understandable.'

'They've decided to replace Ranjana with Preeti, her stylist,' Prachand said, 'for the remaining shots. They'll do some computer business after that. Paramveer Khattar seems pretty confident about pulling it off.'

'Hmm. Talking about Paramveer Khattar, what sort of a man does he strike you as?'

'Ruthless, ambitious, entitled.'

'Capable of murder?'

'I'm not sure yet,' Prachand concluded after a long pause.

'Okay,' Inspector Gupta said. 'I have some news to share.'

'You heard from Dr Wadia?' Prachand sounded eager.

'Yes, I did,' replied Inspector Gupta, surprised at the telepathy. 'Ranjana Jha was indeed drugged.'

'Really!' Prachand spluttered. 'Heart attack, head wound and drugs. What a confused murderer and what an odd mystery this is turning out to be. What drug was it?'

'They don't know yet.'

'Did you know that poisoning is still quite a prevalent practice, Guptaji? Back in Kanpur, I was approached by a lady who suspected someone was trying to make her daughter sick. The culprit turned out to be the stepfather! We caught him red-handed.'

'How did he do it?'

'Slow poisoning, to weaken the system first. He used to take her out for treats when the mother wasn't around. We laid a trap to nab him.'

'I wonder who poisoned Ranjana. How and why? I mean, there are easier and less-suspicious ways to kill someone. Clearly, the murderer tried them all. Why poison as well? Something doesn't make sense, Prachand. Maybe there's two of them?'

'I would approach the problem in another way.' Prachand suggested. 'My Ammaji always says "*Buri museebat ki naak ulte haath se pakdo.*" Let's think of it this way. Who could possibly have easy access to poison or drugs amongst all our suspects? Once the opportunity is clear, the motive will appear. It's being a bit of a shy bride at the moment.'

'We will have to wait for a further analysis. It's important to know what poison was used.'

'Guptaji!' Prachand suddenly exclaimed. 'I just remembered!'

'Something else Ammaji says?'

'No. Where do most poisons come from?'

'Shops?'

'No. I'm not talking about where they are sold, but how they are made.'

'From what I've heard, they could come from spiders, animal droppings, even mercury, but largely from plants.'

'Right. And other than the local vaid, who is that one person who has a good knowledge of plants and herbs, has access to all the homes in the area and will never be suspected of causing harm?'

It took a few seconds for Maya Gupta to process the information before it dawned on her. 'Bhutaari Baba.'

CHAPTER 39

All Aalok Kumar wanted was to finish this film, but the universe was conspiring against his ambition by sprinkling bodies, camels, tantrics and the police in his path.

The day had begun with a heated discussion on how Ranjana Jha's remaining scenes would be shot. Paramveer Khattar had recommended that Ranjana's stylist, Preeti, step in. As it turned out, the perky young girl was an aspiring actress herself.

'C ... casting is not your responsibility,' Aalok Kumar told Paramveer Khattar.

Paramveer Khattar, meanwhile, took a long drag from the pipe he was smoking and glared at the rotund young man with distaste. 'And I suppose you have many options? What will you do? Hold auditions? Oh, yes. Aspiring actresses, please report to the cursed ruins of Kuldhara to fill in for the murdered lead. Terms and conditions apply.'

Aalok Kumar turned a strange shade of indignant purple. 'B ... be that as it may, it is my creative decision.'

Ramnarayan Rathod, who was sitting in his favourite chair by the window, drolled. 'Param, I had an ingenious idea. Perhaps we can cast your bhabhi in the role? I see an uncanny resemblance with Ranjana. Don't you? Besides, she is naturally prone to drama and histrionics. What say?'

Padmini Rathod, who was polishing some silver bowls on the dining table, looked up for a few seconds but didn't respond to the obvious and demeaning provocation.

Prachand was watching these proceedings from across the sitting room. He took in Padmini Rathod's small, graceful movements. There was an innate poise and patience in the way she conducted herself.

'Why not Vidya Bhabhi then?' Yatish chimed in. 'She played Shakuntala in her college play. Why, she has even played Manthara in school, right, Bhabhi?'

Vidya scowled. 'I was filling in for Manthara, who was absconding. It was a last-minute decision and I decided to help out of magnanimity.' The fact that she didn't want to highlight being cast as the hunchbacked and most despised character from the Ramayana was lost on Yatish.

'My decision is final,' Paramveer announced, holding up his hand. 'It is in everyone's interests. You'll see, she is most accommodating.'

'Well, this is on record,' Aalok scowled. 'That you are t ... twisting my arm. I will g ... give it a go because there is a p ... paucity of options and we must finish the film. B ... b ... but I make no promises. If she is no good, she is out. And when there is no one left to consider, I will f ... finish this schedule, even if I have to wear a salwar-kameez and wig myself,' he said and called out to Venky, his DOP. 'Let's talk to the special effects team back in Mumbai. We will need to do some heavy d ... d ...uty work on parts of the film! I suppose I'll have to finish my sketches as well,' he rued. 'It's hard being avant garde when fate is insisting on toying with us.

The stylist and soon-to-be-celebrity was summoned an hour later. By force of habit, Preeti came armed with her wardrobe, make-up kit and hair brushes. She complained about receiving an unkind call from Ranjana Jha's mother who labelled her an opportunistic vulture. Of course, she was too jubilant about the providential change of tides to care. It only took her a few minutes to step into the late actress's clothes, literally. She was about a size smaller than Ranjana Jha, and not as well-endowed, but she winked and said that the matter 'could easily be fixed.'

The shooting commenced and Vikas Kishen prepared himself to film a scene with his new leading lady who barely reached his shoulder despite wearing heels.

'Another quick fix!' she winked and batted her eyelashes, looking up at Vikas Kishen who coloured a little and nodded. Aalok Kumar groaned audibly and asked for a stool.

That's when Prachand, who was watching this drama unfold from a distance, noticed Paramveer Khattar moving hurriedly towards the main courtyard. On instinct, Prachand decided to follow him, but fell behind.

Yatish caught up with him. 'Prachand Da, are you looking for Paramveer Khattar?'

'Yes.'

'Well, he just pushed past me and rushed out.'

'That way,' Prachand said, pointing in the direction of the woods. 'Let's go.'

As they walked hurriedly, trying to catch a glimpse of the man they were following, Prachand almost tripped. 'Yatish, please let go of my shirt.'

His childhood friend looked around anxiously. 'These trees give me the creeps now, Prachand Da. Remember how I used to refuse to cross that *kabristan* on the way to Naveen Market when we were small? I feel the same way about this place.'

'Yatish, this is no kabristan. What we need to be bothered about are the living who are causing trouble.'

They had reached the clearing by now. 'Look, there they are!' Prachand said. Paramveer Khattar and the driver, Chintan, both had their backs to them. There was a familiar looking box in their midst. They seemed to be arguing.

As Paramveer Khattar snatched the box from the driver, Prachand stepped into the clearing. 'What's going on here?'

CHAPTER 40

Paramveer Khattar hissed. 'Why do I owe you an explanation? This isn't any of your damn business!'

Yatish, bristling on behalf of his friend, intervened. 'Oh, it is! You're the one lurking around a crime scene, suspiciously, if might I add.'

'And like I said, that's none of your business!' Paramveer Khattar growled.

The driver found his tongue. 'It's all him. He made me do it.' He was pointing right at Paramveer Khattar who brushed away the hand that was levelled inches from his face.

'Enough!' Prachand went straight for the box in the driver's hand, lifting the lid. 'I've seen these before.' he said, frowning at the colourful little vials, about ten of them, neatly lined up inside. The rest of the empty space was filled with thermocol and clumps of paper. He looked Paramveer Khattar straight in the eye. 'You brought these to my office as well, if I remember correctly. What's in them?'

Paramveer Khattar looked like a deer caught in the headlights but forced out a mirthless laugh. 'Now I suppose you'll accuse me of carrying poison or something as absurd as that? One sinister theory after another.'

Prachand narrowed his eyes. 'So, is it? Poison?'

Something in Prachand's expression made Paramveer Khattar abandon the brashness and pause. 'Ranjana Jha was poisoned, was she?' he asked slowly.

Prachand nodded. 'Yes, but that information was only given to the police and me.'

The implication of this statement wiped out any leftover trace of indignation. Paramveer Khattar pleaded before the detective. 'I ... I swear I just blurted that because I was irritated. I had absolutely no idea that she was poisoned. Believe me.' Pointing to the vials, he said, 'This is not poison.'

'Then what is it?'

Paramveer Khattar looked back and forth from the vials to the driver, who seemed equally frazzled. Prachand kept a stern expression trained on him. 'You can either tell us on your own or there is always the other option of letting the police get it out of you.'

'It's my favourite way of passing time!'

All four of them turned around to see Inspector Gupta approaching them with her deputy, Brijesh.

'Why is it that for some or the other reason I always find myself returning to this spot?' she said as her eyes swept the surroundings. Then she turned and picked up one of the vials. 'And the person I find myself returning to is you. You love being in the limelight, don't you?'

'Inspector Gupta, I swear what you're holding has no poison in it. And I had nothing to do with Ranjana's death either.'

Inspector Gupta picked up some more vials for inspection. 'Well. Here are the facts. You have no real alibi for that night, you were in constant friction with the deceased and all you clearly care about is finishing this film. I'll ask you one last time, Mr Khattar. I promise you.'

'This looks like the medicine our vaidji used to prescribe in Kanpur. He once gave me a bottle with a yellowish liquid for my nani's constipation. She accidentally had the whole bottle and you can imagine how ...' Yatish stopped his inane rambling when Inspector Gupta raised her hand impatiently, brow furrowed.

'It's a medicine really,' Paramveer Khattar confessed, his shoulders drooping. He walked to the well and then turned around. 'I ... I used to do drugs in college. People think I was born with a silver spoon in my mouth, like I had it all. What no one saw was the loneliness and the expectations inside a glass palace, where the silver spoon can end up choking you.'

'Mr Khattar,' Inspector Gupta interjected. 'I don't mean to be unkind, but I'm not a very patient person, so you'll have to save your speech for another day. Also, you waxing on about your struggles is not explaining the presence of illegal drugs in your possession, drugs that could have killed Ranjana.'

'Just let me explain!' Paramveer Khattar barked. 'My father is not the most compassionate or indulgent person. In fact, the pressure he created to mould me into the perfect successor drove me to drugs.'

Prachand was the only one with an empathetic look on his face. Paramveer Khattar's story was bringing back memories of the years he had spent being a disappointment to his father as an IIT failure. But the hardened inspector didn't look like she was buying into the sob story of the poor little rich boy.

Paramveer Khattar held up one of the vials. 'This is methadone. It was prescribed to me by a family physician when I was falling back into the habit. It's supposed to ease withdrawal symptoms, but I ended up getting addicted to it. It's very hard to source. That's why I needed a local to help,' he said and glanced at Chintan.

'Can an overdose of this ... thing ... be fatal?' Prachand inquired.

Paramveer Khattar shrugged. 'I suppose an overdose of any drug can be fatal.' He narrowed his eyes and asked, 'Are you implying that I supplied drugs to Ranjana?'

'Did you?' Inspector Gupta seized the opportunity and pounced on him. 'Or did she threaten to expose your addiction? Was she blackmailing you? Is that why it was important to get rid of her? So that daddy dearest wouldn't come and wring your neck, or have you thrown out on the streets with no one to finance your *aiyashi*?'

Paramveer Khattar sniffed, his eyes darting from one person to another, looking like a trapped animal. 'You can't pin this murder on me. You have no evidence. I know that.'

'Oh really?' So, this was not a vicious, premeditated crime to to get rid of someone you argued with incessantly, someone you hated who was now a liability?'

'I doubt he hated her,' Prachand said.

Inspector Gupta looked at Prachand with a scowl, annoyed at her badgering tactic being interrupted. 'What do you mean?'

Prachand took his time to respond. 'He was having an affair with Ranjana Jha.'

CHAPTER 41

A sudden dust storm drove the conversation indoors. They all walked back to the haveli, with Inspector Gupta and Prachand trailing behind, deep in conversation, something that Vidya Tripathi noticed immediately.

Dinanath Tripathi, who had decided to take a short stroll and was ready with his shoes on, sat down grumbling in a rickety chair by the main door. 'This weather is a joke. *Kabhi baarish kabhi dhool!*'

'The desert can be as temperamental as us human beings, Mamoji,' Arjun Prajapati smiled indulgently at the old man.

'It's just that the villagers say unpredictable weather is a bad omen, especially this sort that blots out the light,' said Arjun Prajapati.

'Believing in nonsense like that is what will ruin this country,' Inspector Gupta commented while walking towards the makeshift interrogation room. Arjun Prajapati, bewildered after seeing her, bowed and turned in the direction of the kitchen. Inspector Gupta watched him scuttle away, her eyes lingering for a moment. She gestured for her deputy who came running. 'Yes, Madamji?'

'I do remember speaking to him but have you looked into him properly? He was very much in the haveli that night.'

'Madam, let me check.' Brijesh pulled out a long notebook from the cloth bag hanging around his shoulder. The rabbits and elephants illustrated across the cover of the notebook caught his boss's eyes. 'I borrowed it from my daughter,' he said, smiling sheepishly. 'I've made an exhaustive list of all the people we have covered between us. Just give me a minute, please. He was one of the first few ones, so I can't remember.'

Inspector Gupta looked on with pursed lips as he proceeded to put on his glasses and turn over some pages, licking his finger every time he did so, looking more like a moneylender than an investigating police officer.

'Maharaj Chitragupta, if your perusal of your *khaatas* is done, may I have my answer?' asked an irritated Inspector Gupta.

'Yes, Madamji, here it is!' Inspector Brijesh exulted, taking his glasses off. 'Arjun Prajapati was with his wife in their room on the night of the murder. They live in an outhouse on the property. He didn't wake up till he was called in to search for the missing actress early in the morning. He was the one who discovered the body along with the detective.'

'Hmm. Yes, I remember.'

'Any problem, Madamji?'

'No, not yet. His tantric friend is absconding because he clearly has something to hide, but go grill Prajapati again about being Bhutaari Baba's alibi on the night of the murder. You never know what comes up.' Inspector Gupta gestured with her head for Prachand to join her in the interview room. She noticed Vidya muttering something to him while looking in her direction, making her oddly self-conscious. She smoothed her creased uniform and pretended not to notice.

When Prachand joined her, Inspector Gupta asked, 'All okay?'

'Oh yes, Guptaji, not to worry. All's okay,' Prachand said with a smile.

'Tell me your theory about this affair, which he has now admitted to. I wanted to hear the facts from you before that wily man manufactured his own, and I also want you to tell me why you withheld this information from me.' She popped a chewing gum into her mouth and leaned against a wall, arms crossed over her chest.

Sensing trouble, Prachand tried to formulate a response. He cleared his throat. 'Guptaji, you must believe that I had no bad intentions. It was merely a sliver of a suspicion at the time, so I had no reason to come to you. You see, something I truly believe is that when you try and read a person, you don't have to entirely rely on their words. Ever since I stepped on to this set, I have been doing just that. Yes, Ranjana Jha wasn't the nicest person. She was argumentative and high-maintenance in general, but even more so with Paramveer Khattar. It was almost as if she was deliberately trying to get his attention, sometimes acting coquettish, sometimes impossible. It was all volatile, the kind of volatility and capriciousness you expect between lovers, not foes.'

'So, purely based on observation, you deduced that they were having an affair?'

'There was something else,' Prachand said. 'When Ranjana Jha's body was discovered, her mother had claimed she had taken insulin shots earlier. The police hadn't arrived by then and I merely wanted to check whether she had died of a possible overdose. I mean, I am no doctor but mere curiosity took me to her room ... and then her dustbin.'

Inspector Gupta's eyes widened. 'You rummaged through her dustbin?'

Prachand's eyes lit up. 'Oh, yes. A person's waste is often a treasure trove. I have solved quite a few cases by rummaging through dustbins. They are laced with remnants of our lives, all that we use and discard, tiny pieces of our everyday, things we remember and want to forget.'

'Interesting,' Inspector Gupta remarked and sat back in a chair, glancing momentarily into the dustbin she had thrown the chewing gum wrapper in, wondering what other mysteries of life lay in its smelly depths. 'You are quite the philosopher! Now, going back to one particular dustbin.'

'Yes. Ranjana Jha's. The dustbin by her bed helped me understand her state of mind on the day she died. It did have insulin vials, a crushed rose and a torn-up card, you know the small paper ones you see with bouquets? There was also an empty strip of Disprin, which is usually taken for headaches. All of these things, the poor mauled rose, the headache tablets, the torn-up note, etc., indicated that she was distressed.'

'What does that have to do with Paramveer Khattar.'

'There was a faint but distinct smell of tobacco lingering on the card, left by whoever the writer was, the sort that Paramveer Khattar smokes all day long.'

'I see. Why didn't you share this information with me earlier? It would have given us a clearer motive. They were clearly quarrelling about something. In fact, I remember inspecting the room myself, but the dustbin was empty.'

'Exactly, Guptaji. I overheard you telling your deputy that you had checked the room and found nothing of consequence. I even sneaked in again to find the dustbin empty. How could I approach you with missing evidence that I wasn't supposed to find in the first place? Once I saw an opportunity for a confession from Paramveer Khatter today, I mentioned what I knew, the veracity of which was writ large on his face. He did admit it.'

'Even between lovers, a quarrel means heightened emotions. Perhaps he flew into a rage and lost control.'

'I thought of that angle, Guptaji, but other than the fact that he is ambitious and selfish, he clearly was distraught at her passing. The expression I saw on his face when he was with her body, that was no acting.'

Inspector Gupta's furrowed brow seemed to be straightening out, but her sharp gaze stayed on Prachand. 'All right, but no more secrets. Now, is there anything else, absolutely anything else you need to tell me? And I don't care if the evidence or the person has disappeared.'

Prachand was about to shake his head when Aalok Kumar's candid confession came to his mind. Guessing that this information would create further friction later, he decided to reveal all. He gulped and spread his fingers on the table in some abstract gesture of submission. 'Well ...'

'Yes?'

'There might be a little something.'

'Now what?'

'Aalok Kumar.'

'The director? What about him?'

'He ... he might have come to me the day after the murder.'

Inspector Gupta's eyes narrowed. 'And what might he have said to you?'

Prachand conjured the fakest smile he could muster and said in a jovial tone, 'Oh, nothing of consequence, really. He told me that he might have accidentally killed Ranjana Jha.'

The stern expression on Inspector Gupta's face made Prachand want to run to the bathroom.

CHAPTER 42

'Why did you lie to me?' Inspector Gupta was in no mood to mince words.

Aalok Kumar fidgeted with his shirt, his eyes darting nervously from the buttons to the officer.

'I d ... didn't lie. I t ... told you that I used to go for w ... walks in the woods to clear my head. That's all. I had n ... nothing to do with the murder.'

'We'll get to that in a bit. I would like for you to tell me about the nature of your relationship with Ranjana Jha.'

Aalok Kumar blew his nose noisily and wiped it with a damp handkerchief. 'Th ... that's an odd question. I was directing her, of course.'

'She wasn't a great person to work with, I hear. Tantrums, complaints being the order of the day. Must be infuriating, right?'

Aalok Kumar smiled. An eerie, ill-timed smiled. 'I s ... see what you're doing there. My mother used to do the same. T ... trap me into admitting things I d ... id. Women seem to employ s ... similar tactics.'

Inspector Gupta shrugged. 'And I've met scheming men that would put both genders combined to shame. But that's not what I am here to debate with you. I've heard Ranjana Jha insulted you publicly a few times. Even called you a ...' she looked down at the file she was referring to, '... "haklu" and laughed at you.'

Aalok Kumar looked away. 'Yes, she did. She was a d ... decent actress but a horrible person. B ... but I am not the only one who didn't like her. Ask the producer and his pal, Ramnarayan Rathod, or even his wife, they'll all t ... tell you she was nuts. B ... but that doesn't mean I killed her.'

'Well, it seems that you were convinced, only a few days ago, of having murdered her by mistake.'

Aalok Kumar wiped his forehead again. It seemed as if the Ganga and all its tributaries had decided to converge on his brow. 'I know what it looks like, m ... my walking into the woods, Ranjana Jha being murdered. The profile fits, I'm nervous, irritated with the actress, I k ... kill her and run back to the house.'

'Why does it always sound like you're narrating a screenplay?'

He took a big gulp of water. 'Look, I am a c ... c ... creative guy and we have a l ... lot of nervous energy. Especially me. When a project is going on, I need time and space to think, to talk aloud, to vent my frustrations, to clear my head. It's a p ...process,' he shrugged. 'I used my evening walks for this purpose. Whatever that lady would say to me, or for that matter anyone, I would dump it all in the woods. Unfortunately, on the night of the m ... m ... murder, I got delayed due to the thunderstorm. I heard a noise through the trees near the clearing and got startled. I threw a rock in that direction and ran back. Prachand Tripathi was convinced I couldn't have k … killed her. He measured the size of the rock, distance and …'

'Let the police be the judge of that.'

'Fine.' Aalok Kumar lapsed into a sullen silence. Inspector Gupta watched the curly haired director wriggle under her gaze. Was this untidy and timorous man really capable of murder? In her experience, the arty kinds like this city boy were prone to whimsical temper tantrums, but all she had against him was his proximity to the murder scene. While he didn't have an alibi for that night, no one had really reported seeing him after he retired for the night. And given his portly frame, unless Ranjana Jha had really ticked him off, she couldn't imagine him heaving himself out of the first-floor window and landing nimble-footed on to the ground below like Spiderman.

'C … can I go?'

Inspector Gupta broke out of her reverie and decided to let him go. 'I need something from you. Do you usually shoot extra footage?'

'You m … mean wild takes, extra scenes?? Sure. There's a master shot and then we shoot from different angles. There is plenty of extra footage. Anything s … s … specific you want?'

'No. I just want all the footage from the day of the murder.'

'There might be quite a lot of it.'

'Don't worry about it. My colleague Sarthy will sit with one of your people and look through it.'

'Okay. I'll have m … my AD sit with him.'

'That's all for now. You'll be hearing from me.' Inspector Gupta had reached the door when she heard Aalok again.

'You know, you have a very interesting f … face and jawline. If you ever want to dabble in …'

'Never. Thank you.' Inspector Gupta was quick to respond.

Brijesh was flummoxed. 'Madamji, this is a golden opportunity. This man is saying you can be an actress. Why won't you even consider it? Life *ban jayegi!*' A deprecating look from Inspector Gupta made him hastily add, 'I mean, in your spare time.'

'Inspector Brijesh, if I wanted to sing and dance, I wouldn't have had my hide peeled in the police academy and toiled all these years staving off hormonal bosses in our system. If you're so keen, go audition.' Inspector Brijesh looked nonplussed as she grunted, immediately regretting the outburst. 'Did you speak with Prajapati again?'

'I did, and s … sorry, Madamji, I forgot to inform you. While he maintains he was not with Bhutaari baba on the night of the murder, he looked very anxious when I prodded. We must keep an eye on him. There could be something that he is hiding.'

'Is there anything else you've forgotten to tell me, Brijesh? Like the actual murderer having a *taash* party with you last night after confessing and signing a written statement?' Inspector Gupta snapped. 'When will you guys learn to be professional? Do you want to be stuck here forever?'

Inspector Brijesh hung his head low.

'It's okay now,' Inspector Gupta relented and waved her hand dismissively. 'We can only find out more when we have the wily old man in our custody. Keep looking for him.'

As they left the haveli, she looked around, her eyes searching for Prachand. She found that working with him helped her sift through the flotsam and jetsam of the investigation, something she looked forward to. But this feeling was superseded by the irritation caused by him having crossed the line with her.

As Inspector Brijesh brought the jeep around, Constable Sarthy rode in on his scooter.

'Madamji, I have the report on the shoeprint.'

'I was coming to the station anyway. Why didn't you call me?'

'No signal, Madamji!'

'Anyway, it's good you came. I need you to look through some film.'

'I have to watch a movie?' His eyes goggled at the unexpected possibility of entertainment.

'No. Not a film. Film as in footage from the shoot. I'll brief you,' she said, ignoring the crestfallen face. 'First give me the report.'

Constable Sarthy handed her the thin file with a pale blue cover that was branded with department logos and signatures. She leafed through the pages. 'Each footprint was submitted with a sample shoe, to match against the print, I hope?'

'Yes, Madamji. The technicians took foot and shoeprints to be thorough. According to them, due to the amount it rained and the contamination of the site, it was difficult to isolate, but the one that's the freshest and deepest, and closest to the well, matched with one of the shoes, at least in terms of size. Size 9.'

'Size 9? That must be quite common. Who all from our list wear a size 9? Let me guess. Paramveer Khattar.'

'No. He actually wears a size 10, and mostly boots. The print found was a very specific kind of make and design. We did find someone who wears that size.' Constable Sarthy's eyes gleamed with the promise of precious information.

'Well, who is it?' she asked.

'Ramnarayan Rathod.'

CHAPTER 43

After days of frenetic activity, the film was finally nearing completion. Elated with the possibility of an end in sight, Paramveer Khattar had announced a mandatory rest day for the cast and crew.

The haveli was enveloped in silence. The birds trilled louder than usual, reclaiming their right to suffuse the air with their curious chatter while the desert breeze wafted in from the mighty Thar in gentle gusts.

Padmini Rathod and Vidya were sitting in the verandah sipping tea. Chachu Tripathi, now proficient at the art of sniffing out the special adrak-waali-meethi chai, had joined them. He used the opportunity to vent.

'The police seem to have settled here with bag and baggage. Don't they have anywhere else to go?! What did you drink, what did you eat, what position did you sleep in, what time did you go for potty? Asking the same questions over and over won't change the answers or bring the poor lady back from the dead. Even on a day off they have to come back. Now they have your husband inside for the last one hour,' he said to Padmini Rathod who had a faraway look in her eyes.

Multiple murder theories, sordid affairs and now added conjecture about the poisoning had become a constant hum of conversation. Given that the murderer was assumed to be amongst them, every cup of chai was regarded warily, incensed cooks were asked to try their own food before serving it and no one wanted to be alone. Yatish had threatened to leave if Chachu Tripathi did not stop requesting an escort for all his bathroom visits. In this air of suspicion and uncertainty, despondency hung like cobwebs.

'Men are strange creatures, aren't they?' said Padmini Rathod. 'All brave and honourable on the outside but opportunistic and manipulative when it comes to saving their hide.'

'Well, when it comes to self-preservation, won't any person do whatever it takes?' Dinanath Tripathi asked on behalf of all menfolk. 'Look at me. A simple, God-fearing man, but when it came down to saving myself from Ammaji's *chappals*, I used to lie through my teeth. Saving one's skin is a compelling force.'

Padmini Rathod turned towards the elderly man. 'I'm talking about extremes. About the people who would throw their loved ones to the dogs, who would trundle on the feelings of others to serve their selfish desires and fake pride. On one hand we have people building temples dedicated to goddesses and brave women like Rani Sati, but these same people suffocate the women in their homes,' she said, her eyes ablaze with an unfathomable fuel. Vidya was surprised to see the usually placid sea brimming with emotion, but could also understand why this was happening.

Inspector Brijesh, now Prachand's friend, had told him in confidence that, while defending his alibi, Ramnarayan Rathod had ended up discrediting Padmini. He revealed to the officers that her nightly alcoholic indulgence had compromised her memory. Vidya shuddered to think how it might feel if Prachand bared her secrets to the world, like how she could shame a mule with the amount she kicked while sleeping, or that the deafening snores that gave the Tripathi household sleepless nights emanated from her and not her husband. The chamber of secrets that marital threads bind is filled with a heady mix of mortifying matters that should remain under wraps.

'I'll never understand men,' Padmini Rathod said shaking her head.

'Well, some are easier to read than others,' Vidya said, locking eyes with Prachand who was walking towards them. He shot her a dazzling smile and her heart skipped a beat, as it always did at the sight of the simple, honest and lovable man she had married. She did not smile in return, given the nature of the conversation they were having.

'You deserve so much better,' she said, looking meaningfully into Padmini Rathod's eyes. She saw a sad capitulation, a mockery of all that her place and title in the haveli stood for.

'Sometimes, circumstances render us helpless, my dear friend,' said Padmini Rathore.

'I hope I'm not interrupting?' Prachand was about to occupy the chair next to his uncle when he saw the expression on Padmini Rathod's face and paused mid-air, his posterior hanging about in abeyance, unwilling to intrude.

Registering his presence, Padmini smiled. Vidya looked at her for residual traces of their conversation, but the expression on her face announced that she had moved on from her musings, and that Vidya would have to do the same.

'Did my husband have anything else to add? Is he cleared from suspicion?'

Prachand looked around awkwardly. Vidya read his mind and placed a hand on his. 'Oh, come on, Prachand! This concerns her husband. Besides, nothing remains a secret here for long.'

Prachand gave his wife a withering look. 'Padminiji, do you mind if I ask you a few questions?'

'My opinion hardly seems to matter these days, so this should be welcome,' she smiled wanly.

'Would you remember where your husband was on the day of the outdoor shoot, when it rained? He told the police that he was at home, working in his study.'

She shrugged. 'I'm honestly not sure, but he did ask for his lunch to be sent up.'

Prachand nodded slowly. 'I see. And does Arjun Prajapati usually see to your husband's wardrobe and personal grooming needs, or is it you?'

'Well, it's the both of us really. Depends on his moods. He is quite temperamental as you've seen.'

Prachand narrowed his eyes as if trying to frame the right question delicately. 'Would you be aware of all the shoes in his collection?'

If she was surprised by this question, Padmini didn't show it. 'I can recognize it if I see a pair. But I'm not sure if I know each one. He is quite finicky about his shoes and gets them custom-made.'

'I see,' Prachand nodded slowly, digesting the information. Just then, Arjun Prajapati appeared with a glass of chaas that Prachand had requested. He ensured Prajapati was out of earshot before continuing, 'Inspector Brijesh seems to think they've been through his entire collection, but there is a pair missing from his rack.'

'The pair they think they identified at the murder scene?' she stiffened.

Prachand explained as gently as he could. 'They have to explore every angle, Padminiji. That doesn't necessarily mean he is guilty. Just cooperate with the police and they will be out of your hair soon. I wish your husband would comply. Being agitated and confrontational won't help. I mean, that's what Inspector Brijesh tells me.'

Vidya cocked an eyebrow at him as he emptied the glass in his hand. 'Inspector Brijesh seems to be volunteering an awful lot of information this morning.'

Prachand smiled sheepishly. 'Might have to do with the fact that his *mameri behen* is from Kanpur and that he has a particular fondness for *Thaggoo ke laddoo*. I've promised to send him a few boxes. Guptaji is still upset with me, so I had to be enterprising,' he shrugged. 'I've actually had a spot of luck while going through the footage. Found something interesting.' He seemed to be looking at something on his phone but didn't divulge any more.

Sensing that he was being watched, he noticed Arjun Prajapati standing in the distance, shuffling from one foot to another. He excused himself and walked up to the man who was clad in a stiff grey safari suit.

'All well?' Prachand asked.

'Prachandji, please help me. I've goofed up! I didn't mean any harm. *Kasam Bhairon Baba ki*!' he spluttered, folding his hands.

'Please don't tell me you murdered someone by mistake.'

'No, no!' Arjun Prajapati's proud moustache quivered as he shook his head vehemently. 'I just want to talk to you about ... Bhutaari Baba.'

'What about him?'

'I've known him for years. He ...' dropping his voice, Arjun Prajapati came close till he was just an inch away from Prachand's nose, '... he came to me today, to ask why I denied meeting him on the night of the murder.'

'You mean you lied? And he just came to the house? Why didn't you tell the police? Everyone's been looking for him. And if you are indeed his alibi, you should have spoken sooner. That would have cleared your friend.'

'I didn't want to get involved!' Prajapati moaned, covering his face. 'He stormed in today, boiling with rage, and then left, swearing that he had nothing to do with the murder.'

'Of course, he would try to reach you. That's entirely justified.'

'You know that police Madamji well. She unnerves me. If you could just tell her on my behalf, in your own way ...'

'Oh no, I won't! I'm already in trouble for doing something similar and I will absolutely not become a messenger again.'

Ten minutes later, the gullible Prachand Tripathi made his way to the interrogation room where Inspector Gupta was conversing with her colleagues. He promised himself that once they were back in Kanpur, he would take some lessons from Vidya on the fine art of learning how to say no.

Seeing who was coming her way, Inspector Gupta pretended not to have noticed.

'Namaste, Guptaji.' Prachand smiled. She gestured to her colleagues to wait for her outside.

'Yes?'

'I have a few updates.'

'I'm sure you do.'

He looked at her apologetically. 'I promise you I will never make that mistake again. In fact, Arjunji has some important information that might help you make your mind up about Bhutaari Baba.'

'Really?' she cocked her eyebrow. 'And again, he came to the saviour of the world instead of the police.'

'I believe all that will cease to matter when I show you what I found in the footage from the shoot.'

'And what the hell were you doing with the footage?' Inspector Gupta shot an irritated look towards the door. Constable Sarthy, anticipating trouble, hurried out faster.

Prachand produced a frame he had captured from the footage. It showed Ranjana Jha and Vikas Kishen at the outdoor shoot.

'What am I looking for?' Inspector Gupta peered into the picture. And then she saw it. It was a man not very far from Ranjana Jha, hidden behind a tree. What struck her was the intensity and hatred on the contorted face that was keenly focused on the actress. 'That's Ramnarayan Rathod!'

'Yes!' Prachand trilled, his voice high-pitched with excitement. 'According to his statement, he was nowhere near the shoot that day.'

Inspector Gupta looked pleased. 'Got the lying bugger. I'll pin him down this time.' She hesitated and then looked at Prachand. 'Thanks. This helps.'

Prachand beamed at her. 'Does this mean I've redeemed myself? You don't want to kill me any more!'

Before Inspector Gupta could respond, the smile on Prachand's face crumbled into a grimace. In perfect slow motion, he fell to the ground, unconscious.

CHAPTER 44

'I knew this would happen. The spirits are restless. They have possessed the poor detective!'

'You seem to have a direct line with the other world. How do you know it isn't Mahua who has possessed him?'

'How absurd! There are rules in every world. Daakans inhabit women, not men. Have you ever seen a woman go into a men's loo?'

This intellectual debate broke out between Arjun Prajapati and Vikas Kishen, in the corridor where everybody had crowded, waiting for news of Prachand. Dr Sisodia, the family doctor of the Rathods, had been summoned hurriedly when all attempts to revive Prachand had failed. While Vidya and Yatish were with the doctor inside, Paramveer Khattar was pacing the living room where Ramnarayan Rathod had surfaced upon hearing the news. There was a deep crease on his forehead.

'This shoot of yours is turning my home into a disaster zone. What is going on, Param? I tried to help you and now I'm regretting my decision.'

Paramveer Khattar seemed uninterested in any mollycoddling. He scowled and said, 'Stop over reacting. He fainted, that's it.'

Ramnarayan Rathod held his tongue, which he only did in his friend's presence.

No one noticed a pale-faced Maya Gupta wringing her hands in the police jeep parked outside. Despite repeated requests from her colleagues, she sat stubbornly in her vehicle, too tense to even walk into the house. She was consumed with remorse. Prachand had only been helpful and she had been pretty nasty to him.

The object of everyone's concern finally woke up. The first person Prachand laid eyes on was a bespectacled old man whose face was an inch away from his own. 'The patient is alive and awake,' he announced redundantly.

An ashen-faced Vidya, who was sitting quietly at the foot of the bed, rushed to Prachand's side, almost knocking over the doctor who looked frail enough to disintegrate on any kind of physical prodding. Vidya swept her hand over Prachand's forehead, her eyes brimming with tears. Prachand managed a weak smile.

'The last time I saw you crying was when your secret stash of guavas was discovered by Ma and distributed to the Gwaltoli Gilehris with *namak and mirch*. Am I dead?'

'Don't you dare!' Vidya hissed. She looked at the septuagenarian doctor who was hovering behind her. 'What happened to him? Is he okay now?'

'Hain?' The doctor cocked his ear closer to Vidya.

'This man needs a doctor himself,' Vidya muttered to Yatish and then repeated her question.

In response, he coughed repeatedly, his eyes bulging in their sockets. 'Apologies. It's a chronic allergy. Nothing infectious. This changing weather doesn't help. I'm okay,' he said reassuringly to Vidya who wasn't the least bit interested in how he was feeling. 'Your husband seems fine. He was groaning and holding his stomach as he slept. It's probably something he ate. I've given him a medicine to help him flush his system.'

'Why would he faint because of it?'

The doctor hacked yet again. 'I'm not sure. But his BP is a bit low. He should rest. Make sure he has plenty of fluids.'

Once the doctor had been escorted out, Vidya marched up to Paramveer Khattar and Ramnarayan Rathod who were still in conversation.

'We are leaving,' she announced.

Paramveer Khattar's face paled. 'Please don't say that. Dr Sisodia mentioned that this might have been a stomach upset. Why do you want to leave?'

'Are you serious, Mr Khattar? Even after a murder, we stayed back to fulfil our promise. To do right by you. But I will not stand and watch my husband coming to harm. What if that Bhutaari Baba is responsible? Wasn't he lurking around? What if it was one of your staff? Point is, we will never know and it seems to be too dangerous here.'

'Please, Mrs Tripathi. With Ranjana gone, this shoot needs you both even more. We are almost at the finish line. I'll speak with Venky to hasten up whatever remains.'

Vidya felt weary and drained, but the defiance remained. 'I have my conditions. We need more guards; I want security cameras installed and a doctor needs to be on the set till we leave.'

'Security cameras? I'm not having imbeciles and labourers traipsing through my home, digging holes in these ancient walls. It's crowded enough already,' Ramnarayan Rathod piped up.

Paramveer Khattar shot him a vexed look and returned his attention to Vidya. 'The cameras won't be possible, I'm sorry. I really don't have the budget for it. But I can assure you that I will beef up the security and have a doctor on call at all times.'

'If by a doctor you mean the one from the Stone Age who just saw Prachand, I'd rather turn to Bhutaari Baba.'

A few more negotiations later, Vidya made her way back to Prachand. She bumped into Inspector Gupta on the way and was rather surprised when the stone-faced inspector gently laid a hand on her shoulder. 'I can see why Prachand speaks so highly of you. I, for one, would love to have you in my corner in any situation.'

Vidya smiled, wiping away a stray tear.

'Don't worry. I'll speak with Dr Sisodia,' Inspector Gupta reassured Vidya. 'We must try and find out what happened to Prachand. I suspect there's more to this than meets the eye.'

Back in the room, Inspector Gupta's words were still ringing in Vidya's ears. Chachu Tripathi was beside himself with worry and lamented to Yatish. 'I know why this is happening. I abandoned my role as Jambavan for the glitz and glamour of films. I have invited the fury of the gods.'

'What nonsense, Chachu. God is not vindictive.' Yatish tried his best to placate the old man.

Hours later, when the commotion had dissipated and the haveli was quiet once again, Prachand woke up with a start, with an urge to go to the bathroom. It took him some time to gingerly pry Vidya's fingers wrapped protectively around his forearm. He tucked a stray strand of hair behind her ear and left a soft kiss on her head.

The floorboards creaked as he made his way to the bathroom. Switching on a dim light, Prachand, still weak, used the wall to steady himself. When he turned, he saw a flash of colour on the bathroom mirror. As his eyes adjusted to the light, he moved closer and realized what he was looking at.

Right in the middle of the wrought iron mirror was a familiar sight that made the blood of the otherwise practical solution finder run cold. Small and bloody handprints. He knew he had to wipe them away before they caused more panic. Someone was trying to tell him it was his turn.

CHAPTER 45

With his nostrils filled with the tantalizing aroma of food, Prachand walked to the table as his mother gingerly lifted the lid off a large pot. 'See what I've made for you!' she said, her eyes shining with excitement. To his horror, there were two heads bobbing inside the gravy. It was Paramveer Khattar and Ramnarayan Rathod's heads that announced in unison, '*Khammagani!*'

Sweating profusely, Prachand woke up to find himself alone in bed. He wiped his forehead with his sleeve. 'This case is clearly getting to me.'

As he got up and headed towards the hall, he could still smell food. And then he heard a voice that made him abandon his sleepwalking theory.

'Aye, Rachna, *dhukariya ke tani kuch khaee ke de deo.*'

'Ammaji!' he shouted.

He ran the remaining distance to take in an astonishing sight. Ammaji was laid out on the long divan in the living room, his mother was in conversation with Padmini Rathod and Vidya was at the dining table with Chachu Tripathi, Yatish and Bhushan, cackling about something.

'How on earth did this happen!' he expostulated.

'*Hamaar bitwa*!' Ammaji exclaimed with such emphatic delight that her dentures came flying out. Prachand caught them just in time and melted into her arms. She smelt of home and happiness. After much hugging and jubilation, a crease broke across his broad forehead. 'How did you all get here? I mean ...'

Arjun Prajapati materialized out of nowhere. 'I ... erm ...you see, I was contacted by your brother. They wanted to surprise you and I couldn't help but ...'

Prachand didn't usually succumb to emotional outbursts, but in that moment he felt a surge of something molten in his nerves. 'Arjunji, you are well aware of the ... situation ... here. Even then?'

Vidya squeezed his shoulder. Her voice was low. 'I know, Prachi. But I truly believe his intentions were right. He assumed you needed the comfort of family, that it would help.'

With great difficulty, Prachand tore his eyes away from the quaking man.

Rachna Tripathi had cocked an eyebrow. 'What is this *khusur-phusur*?'

Prachand smiled, taking in the silver streaks, the web of aggressive wrinkles and the eager face of his mother. 'Nothing!' he said drawing her into a bear hug. 'How did you decide to come?'

'Some nerve you have asking me that!' She whacked him on the arm. 'No one seems to be interested in taking my calls or telling me what's happening. I had to come!

Besides, something terrible happened the other day.' Her lips quivered.

'What? Is Pitaji alright?'

'Pooh! What will happen to him? I was cleaning your room when a lizard fell on my head!'

Registering both Prachand and Vidya's blank expressions, she grimaced. 'It signifies death! I called the panditji, got a puja done and came here with the *bhabhuti* for all of you.'

'Maaji, what if the lizard had fallen on my face?' Bhushan inquired with a straight face.

'Simple. It means relatives are dropping in for a visit.' Rachna Tripathi shrugged. Noticing the sniggering, she threw a cushion at him. 'Don't you dare laugh!'

Prachand chuckled heartily, wiped his eyes and hugged his mother. 'Many thanks to that lizard then. I am so happy to see all of you!'

His mother squirmed. 'That car journey has already squeezed most of the life out of my limbs and you're claiming whatever is left. This dadi of yours didn't rest her mouth for a second. How can one frail woman pack in so much food?! Then there's her bladder.'

'Oh ho! Forget about all that. What matters is that you're here,' Prachand said cheerily. 'Bhushan, what happened to your play?'

Bhushan looked pained, like a festering wound had been fingered. 'Don't ask, Bhaiyya. That production was cursed. From disappearing wigs to falling lights to actors leaving to people falling sick, it was as if an unseen negative energy had enveloped it.'

'All superstitions, Bhushan. Why shut down the entire play?'

Bhushan then went on to narrate how Bhalla Uncle, who was playing Pawan Putra Hanuman, had accidentally put the set on fire with his tail. Panicking, he had thrown the flaming tail on to one of the curtains. The tailor had later admitted to using a lot of cheap and flammable cloth. 'Lanka was saved, but the production was ruined. The producer didn't have the funds to reinvest,' he lamented.

'That's sad,' Prachand clucked. 'Worry not. Bholenath will find another channel for your creativity.' He patted his brother's back affectionately. 'The biggest surprise is how Pitaji agreed to let you all travel.'

'Oh, this old woman still has a few tricks up her sleeve,' winked Rachna Tripathi.

'Breakfast is served!' Padmini Rathod announced. 'Maaji, thank you so much for teaching me your special recipe for mirchi ke pakode.'

Rachna Tripathi beamed at her like a proud peacock, ecstatic about this validation from someone belonging to the upper echelons of Rajasthani society.

As the food on the table was polished off greedily, Arjun Prajapati announced a visitor.

'It's Inspector Maya Gupta, Prachandji. She came asking for His Royalness, but he isn't home. Will you please meet her?'

Bhushan looked around the table. 'Inspector? What are the police doing here?' he asked.

'Police? What police?' Yatish giggled nervously.

'The police ... in the hall,' Bhushan said.

Rachna Tripathi looked at Prachand across the table. 'Beta, what is it? Everything okay?'

Prachand took a few seconds to respond. 'Ma, don't get too worried, but there is something going on here.'

Rachna Tripathi's eyes swept across the hall, to the ceiling and back. 'I know, Beta. It seems as if this *khandahar* ... I mean, this haveli ... is in the middle of some badly needed renovation work. Right? We understand. Such a heritage property must be hard to maintain,' she smiled and looked at her host.

'No. What I mean is that a crime has been committed.'

'What! Oh no! Have the labourers made off with something? Scoundrels. Do you recollect, when we were getting the terrace fixed back home and those two workers stole cement sacks? The construction industry is full of these ...'

'Ma! Listen to me. The police are here because we are in the middle of a murder investigation.'

CHAPTER 46

'Digoxin. They found it in her blood. That's what the toxicology report says,' Inspector Maya Gupta poured some tea in a saucer and sipped from it. A debilitating headache had kept her awake for most of the night. 'Taken in large quantities, it can be fatal to certain constitutions.'

'Didn't you mention that you suspected Bhutaari Baba?' Vidya asked. 'Isn't this a bit high-tech for a tantric? I was thinking insects and lizards were more his territory.'

'Well, it's a medicine used for heart troubles. The interesting thing is that a lot of medicines are derived from plants and there are enough people in the village who swear by the herbaceous pills and potions that he carries with him. He does have an alibi for now, but we can't be sure if he was annoyed enough to kill her and clever enough to fool his friend and hide it. To explore this angle, we need to locate him. And his goat.'

They were sitting in the verandah and Prachand was in deep thought. His lips were moving ever so slightly, discernible only to Vidya who knew he indulged in subsonic mumbling when he was thinking hard.

Inspector Gupta continued. 'We have questioned Ramnarayan Rathod a few times, but he remains mulish and uncooperative.'

'Could he explain what he was doing on the sets, and why he lied about it?'

'It's always the same response. It's his house and he doesn't need anyone's permission to walk around his property. Until I have some concrete evidence, we can hardly hold him.'

'Did you know that, right now, we are surrounded by debilitating poisons?'

Both Vidya and Inspector Gupta looked at Prachand curiously. He still had a faraway look in his eyes and was drumming his fingers together. When he knew he had their attention, he leaned back in his chair. 'I bet that in our vicinity there are at least fifteen to twenty substances that are potent enough to kill. A lot of these provide the foundation for popular medicines and drugs.'

When neither of them said anything, Prachand stood up.

'Come with me,' Prachand said. The two women followed him as he walked towards a circular patch of vegetation a few yards from the main entrance of the haveli.

'You see that plant?' Prachand pointed to a shrub of white and yellow flowers. 'Oleander, locally known as kaner. Very poisonous.'

'Really? Chachu plucks these everyday as an offering to Bholenath,' said Vidya.

Prachand started circling a short tree. 'Saptaparni. Usually unsuited to this climate, but it's been carefully cultivated here. Also called the Devil's tree,' he said and pointed to another plant. 'This is a castor oil plant. Its seeds are very poisonous. This other one here, jimson weed, also known as dhatura, is poisonous as well.'

Inspector Gupta gave him a look mixed with surprise and admiration. 'How do you know so much about shrubs and plants?'

'When Pitaji used to drag me to the leather shop every day, I would slip out and spend time with Bihari Kaka who lived next door. He is a botanist and knows more about plants than anyone I have ever met.'

'Oh!' Vidya tittered. 'Wasn't he the one who gifted us a clock that had Bittu weds Gudia written on the dial?'

'Come on, Vidya. Poor fellow. He is known to be absent-minded.'

'What is your point here, Prachand?' Inspector Gupta interjected. 'Are you saying that it isn't Bhutaari Baba but someone else who is responsible for the poisoning?'

'All I am saying, Guptaji, is that this patch of carefully cultivated land in this otherwise poorly maintained place is very much on Ramnarayan's property. We shouldn't rule him out too quickly, even if there is lack of evidence for now. These poisonous plants haven't just congregated here for a herbal party. This looks deliberate.'

Inspector Gupta nodded. 'We should chat with the gardener. Not that I've seen him mentioned in the list of people Brijesh has pulled out.'

'Padminiji did mention him in passing,' Vidya said. 'Apparently the last gardener was fired almost six months ago for some theft. He has been absconding since. She herself does the bare minimum of watering the few plants on the property while on her morning walk. She doesn't seem very keen on maintaining the garden, and it is hard to hire people here.'

They made their way back to the main hall to find that the remaining Tripathis had moved base from the dining room.

'Rachnaaaaa, mukhwas *lao*,' Ammaji hollered from the divan that seemed to be standing in for her favourite charpai in Awadh Niwas.

Rachna Tripathi made big eyes at Chachu Tripathi. 'You'd think that by now she would have figured out that she's the one who is deaf.' She then looked at Yatish who was just about to settle down in a chair. 'Go get it, please,' Rachna said. 'You know, the red one.

'They're all VIP suitcases, Mataji. Which one?' Yatish pressed on.

'Forever full of questions! Arey, it's the one with the red ribbons on the handle and the Har Har Mahadev sticker. Now get it quickly.'

Prachand cleared his throat. 'Everyone, this is Inspector Maya Gupta, the very capable officer who is investigating the case.'

Inspector Gupta had barely raised her hand in a greeting when a wiry young boy with eager eyes and a wispy moustache appeared before her. 'Hello, Inspector Madam. I'm Bhushan Tripathi. Singer, songwriter, poet, screenplay writer and director.'

Prachand noticed the look of amusement on her face. 'That is indeed a long list of skill sets. Congratulations, young man!' she said.

'You see, I am always on the lookout for new stories and interesting new characters. I was, in fact, thinking of a musical featuring a lady inspector just the other day.'

'Bhushan, please, Beta. Not now,' Prachand said and patted his younger brother's arm.

Inspector Gupta nodded at Bhushan and touched the feet of the elderly ladies. What she couldn't have predicted was the bear hug she got from Rachna Tripathi. While she was figuring out an exit strategy from the unrelenting warmth, a pair of vexed eyes were fixed on her. As usual, the first one to notice was Prachand.

'What is it, Vidya?' he asked, spreading an arm around her slender waist.

'Bhootni!'

'Who?'

'Your new girlfriend in law enforcement.'

'I thought you started liking her. What changed?'

'She is a chameleon. On the one hand she behaves like she is made of stone and then, like Soorpanakha, she tries to dig her talons into my family. What police inspector touches the feet of a stranger's family?'

'Can you please pick one for clarity? Bhootni, Ahalya, Chameleon or Soorpanakha? I personally think she might prefer ...'

'I'm not amused,' Vidya hissed. Prachand Tripathi's smile vanished.

CHAPTER 47

If the bedrock of the Rathod homestead was silent coexistence and order, the arrival of the Tripathis turned out to be the cultural and sensorial bonanza they never signed up for.

Between Ammaji's hookahs, the ear-splitting music Bhushan played and the heady aroma of an always-active kitchen, Naveli Haveli looked and smelt different in just a day or two. Room freshers were rendered redundant as everyone homogenously smelt of masalas, something Ramnarayan Rathod frequently complained about. Prachand couldn't be happier and even Vidya, Yatish and Chachu Tripathi's homesickness seemed assuaged in these temporary transformations. The tricky part was handling Rachna Tripathi.

If her royal dreams had been deflated at the sight of the derelict haveli, they were thwarted further when the shooting resumed a day later and she realized that the venture she had assumed would be a big fat Bollywood tamasha was actually hanging from a shoestring budget. The murder investigation definitely did not boost her mood.

'Behind my back. The whole time,' she complained in a wounded voice. 'All those calls about fancy shoots and the media on the set. A palace grander than our wildest imagination. I was fed lies. By my own son, my brother-in-law, my daughter-in-law,' she said, barely glancing at the accused who were lined up like a row of sentenced convicts, looking everywhere but at the woman behind the angry tirade.

She eventually turned to Vidya. 'I thought you were like my own daughter. I sent you here thinking this change of scenery will help you with ... you know what. I've never pushed you on the grandchild front, but ...'

Vidya's jaw dropped. 'Ma, really? You've made me drink goat milk infused with special herbs, you've had me chew on foul-smelling churan, you even hired some strange woman to perform a "special" massage to activate my reproductory chakras. I don't call that being subtle. If you consider me your daughter then you have to walk the talk and accept me with or without a baby.'

Rachna Tripathi remained defiant. 'I am the most understanding mother-in-law anyone could have. Ask whoever you'd like to in Gwaltoli. So what if I want to play with a grandchild? Is that a crime? I was only trying to help you. On Bimla Auntie's advice I even researched modern methods and asked you to explore the fertilizer thing, but you're so stubborn.'

'Fertilizer?' Chachu Tripathi asked.

'Devarji, it's completely natural. They put fertilizer in the belly if a child can't be conceived. There is a clinic in Rambagh.'

'Good God! I'm not allowing anyone to put any fertilizer inside my wife,' Prachand protested.

'Ma, stay on the topic. Why have you digressed from scolding to farming?' Bhushan intervened.

'Quiet!' Vidya held her hand up. 'Everyone! Ma is talking about fertility treatments. IVF is what she means.'

'Exactly! That's exactly what I said.'

'Stop it, Rachna.' Ammaji, who was parsimonious with her words and reserved her mouth for churan, blew out a thick plume of smoke in her daughter-in-law's face. '*Kok hai ya anaaj ka bhandaar*?' she said and then cocked her head in Vidya's direction. '*Bitiya, jaun toka bhae, taun kar.*'

Trounced, Rachna Tripathi scowled, knowing better than to take on two strong-headed women. She changed her strategy like a seasoned warrior. 'Ammaji, *yahan khoon hua hai, khoooon*!'

'*Aain*? *Kiski patloon*?' Ammaji strained her ear.

Realizing the futility of this conversation, Rachna Tripathi grunted and looked at Prachand. 'This is so dangerous, Prachand! You said the murderer could be living under this roof. And what a roof! Beds that creak, cobwebs and dust balls hang like decorations and the walls look like they were painted when the Mughals were still here. What kind of haveli is this? It's the creepiest place I have ever seen! And that bloody Rathod. Imagine, he had the nerve to tell me that Kanpuriyas seem to carry a certain "smell" of their city with them. The scoundrel! At least we know how to take care of our ancestral property. If he is the half-hearted co-investor in this production, I can see why the film is being shot on such a small budget. I can tell. The director looks like he hasn't ever combed his hair and the heroine is more interested in make up than acting. Instead of preparing for the festival of lights, here we are, stumbling about in this dark, godforsaken place!' She paused to draw a long breath.

'I think Ma hasn't taken some vital medication today,' Bhushan mumbled to Yatish who was watching the familiar proceedings with a smile. 'Now she is blithely moving between murder, decor and make up.'

Prachand pulled his mother to the edge of the bed and sat her down, placing an arm around her. 'Ma, calm down. I apologize for all of it. No one wanted to lie to you. I made them.' His mother gasped at this admission.

'What was the point in worrying everyone?' Prachand continued. 'I can't even imagine Pitaji's reaction. We are already deep in the investigation. In fact, I'm helping the police and we are very close to catching the murderer. You should return to Kanpur. We will wrap up and be back shortly.'

'We can't just leave you all in danger, Bhaiyya,' Bhushan refuted.

Prachand walked up to his younger brother and embraced him. 'Little Bhaiyya, this is my work, my territory. You have to trust me and let me do my job.'

'I am not leaving without my family. That is final.' Rachna Tripathi looked at her son with a militant expression, her arms crossed over her chest, signalling that she would not relent.

Prachand knew better than to consider a mutiny when it came to his mother. This Gwaltoli Gilehri who was a mild and sweet old woman on the outside was qualified for making a living as a mafia strongman given her coercive techniques.

'All right, but this stay is extended on my terms. Pitaji will be kept out of the picture. Thanks to all the political bigwigs involved in this fracas, the media has been kept at bay so far. We should continue to keep it under wraps.' After a few seconds, he turned to Yatish. 'Didn't I overhear you talking to Venky about some lights that need to be replaced for the shoot?'

'Yes. Over the weekend. They will have to be sent to Jaisalmer. The shoot can't resume without them.'

'Hmm. That seems fortuitous,' Prachand smiled mysteriously.

'That the lights broke?' Vidya raised an eyebrow.

'Well, yes!' Prachand nodded. He had now gone and sat next to Ammaji. 'And I have a feeling we might be going to Jaisalmer with those lights.'

'Huh?' Rachna Tripathi's eyes gleamed.

'Ammaji, *kuch ghooma phire jaike hai*?' Prachand hollered into the octogenarian's ear.

The old lady nodded with glee and shuffled towards the exit with great alacrity, leaving everyone in splits.

CHAPTER 48

'What is the real reason behind this trip, Prachi?' Prachand zipped his weather-beaten duffel bag and smiled at his wife. 'You are equally guilty of trying to seek out mysteries everywhere,' he said and walked over to where she sat on the edge of the bed. He ran his fingers down the length of her straight, long hair, clearing out the knots.

Vidya's brows remain furrowed. 'Don't think you can distract me. I know that entertaining your family would be your last priority in the middle of a murder investigation.'

Prachand sighed. 'All right, Feluda. Be patient. There is a reason, but a small one. It is to indulge my curiosity. And I'd rather you concentrate on having fun. This trip has turned out to be nothing like what you expected. Now that there is an opportunity, I order you to think of nothing but relaxing over the next two days. Leave the sleuthing to me!'

'Can we even travel, Prachand? Won't Maya Gupta ...?'

'I've handled all of that. There are perks of having friends in law enforcement,' he said with a wink.

'Don't even get me started!' Vidya grunted.

The ground floor of Naveli Haveli was reminiscent of the chaos at a railway platform. Breakfast was underway in the dining hall, the technical crew was milling about packing and loading the lights into the minibus, and the luggage was being piled up near the main door, drawing curious glances from the staff, wondering whether their guests were leaving for good. Paramveer Khattar seemed unusually chatty as he spoke about the accommodation to Ammaji and Rachna Tripathi, who were decked in their best banarasi silk.

'The bus is at your disposal till you return. The men only need to be dropped off at the workshop and picked up on the way back. I have asked Prajapati to call in advance and reserve rooms in Hotel Sanskaar. The views are to die for!' Realizing his poor choice of words, he hastily added, 'I mean, your family will really enjoy themselves.'

Prachand, always wary of excesses, in material or manner, squirmed at this unwarranted benevolence, but his mother was most approving of the gesture. 'Arey, don't make this Yamraj-like face. Let us feel special, if only for a little while!'

At the dining table, Padmini Rathod ensured Rachna Tripathi felt even more like a dignitary with the lady of the house fussing and fawning over her. When Prachand carried a plate of food to Ammaji, he was received with a grunt.

'*Hum na khaab*,' she said and refused the food, making a face at the plate from behind her dark glasses.

Prachand laughed and nudged the old lady. 'Ammaji, please wear your dentures. I know you like it when Ma serves you, but she is busy being pampered at the moment,' he said and gave her a quick peck on her wrinkled cheek. She grudgingly fished out her dentures from a small potli hanging from her pallu and accepted the plate from her grandson.

In between bites, she pulled Prachand's sleeve. '*Uka khasam hain okey*?' Prachand looked in the direction of her pointing finger. Padmini Rathod was now by Paramveer Khattar's side, fussing over him as he fended off the relentless flow of puris and ghee-laden rotis.

'No, Amma, that is our producer, not her husband. Padminiji is a generous host and takes care of everyone.'

Under the veneer of a smile and small talk, Prachand's mind was hard at work. Ramnarayan Rathod, who was in the hot seat at the moment, refused to meet with his guests. He was spending most of his time either in his room or his office in Jaisalmer, which he visited a few times a week. The sulky driver running his errands seemed to be his most frequent visitor. Purely on instinct, Prachand decided to try and speak with their host before their departure.

It was the first time he was exploring this part of the mansion. Places with history, especially the ones that had suffered abuse at the hands of time, filled Prachand with a tinge of sadness, as if they were bemoaning what they had been reduced to. There was something dark about the energy here and he felt a certain heaviness and foreboding in his heart as he walked on. Unable to explain these emotions, he reminded himself of the directions he had received and reached the room. When there was no response despite several knocks, Prachand assumed that Ramnarayan Rathod was away.

A gust of wind made him look towards the window to his right. He walked up to it and looked far into the distance, beyond the boundaries of the property. Then, on an impulse, he turned his head further to the right, where the abandoned village of Kuldhara loomed not very far from the haveli. The images of the bloody handprints floated unbidden into his head. That was another puzzle. Could he really give any credence to the superstition? Was he really in danger?

'You'll fall!'

Prachand was so startled that he almost lost his balance, leaning so far out of the window. He pulled himself in and backed away from the window, staring into the puzzled face of Padmini Rathod.

'Are you okay?' she inquired.

Prachand nodded and pointed at the door. 'Your husband is not at home?'

A look of unease crossed her face. 'I don't really know,' she shrugged. 'He has been irritable of late and doesn't speak much. I wish I could help you.'

Prachand felt sorry for her. 'Don't worry, Padminiji. I shall pray for this case to be wrapped up soon so that you both can resume your lives. I can understand there has been a lot of upheaval in these last few weeks.'

'I know you might think lesser of me when I say this, but I really do believe there is a shadow looming over us. I've felt it every day, in my breath, as if its infected me and runs in my blood.'

Prachand took his time to respond. 'Padminiji, according to me, our minds and hearts can play tricks on us, but we have to try and look beyond that confounding fog. There is an explanation for everything that has transpired here, and I will try my best to bring them to the fore as quickly as possible. Please don't lose heart.'

'Some *prasad*,' she said and extended her hand that held a few pieces of *mishri*.

'What are you looking at?' she asked when she noticed Prachand's gaze lingering on the mishri before accepting it and popping it into his mouth.

'Nothing,' Prachand smiled and waved his hand dismissively. 'I'm always distracted and thinking of something or the other. Let's go down. Your friend won't leave without saying bye to you and it'll take me some time to herd my big, fat family into that bus! Are you sure you wouldn't like to accompany us?'

She shook her head and returned his smile. 'I think it's time I concentrated on my husband. He needs me.'

After a lot of commotion and heaving, every single person was finally packed in and the creaking bus was ready for a mini adventure. It would be a welcome respite from the innumerable questions, the uncertainty and the confusing threads of the investigation.

The last ones to board were Prachand and Vidya. As he helped his wife in, she lingered at the door and looked back at the haveli. He realized that she was looking at Padmini Rathod standing in the doorway. She was waving at them.

'I can sense her fear. Do you think something will happen in our absence, Prachi?'

Prachand shut the door noisily. 'Let's hope not.'

CHAPTER 49

A change of scene can temporarily douse the fires of the present. Jaisalmer was just the salve that the Tripathis needed. The mere sight of the golden city, crafted with the brush of Islamic and Rajput architects, filled their hearts with an inexplicable joy and dispelled the darkness of the last few days. Mesmerized by the simplicity and the charm of its yellow sandstone houses and multicoloured shops and wares, even Ammaji abdicated her characteristic insouciance and stuck her head out of the minibus with childlike enthusiasm.

Madho Singh, the jovial man behind the wheel, regaled them with urban legends and trivia about the city and its people. Yatish, sitting upfront with Chachu Tripathi, kept up a steady flow of questions. 'If people are still living in the fort, how are structural repairs carried out? These houses look like they are glued to one another.'

Madho Singh laughed indulgently. 'You know, we joke that the brick and sandstone homes here are glued together by folktales and songs, not mud and cement. The Ravs and Bhats, a caste of bards and genealogists, would roam the lands, knitting together the wisdom and experience of the years gone by. That's what runs in our veins as well. Songs and stories are all we need! Tales aside, these walls and our will have prevailed for centuries, be it through invasions, droughts or treacherous weather. Only a fourth of the population resides within the fort. There are newer constructions on the outer rings.' With that, he swerved and narrowly missed hitting a swarm of tourists spilling on to the road. 'You must stay on till Diwali when the fort is decked up like a new bride. It's a sight to behold!'

'It's so romantic, Prachi.' Vidya squeezed her husband's arm. They were driving through the narrow winding lanes and gateways leading up to the fort that sat majestically atop a hill. The sight of the locals going about their day, the street vendors, the walls adorned with hand-printed *daris* and wall hangings stole her heart. When she realized that her husband was muttering and deep in thought, she whacked his arm. 'No, you don't! How can you think of the dead when there is so much life around you?'

Prachand tapped her nose. 'Don't worry, Viddu. I'm right here. You'll just need to cover for me when everyone is at the fort. Only for a little while. I need to zip out for some quick work.'

Vidya frowned. 'No secrets. You promised.'

'No, never. Trust me, Viddu, it's something minor. I'll tell you later. For now, all I need is for you to be with the family and enjoy yourself. That's what you can do for me.'

Vidya's incoming protest was drowned out by some loud swearing from Rachna Tripathi.

'When will these ghosts leave us alone?!'

'Bhoot?' asked Bhushan, pulling out his earphones. He had been relegated to the rear section with the men and the lights.

'What are you saying, Bhabhi?' Chachu Tripathi looked around nervously, checking for any other-worldly presence. Rachna Tripathi was hiding under her pallu.

Madho Singh guffawed yet again. 'I think Mataji is referring to Bhoot Pol!' he pointed ahead at the tall gateway they were passing. 'It's only a door for the humans, not for the dead!'

After dropping off the light crew, the minibus stopped at Jaisalmer Fort for an hour, and then at Gadisar Lake. It wound its way past restored havelis, sandstone homes and temples that stood like beautiful vanguards of a rich and resplendent heritage. It stopped at Manak Chowk for some customary shopping. Ammaji, who was kindly ferried around on chairs, took to the delicate and ubiquitous ghewar with a ferocity that might be expected from an association dating back to previous births. Rachna Tripathi was so alarmed at how much she ate during their lunch stop that she kept Dr Dayal, the diabetologist, on speed dial, expecting some medical emergency.

Bhushan, ever the iconoclast, insisted on enjoying an Italian meal in the most authentic sounding Ristorun Jaisal. He wanted to experience 'more of the world' on his Rajasthani holiday. While his family tucked in to Rajasthani thalis, he ordered from a menu that the Italians would have balked at, comprising Pyazi Polenta and Sarvagun Sampana Spaghetti. Prachand returned by the time lunch was being wrapped up. He winked at Vidya and then froze at the sight of the shopping bags heaped next to her.

Licking her fingers dry, Rachna Tripathi pushed her thali away and reached for the buttermilk. Her own spoils were crowding around her feet, under the table. Within two hours, she had earned the reputation of a wily, predatory bargain hunter. A lookout notice had been issued amongst the merchant community for the silver-haired lady who could put them out of business. 'I think we should head to the hotel, Prachand,' she suggested. 'We still have tomorrow. Ammaji must be tired and ...'

'*Hum na jaab*,' Ammaji declared from behind her dark glasses, wiping out a bowl of ras malai and refusing to budge.

Vidya tried to reason. 'But, Ammaji, you must be exhausted.'

'Hum na jaab,' she repeated with conviction.

Prachand, anticipating friction, stepped in. 'Where do you want to go, Ammaji?'

'*Humka kauna tarah oonth par dhar deo*.'

'But how will you mount a camel, Ammaji?'

'*Hamaar bahut icha baate*,' she said and pouted like a child.

Prachand disregarded the disapproving glare from his mother. His heart had already melted at the sight of Ammaji's cataract-ridden eyes. She had strategically lowered her glasses for better emotional impact.

'Bhai Sa, have you heard of the camel safari?' the enthusiastic server who was clearing up the table leapt into the conversation. Prachand shook his head while Bhushan's eyes gleamed with excitement.

'It's a mere fifteen minutes from here by car. The overnight cost includes dinner, a camel ride, entertainment. All the phirangs do it. Most popular activity here.'

'But how do we take an elderly person with limited mobility?'

'Oh, they will manage. The guy who runs it is a friend of mine. I'll even get you a special discount,' he winked.

'Sleeping in the desert? What will Bade Bhaiyya say? What if a camel runs over us as we sleep?' Chachu Tripathi's fear and foreboding of the world in general had resurfaced.

'As long as Bhushan Bhaiyya promises not to sing, no camels will walk over us,' Yatish tittered, avoiding eye contact with Bhushan.

Rachna Tripathi elbowed her son. 'Beta, what about our morning ... activities?'

The server, who was now comfortably seated at the table, responded, 'Arey, Mataji, there will be a clean bathroom. Don't worry, you won't have to go on the sand like the camels.'

'Someone is clearly gunning for a referral commission,' Vidya said and elbowed Prachand, but he was too distracted by the thought of camels.

'That's it then! I'll call the hotel and tell them we will check-in tomorrow,' said Prachand. 'Desert safari, here we come!'

CHAPTER 50

Sitting atop a prickly camel that plodded languorously across the sand, Prachand stretched his hand skywards, as if in deference to the network gods. Every few minutes, he would bring the phone back down and whack it in the hope that the time-tested Indian remedy for all malfunctioning gadgets would help cough up a few bars. That's when he caught snatches of a conversation between Bhushan and one of the camel handlers

'I refuse! I absolutely refuse. This is animal cruelty. The poor camel started shitting as I tried to mount it.'

'Don't worry' the man said. 'It had a bit of dysentery from before. Your weight is negligible.'

'Are you calling me scrawny?' Bhushan's slight frame quivered with indignation. 'I'll have you know that I am a youth sensation in Gwaltoli. There are hundreds of young Kanpuriyas who aspire to be like me.'

Prachand quickly intervened from his high perch.

'Bhushan, why don't you return to the camp? Or wait with Ammaji? We'll be back soon.'

Ammaji was quick to respond, her auditory faculties conveniently restored. '*Humka oonth par baithan deo.*' All attempts at dissuading her from doing so failed. Finally, with the help of three extra set of hands from the camp who handled her her like she was a ticking time bomb, Rampyari Tripathi took her first camel ride at eighty-eight years of age, her pallu billowing in the desert breeze and a giddily happy expression on her face.

Rachna Tripathi watched the proceedings from her camel and complained to Yatish who was moving like a pendulum, desperately trying not to fall off. 'My camel is obstinate; it spits and farts. Could be Ammaji's Rajasthani twin! Now look at that woman, the sugar high from the ghevars has driven her insane. If she falls and breaks her bones, your uncle will throttle us all!'

Left alone with his principles for company, Bhushan sulked and trailed behind the camels with some of the helpers from the camp. The Tripathis had opted for the short safari, given the geriatric quotient. Despite the more tolerable temperature during this time of the year, the desert was pretty unrelenting and the riders were shielding themselves with caps, pallus, straw hats and pretty much anything else they could grab.

They passed a few villages along the way. The scarcity of resources was evident, but the villagers' cheerful dispositions and the welcoming mandalas drawn outside each home were a testament of their tenacious and hospitable spirit.

Upon their return, tents had been set up for the guests and the tired travellers soon retired to stretch their limbs. Before limping into the tent that she was sharing with

Ammaji, Rachna Tripathi moaned. 'How do I untangle my kidney and intestines?'

In the Thar, the harsh and hot days segue seamlessly into generous, cool evenings. Prachand felt restless as he sat with his heels dug in the sand. Contemplation and recalibration were important weapons in his investigative arsenal. Unfortunately, he had not had much time to himself; his methodical note-taking had suffered as well. He wondered if these were the very reasons responsible for the tardiness of a resolution to this murky affair. All the tiny shards of the puzzle were up in the air with no real answers in sight except the one tiny hunch he was trying to dissect and collate in his head.

The rosy sunset, which was the most gorgeous sight any of them had laid eyes on, had brought with it chilly winds. Lanterns now dotted the camp site. As a group of colourfully clad dancers performed to the *dholak*, Prachand sauntered away to clear his mind.

He was seated some distance away when he felt familiar pressure on his arm and Vidya settled down next to him. Her beautiful face reflected the distant light of the campfire and made him spill the cobwebs cluttering his mind.

'This state of abeyance is making me uncomfortable. It's as if our wheel is stuck with no way out. We have four suspects: Aalok, no alibi, opportunity, weak motive; Bhutaari Baba, a sketchy alibi, opportunity, weak motive; Paramveer Khattar, no alibi, opportunity, motive; and Ramnarayan Rathod, no alibi, opportunity but no clear motive. Though Paramveer Khattar seems to be the likeliest suspect, arguments could go both ways. Plus, all we have is circumstantial evidence. I don't think we can eliminate anyone at this stage. Identifying those shoes and getting the telephone records seems to be our best bet.'

'Their best bet is you! If there's one person here who can catch the bad guy, it's Prachand Tripathi.'

Prachand smiled and drew Vidya closer. 'Now let's enjoy the rest of the night. You won't find network, so there's no point roaming the desert like a lost *chinkara*. Wait till we get back into the city tomorrow morning,' she said.

'Sure,' Prachand nodded. 'I should have packed a sweater. I didn't realize it would get this cold.'

Vidya squeezed Prachand's arm and winked. 'Don't you worry about that. We are cozying up under the stars tonight and you are sharing a mattress with me. There won't be any dearth of heat.'

Prachand's face coloured as he followed his wife back to the camp.

CHAPTER 51

After bidding adieu to the dunes and the flatulent, hairy ships of the Thar, the packed minibus made its way towards the packed streets of Jaisalmer that were bursting at the seams with people on foot or two-wheelers. Diwali festivities were in the air. The occasional tempo that strayed into the wafer thin lanes would be stuck till the choicest of abuses from stranded vehicles behind it, or the helpful directions from residents standing in the balconies above, helped remedy the situation. The minibus met a similar fate, but the Tripathis had their hearts set on breakfast at the famous Dhanraj Ranmal Bhatia sweet shop near Gopa Chowk.

The establishment came highly recommended by the locals and the Kanpuriyas, missing their favourite street treats from back home, had quickly sealed the plan. The shop itself turned out to be minuscule, but the smell of fresh jalebis, kachoris and laddoos that were laid out made their mouths water. Once the famous local gotua laddoos, kesar pedas and pyaz ki kachoris arrived, no one bothered talking;

their tongues were marinating in the succulent flavours of the sweet and savoury treats.

The only person who didn't seem interested in this gastronomical experience was Prachand. All he wanted to do was connect with Inspector Maya Gupta for further news. The sleepless night had done nothing for his mood. Vidya had peacefully snored while he was left to fend off her vicious Jackie Chan kicks all night long. He checked his watch. Nine in the morning seemed liked a respectable time to call the inspector. She received the call almost immediately.

'Guptaji, sorry, we had no network around the camels yesterday.'

'While you were riding camels, a lot happened here, Prachand.'

'Really? Please fill me in!'

'To begin with, Bhutaari Baba has been found. He was hiding at some halwai's place, someone who owed him a favour. Inspector Brijesh arrested him while he was stuffing his face. He isn't as smug any more. Swears on his beloved goat that he is innocent.'

'Then why did he bolt? Innocent folk don't go running off with their bag and baggage.'

'His explanation was a bit colourful. He claims that it all started when he overheard Ranjana argue with someone on the morning of the day she was murdered. She caught him eavesdropping and threatened to report him. This slighted him enough to want to stick around and frighten her, teach her a lesson, as he said. But when the rain disrupted the shoot, he decided to take shelter with Arjun Prajapati as it was too late for him to leave. He waited till everyone was asleep and then slipped out when he thought no one was watching. When Ranjana was found murdered, he assumed his alibi would cover for him. But when the police started looking for him, he chose to go into hiding.'

'And what did he do to make me sick, on the day I felt dizzy ... I mean, fainted ... well, collapsed.' Prachand coughed, embarrassed at having to recall how he had fallen with minimum resistance, like a wet leaf cascading to the earth.

'He point-blank denied having anything to do with it.'

Prachand took some time to cogitate. 'Do you believe him?'

'Well, he doesn't sound like he is fabricating anything.'

'Hmm. Say we were to believe him. Where does that leave the others?'

'Speaking of the others, here's a spot of good luck. We finally managed to get a hold of some call logs. The permissions took forever! The technicians weren't able to unlock Ranjana Jha's phone, which was password-protected. But we have been able to get her call records.'

'And?'

'Just as we guessed, some bit of Bhutaari Baba's story checks out. Ranjana Jha was indeed arguing with Paramveer Khattar on the morning of the day she died. It fits into the time frame and was the longest and only call.'

Prachand's mind was racing, reconstructing the order of events from that fateful night. When he didn't say anything for a few seconds, Inspector Gupta interrupted his mental machinations.

'What are you thinking?'

'A possibility, Guptaji. These arguments with Ranjana, the affair, nothing really proves that he committed the murder.'

'Would you like me to give you something more concrete to hold on to?' Inspector Gupta said and deliberately held her silence to toy with Prachand.

'Please tell me, Guptaji. Don't give me ulcers.'

'Due to the thinner density of towers in the area, signal triangulation wasn't easy, but the service provider's team now has an app to work with. It managed to locate a cell phone that was active and very close to the murder scene that night. It fits into the window of the murder as well.'

'Wow! That's like gulab jamuns topped with rabdi!' Prachand exclaimed. 'Whose cell phone was it?'

'The man you deem innocent. Paramveer Khattar.'

CHAPTER 52

As the Tripathis waited for a room at Hotel Sanskaar, Ammaji grabbed hold of the waiter serving welcome drinks and placed an order for mirchi ke pakode. Rachna Tripathi shook her head in disbelief. 'As a child, I would always hear that old age is the station when you start preparing for your final journey, when you withdraw from worldly pleasures. This woman however, won't leave for heaven till she is promised a fried food stall up there.'

'Don't worry. Let her enjoy,' Chachu Tripathi coaxed his sister-in-law and then stood up to stretch. 'Let me check what the hold-up is.' As he walked towards the reception, he looked around and took note of the high ceiling and the golden chandelier that hung majestically over the mosaic floor. The walls were covered in stained glass artwork interspersed with locally made colourful tapestries. The opulent surroundings made him subconsciously ease out the crease on the Nehru jacket he had managed to crumple. He sighed at a passing reflection of himself, thinking of the three times he had worn this very jacket when he was visiting prospective brides in his youth. Now here he was, many years later, still a bachelor sporting the same jacket. Life had squeezed him dry of his deepest desires like a lemon on a lemonade cart, but he still had some pulp left.

'Do we have a reservation, Prachand?' he asked, resting his hand on Prachand's shoulder. He could see Vidya arguing with the receptionist. 'Our tigress is at it. I see.'

Prachand smiled in response. 'This is apparently the hotel the Rathods and Paramveer Khattar have patronized for years. There was a mix-up with the bookings since we were supposed to come last night. They're apologizing but have no rooms.'

Fifteen minutes later, after much grumbling from Vidya, Hotel Star Lovers next door came to the rescue. As they unloaded their luggage, Rachna Tripathi stamped her disapproval instantly. 'Really? Star Lovers?'

'Ma!' Prachand protested. 'Don't judge a book by its cover. It's a decent accommodation. Come in. You'll see.'

'I have already stayed at decent places in Kanpur. I wanted a luxurious hotel to compensate for that khandahar in Kuldhara.'

The lobby was teeming with guests as Prachand finished the check-in formalities. Yatish offered to fill the guest register. He tapped on one page and passed the register to Prachand. 'Look at the entry on the previous page, Prachand Da.'

Prachand squinted in the inadequate light. 'It says "P. Khattar + 1". Single room.'

Yatish nodded. 'Didn't you mention that they only stay in the other hotel?'

'Yes. And if we assume that for some reason he had to stay here due to lack of rooms there, who was with him? He doesn't seem like the sort who would be keen on sharing anything, let alone a room. What date was this?' His finger traced the entry backwards towards the serial number column. 'Here it is. Isn't this the day when we took a break and shoot was cancelled?'

Yatish nodded.

'Mr Khattar has been busy. I was wondering why he was so keen on everyone taking an off. When I was chatting with him the day after that, he said he was under the weather and had to go see a specialist doctor. Why would he lie?' Prachand's lips started moving again as he silently worked at a knot in his head. He called out to the man behind the desk. 'Can you please tell me if Mr Paramveer Khattar frequents your hotel?' Prachand asked, trying to sound as casual as possible. 'He is a friend.'

The man's expression became guarded. 'Well, perhaps you can ask your friend yourself when you meet him next. He is one of our privileged guests,' the man said with a bow and ended the conversation.

'Looks like we have to dig deeper to find out why Paramveer traded his sanskaars for some "star loving",' Yatish said with a wink and looked around. 'This fatty won't say anything. Let me try and chat up some staff.' He walked off, whistling.

Prachand walked around the lobby collecting his thoughts. That's when he noticed a small boy who was hovering around the tourists, trying to earn a quick buck. The foreigners were indulging him, but the desi guests kept shooing him away. He followed the boy to a paanwalla outside the hotel. 'Busy boy, aren't you?' he asked.

'What do you want, Sahib? Khana, books, tickets ...' he said. And then, with a wink, he asked, '... *chokri aur pudiya bhi milegi.*'

It took Prachand a moment to understand the reference to the illicit items that some guests probably requested. 'Shouldn't you be in school? Or at home?'

The boy, who looked no more than eight years old, knocked back tea from a small cup and shrugged. 'These streets are my home now. And I'm happy here.'

Supressing the twinge of sadness in his chest, Prachand joined the boy on the slim bench and asked him to order whatever he wanted. The boy looked at him warily. 'First you tell me what you want in return.'

Prachand shrugged. 'Nothing, Beta. I just feel like giving you a treat,' he said and watched the boy gobble down tea and samosa.

Minutes later, and after a satisfied burp, the boy leaned in towards him. 'You be careful about that hotel. Lots of *gadbad-ghotaala* happens in there.'

Something struck Prachand as he pulled out his phone. 'Have you seen this man recently?'

The boy looked at Paramveer Khattar's picture and nodded. 'Yes, I saw this hero a few days ago with an auntie.'

'Auntie? You mean he wasn't with another man?'

'No, he stayed with an auntie. I'm sure of that. I carried her shopping bags from their car.'

'Oh. Thank you, Beta. Can you also help me with a description of this auntie?'

CHAPTER 53

Prachand updated Inspector Gupta about the discovery he had made.

'This man can't seem to keep his jewels tucked in his treasury box, can he? First Ranjana Jha, now Preeti,' she expostulated. 'What if they were both in on it?'

'Inspector Brijesh told me earlier that Preeti's whereabouts were checked on the night of the murder. She has an alibi.'

'Being complicit doesn't necessitate physical presence.'

'In the same vein, being a philanderer doesn't make one a criminal,' Prachand quipped.

'But it does give him a motive,' Inspector Maya Gupta countered. 'Remember what Bhutaari Baba said? Ranjana was arguing with him. There was another woman. What if he was tired of Ranjana and both Preeti and him decided to get rid of her?'

Prachand replied after a few seconds. 'Yes, that is plausible. But what about Ramnarayan Rathod?'

'He is an unexplained variable so far, without a motive. On the other hand, I have a man with a motive and at least some evidence placing him near the crime. It's clear to me where I am heading now. I'm going to press in on Preeti as well. She might spill the beans under stress. I'm done chasing ghosts.'

This was Prachand's cue to hold his reservations and let the officer do her duty. What she had said was logical, but something still rankled within him. Was he to trust the evidence that was beckoning him in one direction or should he go with the amorphous yet reliable instinct that had come to his rescue so often?

He had to park his turmoil away as he rejoined his family for the cultural performance they had decided to experience on their last night in Jaisalmer. A makeshift stage had been set up in a ground near the hotel. The ticketless, free-for-all event, thronged by locals and tourists alike, was hosted by the Desert Cultural Centre. There were dancers, puppet shows and skits depicting popular folklore; a total sampling platter of Rajasthan packed into two hours, some of which Prachand had missed already. He reached the seats occupied by his family as the puppet show came to an end.

Vidya patted the seat next to her but found him squinting in the direction of the stage.

'Is that ...?' he pointed.

'Umm, yes. That's Bhushan in the wings. He convinced the organizer that he was a seasoned performer, a teen sensation from Kanpur and that they should take advantage of him being here.'

'It will soon be clear who is the one taking advantage.' Prachand shook his head and then sniffed. 'What is that fragrance? It seems familiar.'

Vidya held up her wrist with excitement. 'It's from the hotel. All the rooms have a small bottle. Lovely, isn't it?'

Looking at Prachand's face, Vidya dew a sharp breath. 'I can see your mind is elsewhere. You have this weird expression.'

Prachand nodded. 'You know me too well. No matter who else is a person of interest in this investigation, Paramveer Khattar has the inspector's complete attention for now, what with the new evidence, his prevarications and now this Jaisalmer angle with Preeti.'

'Here, have some chaas.' Chachu Tripathi was passing along glasses of the desi cold drink.

Vidya emptied half her glass. 'I'm curious about why you are trying to defend that scumbag.'

Prachand took a big sip and placed the glass between his feet. 'You know, Viddu, that prickly sensation under your skin, that despite all the logic before you, something doesn't quite feel right?'

'Speaking of prickly,' Vidya whacked her arm, holding up a mosquito triumphantly. 'Well, I know what you mean. Your instinct is almost always reliable, but you also tend to bat for the undeserving. Don't let emotions cloud your judgement. You must consider all the facts.'

'Exactly. And here are some for you.' Prachand finished the last of his chaas and wiped his mouth with the back of his sleeve. 'Does Paramveer Khattar come across as an intuitive and clever criminal or a manipulative and entitled middle-aged guy?'

'The latter. But what does that prove?'

'I'll tell you,' he said and stood up abruptly, pulling at Vidya's arm. 'First, let's take a walk. It's stuffy here.'

Once they were on the road that led to their hotel, he locked his arm in Vidya's. 'Paramveer Khattar is the sort of person who is used to getting things done for him. He has no money, no career, but Papa comes to the rescue. No place to shoot a film, a friend comes to the rescue. He can't get rid of his addictions, the driver comes to the rescue. He likes the good life. Why would he complicate it with a murder? I don't even think he is capable of a crime of passion, which Ranjana's murder could well have been. His kind relies on wit, charm and wavy hair.'

'I get it,' Vidya nodded. 'But your ACP Pradyuman profiling still can't ignore the fact that he was near the murder scene.'

'Okay, here.' Prachand stopped in the middle of the road and faced Vidya as some passers-by bumped into him and scowled. 'I am Paramveer Khattar. I am having an affair with Ranjana and am now stringing along Preeti as well. On the night of the murder, I follow Ranjana into the woods because she is threatening to confront Preeti. I reach up behind her and whack her on the head. She falls to the ground. I decide to get rid of her body by tossing it into the well, but then I just leave it on the ground, so her body is found sooner? Remember, Viddu, this man trains as a wrestler. Ranjana Jha was half his size. Why would he not finish the job? Besides, we haven't been able to explain the poisoning. Can you see the number of ifs and buts in this theory? Ramnarayan Rathod, on the other hand, gave us a false alibi and is refusing to divulge any more details. Who seems more suspicious to you?'

'Everyone at this point,' Vidya said distractedly.

Even Prachand was finding it hard to concentrate as the crowd on the street started swelling. He scanned the apparel shops bursting with customers. In one particular store, a fat salesman was trying on a fuchsia pink sari for a foreigner. Some tourists sitting in a tea shop were laughing raucously as two kids raced past them towards a firecracker display. He couldn't help but notice the incongruity of the dark and dangerous place not very far from here, presenting a sharp contrast to the festive atmosphere that had percolated to every corner of the city. That's when he heard a familiar sound that could best be described as coming from a distressed werewolf on a full moon night.

Vidya froze as well. 'Is that who I think it is?'

Prachand caught her elbow. 'Viddu, Bhushan has managed to grab the mike. We need to get there before he unleashes the full force of his charm. The poor audience needs some saving!'

CHAPTER 54

By the time the Tripathis returned to Kuldhara the next morning, the police had been busy for hours. Paramveer Khattar had been picked up and taken to the police station. Preeti had been brought in as well with her carefully applied Multani mitti pack still on her face.

Prachand hurriedly made his way to the police station, requesting Arjun Prajapati to drive him there on his scooter. As luck would have it, on his way out, he bumped into the very man he had been wanting to meet before leaving for Jaisalmer. Ramnarayan Rathod was sitting on his favourite chair, gazing at his ancestors. Prachand sat close to him, but Ramnarayan Rathod did not shift his gaze.

'No one had the audacity to question these men. And look at the emasculated Ramnarayan Rathod. Relegated to a crumbling mansion, plagued by the nagging of a wife who doesn't care, and now being hunted by a strange woman who dares to question me while standing on my own property!' Every word he uttered was like a venomous hiss.

Prachand measured his words. 'Rathodji, don't fight the police. They are only doing their job. Cooperate with them and they'll be out of your hair.'

'So what if I was curious and popped in to see the shoot, to get some fresh air and to clear my head? Is it a crime if I left for a walk at night? Are these punishable offenses?'

'No, Rathodji. But can you tell me who you were arguing with late at night, just a few hours before the body was found?' Prachand knew he was shooting in the dark, but he decided to follow a hunch.

'I ... now you have brand new accusations.' Ramnarayan Rathod looked flustered and stood up. 'You're no different. I have nothing to say to you.'

As Ramnarayan Rathod walked away in a huff, Prachand realized that he might have unearthed the identity of at least one of the people involved in that late-night scuffle. Could he have been arguing with his wife? From what he could recall, they were male voices. He knew he had to park these questions aside and rush to the police station. Arjun Prajapati, waiting by his scooter, looked rather pale.

'Are you all right?' Prachand inquired, placing a hand on the man's shoulder.

'Ji, hukum,' he said and bowed. 'P ... police station, right?'

Prachand nodded and they drove down the bumpy road, their bones rattling with the motion.

For once, the police chowki was a beehive of activity. The boy who delivered tea was in a tizzy, supplying more than his usual order and wondering why the station that was usually deserted, barring the few familiar faces, was suddenly buzzing with people. The news had spread and there was a row of curious spectators squatting at a safe distance, hoping to see some 'phillum stars' emerge. Inspector Maya Gupta had called in for some backup from the next station.

During the interrogation, she came down heavily on the two lovers sitting across her table. Prachand, as an exception, was allowed to sit in the small antechamber to listen in without interfering. Preeti, who had thankfully washed her face, sat with a rosy complexion that would do her no good in a prison, crying copiously and swearing innocence.

'Yes, we are having an affair, but I had nothing to do with Ranjana Ma'am's murder.'

'She was nasty to you and you wanted Paramveer all to yourself. You convinced him to help you kill her. Admit it!'

'No, Madamji. Mother swear! Why would I kill someone for this guy? I'm not stupid. He amuses me and buys me things. That's all.'

Paramveer Khattar kept his eyes lowered, not reacting to this none too flattering confession.

'I suspected that he had some *chakkar* with Ranjana Ma'am, but he told me it was over. I couldn't care less anyway. She was quite a witch to me,' Preeti continued and glanced at Inspector Maya Gupta. 'That doesn't mean I killed her! Check with Asha from the crew. After the shoot was called off, she was with me the whole night.'

'That throws you to the wolves, Mr Khattar,' Inspector Gupta drank from a glass of water and banged it purposefully on the table, making both Paramveer and Preeti jump.

Paramveer Khattar trained his tortured eyes on her. 'Yes, Ranjana and I had an argument that morning. Yes, I stepped out at night. But onlyonly for the drugsfrom the driver. It's a well-hidden spot and seemed appropriate since people could still be milling around the haveli. You can ask him. I never called Ranjana. I have no idea why she was there.'

'You were right there! Where she was murdered.'

Paramveer banged his fist on the table. 'It was a terrible coincidence that I happened to be there, picking up my stash. I wish I knew! I might have been able to save her,' he said and covered his face.

'Did you happen to see Ramnarayan Rathod when you were out in the woods? He was apparently seen heading there at approximately the same time as you.'

Paramveer Khattar's face froze for a fraction of a second, but not before Inspector Maya Gupta noticed his reaction. 'See? Right there. You shake your head, you say you don't know, but both you and that man are hiding something. Whatever it is, is it worth going to prison for, huh? Your daddy won't be able to save you.'

Fanning his fingers on the table, Paramveer Khattar drew a long breath and leaned back in his chair. 'You have no real evidence against me. The affair, my argument with Ranjana, my presence in the woods, all of it is circumstantial.'

Inspector Gupta's steely gaze settled on him. 'I can always book you for illegal possession and consumption of narcotics. Oh, and please don't forget that I know you tampered with evidence. All easy charges to hold you on.'

'What evidence?'

'After Ranjana's body was discovered, you went to her room, rummaged around for anything incriminating and cleared the dustbin of the card and flowers you had given to her, didn't you?'

'But ... how ... I mean, how can you ...'

'We had someone helpful point it out to us.'

Paramveer Khattar curled his lip and looked towards the antechamber where he knew the detective was waiting. 'Bloody nosey Kanpuriya.'

'There are more things you need to worry about than that Kanpuriya. I assure you.' At this point, Inspector Gupta was interrupted because of a commotion in the adjoining room. She scowled and gestured to her deputy to check what the ruckus was about. Inspector Brijesh poked his head in a few seconds later.'

'Madamji, Mr Prachand is asking for you outside.'

'This better be good!' She raised her voice and strode outside to where Prachand Tripathi stood with Arjun Prajapati.

'Well?'

'Guptaji, Arjun Prajapati has some vital information to share.'

'Again! You're like the neighbourhood barber who has news from all over the village. Now what?'

'Go on, don't be afraid. Tell her.' Prachand nudged Arjun Prajapati.

'I ... I don't want to betray my master, but I can't be involved in a murder either,' Arjun Prajapati said and burst into tears.

'Please calm down,' Inspector Maya Gupta said and handed the quaking man a glass of water. He gulped it greedily and confessed, his wet moustache quivering and twitching. 'On the night Ranjanaji was murdered, Rathod had gone for a walk. When he returned, he looked terrified.' He paused to take a gulp and then added, 'He ordered me to wipe the floor, wash his shoes and return them to him immediately.'

Prachand and Inspector Maya Gupta exchanged a look.

CHAPTER 55

'An actress is dead. You were poisoned. The producer is a druggie and a murder suspect who can't keep his pants on, and now our host has gone missing. Is there any heart-warming detail I'm missing?'

Prachand shifted uncomfortably in his chair under his mother's scrutiny. She had a knack of making him feel like an errant child instead of a grown-up man in his thirties. 'I understand things are not as you hoped, but this is not a situation of anyone's making, Ma,' he said with a shrug. 'I've advised you repeatedly to head back.'

'Come sandstorms, camels or murders, Tripathis stick together,' Chachu Tripathi concurred dramatically, harbouring no further hopes of acting in the production as his character had been dropped from the script, much to his chagrin. He had taken particular exception to the undignified manner his character was made to exit, by electrocution. In the only movie of his career, the last endearing memory of him would be that of a charred piece of meat.

Prachand smiled at his uncle, but his mind was elsewhere. After Arjun Prajapati's revelations, they had raced back to the mansion to find that Ramnarayan Rathod was nowhere to be found. Padmini Rathod was sobbing quietly, her humiliation evident. She declared that she had no clue about her husband's whereabouts.

Inspector Gupta hadn't wasted time empathizing. 'These people in high places have informants placed like invisible termites in wood. Looks like he got a warning from someone and made a run for it. For now, search his room and belongings again. Those shoes have to turn up somewhere.'

She observed that Prachand was in deep thought. Having come to respect his quiet ways and the astute machinations of his mind, she felt a pang in her heart, realizing that they were nearing the finish line and that her time with the Tripathis, especially Prachand, would soon be a strange yet indelible memory. 'What are you thinking?' she asked.

Prachand shrugged. 'I met Bhutaari Baba a few hours ago.'

'That man is back here? My team is utterly useless! We should investigate and press charges against him for trying to poison you, even if he has an alibi for the night of the murder.'

'Fear makes fools of us all, Guptaji. He was cornered and desperate.'

'I feel that way sometimes. Especially when my seniors come visiting. That doesn't mean I will go about poisoning their food and then show up for work the next day with a smile,' she grunted. 'I had to release that Khattar and his bulbul as well. I couldn't hold them any longer, otherwise he would have lawyered up.'

Preaching to a police officer doesn't augur well, so Prachand chose his words carefully. 'I find that empathy helps me think clearly. It helps the unimportant layers peel away. Think about it, Guptaji, take Bhutaari Baba for instance. A criminal would be more bothered about hiding his tracks than turning up repeatedly to check if his alibi is backing him up.'

Inspector Gupta didn't respond.

'In my mind, of all the things we can accuse him of, Ranjana Jha's murder isn't one of them. No prints, yes, a possible connection to poisonous plants, but no other evidence. And a bleak motive of a fall-out with Ranjana. I think his actions were driven more by fear than evasion. Same for Aalok, wrong place, wrong time. That's all.'

'I get what you're saying, but in a policeman's book everyone is under suspicion till the very end. Till we have a culprit.'

'Woman.'

'Huh?'

'Policewoman, not policeman.'

Inspector Gupta gave a wry smile. 'You hear it enough and it becomes a reality. I was always told this job wasn't meant for women,' she said and shook her head. 'Anyway, it looks like you clearly have a new theory in your head. I can tell something's cooking. You don't think Paramveer Khattar and Ramnarayan Rathod, the *good friends,* are in cahoots with each other on this one?'

'I do have a theory, but it's only conjecture at this stage. Give me a little more time.'

With the search complete, Inspector Gupta's team returned to the living room to report that a thorough scan of the grounds and mansion had revealed no trace of the man at large. Two officers were dispatched to his office in Jaisalmer, even to acquaintances, but no one seemed to have a clue.

'That man must have trained under P.C. Sorkar,' muttered Inspector Gupta. Then she barked at Inspector Brijesh. 'Trace his phone. And this once, kindly do it before this case is closed. I don't want any excuses.'

Inspector Brijesh scurried away on the double. On the way, he collided into Vidya who was holding an armful of clothes. As they dropped to the ground, he gathered them hastily, apologized and left Vidya muttering. 'No one seems to have their heads screwed on right today. Someone won't walk with their eyes open, another adds chilli to the halwa, and I'm holding a stack of oversized clothes that aren't even mine!' She looked in Prachand's direction and held them up. 'I have enough to do. Please locate the owner of these clothes. They got mixed up with my laundry.' She walked over, heaped the clothes into Prachand's lap and left.

'You seem to have your hands full with important work. I'd better go check in with my team.' Inspector Gupta had a mischievous twinkle in her eye as she addressed Prachand.

He smiled sheepishly, looking like a dhobi collecting clothes from a client. 'Just between you and me, have you ... had ... I don't know how to ask you ...' Prachand looked at her quizzically.

She cleared her throat.

'Have you experienced something strange or inexplicable ever since you got here?' she asked. Prachand's mind was flooded with images from the afternoon at the well, the whispers, the scream Vidya had heard and the bloody handprints, but he divulged nothing. 'Have you?' he asked in turn, sensing that something was bothering the inspector.

'Let's just say that this part of the world can play tricks on your mind. I just wanted to check with another rational mind before declaring myself a lunatic,' she said, lowering her voice and looking around.

Prachand smiled. 'Guptaji, if we could claim to understand everything that happens in this world, it would be arrogance on our part. Besides, tomorrow is bound to be a test of everyone's patience and faith. I'm anticipating, nah, very much expecting unusual events.'

'Why? What's tomorrow?'

'The last shoot sequence. In the cursed ruins.'

CHAPTER 56

Some days seem marked, deliberately crafted as a canvas for events to unfold with just the right amount of climatic drama. The sun was eclipsed behind a gloomy sky and there was no wind. Not even a leaf strayed from its position, as if holding its breath for what was to come. Even the usually cacophonous crew was on tenterhooks, their hearts filled with foreboding. They scuttled about the ruins, nervous and edgy.

Over the last few days, the villagers had banded together and expressed their apprehensions to the local MLA. They didn't want the ruins disturbed for a shoot, but since the MLA was a friend of the Rathods, this discontent was waved off without much effort. To appease the villagers, a unique 'set shanti' puja had been organized, performed by the freshly reinstated Bhutaari Baba.

Not to be upstaged in religious matters, the Tripathis pulled out their heavy arsenal and chanted the *Ram Raksha Stotra and Mahamrityunjaya mantra* in various corners of the house. Ammaji opted out of these arduous pursuits and settled on praying with the beads of her rudraksh mala.

Such was the sense of disquiet in the air that even the optimistic Prachand Tripathi felt a chill in his bones, his stomach gurgling with some sort of prescience about things to come. Ammaji called out to him and he touched her feet before sitting down. '*O badmaas mil jaavego. Phikar na kar, bitwa*,' she said as Prachand pulled her into an embrace. He smiled thinking of how she always read his mind accurately.

As he walked out of the door, Vidya caught up with him. 'You didn't eat much breakfast. Are you feeling okay? The doctor said we should watch you for a few days.'

'I'm absolutely fine, Viddu. I need to walk about the set once to clear some cobwebs in my head. That's all. I'm headed there.'

Vidya squeezed his arm. 'There's something not quite right about that place. How can you go alone? I'll come with you.'

'Alone? There are more than twenty people milling about. You should try and be with Padminiji. Poor thing. She looks so out of sorts these days.'

'You're right. Well, hurry back.'

'I will.'

Vidya watched Prachand as he walked towards the woods. 'Bholenath, please let this day finish without any more drama,' she mumbled with folded hands. That's when she noticed that Prachand had turned in the opposite direction. 'Where on earth is he off to now?'

If the abandoned village seemed ominous during the day, the spectacle it presented after sunset was scary enough to send the toughest bravehearts running to their mothers. The cold, moody skies brought back distant claps of thunder yet again and made the crew move faster. Everyone seemed jumpy, seeking company, unwilling to stare too deep into the ruins that had driven a stake of fear into their hearts.

While Paramveer Khattar and Preeti had returned to the sets, they were maintaining a distance, aware that their personal dalliance was public now and that they were the cynosure of all eyes. Aalok Kumar and Venky broke out into frequent arguments, something that Chachu Tripathi identified as the result of paranormal activity.

'You see, when there are invisible energies around us, they confuse and confound us, making people irritable and irrational, because our bodies can't make sense of it.'

'Chachu, I had no idea you had completed a PhD on the subject,' Vidya quipped.

'Speaking of confounding things, I can't believe that Bhabhi opted to come to the ruins instead of staying back with Ammaji and Padminiji at the mansion,' said Chachu Tripathi.

Vidya looked in the direction of the snack table loaded with munchies. Her mother-in-law had already picked up some food and beverages and was precariously balancing it all as she made her way back to them. 'She said no force, human or otherwise, could keep her from the set since this was the last sequence to be shot,' Vidya said with a giggle, but her smile faltered as her gaze lingered on the temple she had visited with Prachand only a few days ago. An unusual afternoon where the sequence of events was foggy and made her uncomfortable.

'Are you okay, Vidya *Bitiya*?'

She looked into Chachu Tripathi's concerned face and nodded. 'I'm fine, Chachu,' she said and drew her shawl closer.

'Sileeeeeeence!'

Aalok Kumar's voice tore through the din. 'Roll camera. Sound. Ac ... ction!'

Vikas Kishen stood by a ramshackle structure that looked like an erstwhile home, only four disconnected walls remained.

'Viddu, where are you? We need to head back to the palace!' he called out, very much in character, looking for his amour who had disappeared into the ruins. He then trained his eyes on the house next to him. 'Who is in there? Come out right now!'

'Cuuuut!' Aalok threw his hands in the air. 'Why are you improvizing? Just say your dialogues, man!'

Vikas stood shell shocked, white as a sheet. 'I ... swear someone was in that house.'

The AD came running and checked the house. 'There's nothing in here,' he assured the actor who was shaking like a leaf. 'Let's roll again. It could rain any time,' he said and clapped in an effort to silence everyone.

'Roll camera, and ... action!' Aalok Kumar roared.

'Bhoot pisaach nikat nahin aave, Mahavir jab naam sunave ... nasee rog hare ...' prayed Vikas in a trance-like state.

'You have got to be kidding me! S ... s ... someone get the man a glass of water.'

Chachu Tripathi, feeling vindicated, whispered to Prachand who had finally taken a seat. 'See? I told you.'

Prachand leaned in to whisper into his uncle's ear. 'People are scarier than ghosts, Chachu.'

Giving his nephew a withering look, Chachu Tripathi said, '*Prachand ki paheliyan Prachand hi jaane.*'

'Let's try this one last time,' announced Aalok Kumar. 'Our poor heroine is waiting for her entry from the temple. P ... Preeti!' he spoke into the microphone. 'Sorry about this! One last take followed by your entry, okay?'

There was no response. 'Preeti?' he asked again. All eyes turned to the temple, now flooded by lights.

In a dramatic, almost preternaturally created frame, the actress emerged from the dark belly of the temple and paused on top of the steps. One of her arms was raised and the other clutched her neck. As lightning ripped through the sky and highlighted her voluptuous body with a spectral incandescence, Prachand and Paramveer Khattar rushed towards her. Prachand, reaching first, broke her descent and was struck by the look of agony and terror on the actresses' heavily painted face as she crumpled into his arms without a sound.

CHAPTER 57

'Doctor Saab, is she alive?' Paramveer Khattar asked with a tremor in his voice.

Dr Sisodia, looking discombobulated, rubbed his eyes. 'Yes, she is. But the rate at which people drop like flies on this set, I will certainly be going to my grave earlier than planned. I think I need to draw up my will,' he said.

The actress had been laid out on a makeshift bed created using empty equipment boxes. Her eyes were shut and her shoulder and back had been bandaged. The doctor gathered his paraphernalia and stood up with great difficulty. 'She was attacked with a knife, but I've cleaned and stitched her up. Luckily, the wound doesn't go too deep. You will need to bring her to my clinic, but for now shift her to the haveli. I need to give her an injection that is in my car.'

'How is she lucky?' Vidya asked Prachand incredulously. 'This has to be the work of that bloody Rathod. He has clearly gone nuts!' She was clutching Prachand's hand tight, her eyes on the pile of blood-stained gauze.

Prachand put his arm around her. 'We need to be careful, Viddu. The attacker could not have gone far. I've called the inspector and the police are reaching with backup. The actors and crew have gone to the haveli to pack. I overheard that they have threatened to call the union if Paramveer Khattar forces them to stay.'

A breathless Yatish joined them. 'I'll take Maaji, Bhabhi and Chachu to the haveli. Bhushan had gone to check on Ammaji and Padminiji, so I told him to wait there.'

'Thanks, Yatish.' Prachand looked at his friend gratefully. 'Viddu, why don't …'

'Don't you dare start treating me like a damsel in distress. I'm staying right here with you!' Vidya's eyes flashed and conveyed her determination, something Prachand and Yatish had learnt not to question.

As Yatish sped back to Naveli Haveli, Vidya turned to Prachand. 'I saw you. You were sniffing her.'

Prachand was filled with uxorious pride as he looked at his sharp-as-a-needle wife. 'Yes, I did. That's because I caught a whiff of something familiar.'

'Let me guess, you're going to be secretive again,' Vidya said in an accusatory tone. 'I don't appreciate how you've been withholding information from me on this case. Isn't my opinion valuable to you any more? Only Inspector Gupta matters? We are partners, remember?'

Prachand held his wife's hands. 'This is the last mile, Viddu. I'm almost there. I just need to … look Inspector Gupta is here.'

Prachand hurriedly walked over to Inspector Gupta who was in conversation with Paramveer Khattar. She looked at Prachand searchingly as Paramveer Khattar complained.

'This is ridiculous. Another attack? With a police detail nearby and a detective on the sets? And you've been trying to pin the blame on me? How could I have orchestrated any of this? I'm at least trying to do my job unlike the both of you,' he said with a grunt, defiantly staring Inspector Gupta down.

'I don't have time for this crap,' she snarled. Turning to Prachand, she asked, 'Was everyone on the set?'

Prachand nodded. 'As far as I can tell. Well, except Ammaji, Padminiji, Arjun Prajapati and the absconding Ramnarayan Rathod.'

Inspector Gupta pulled out white, disposable gloves from her pocket and snapped them on. 'Please take me to the scene of the attack. I need to take a look before we head back to the haveli. The team has spread out. Whoever is responsible will be in our custody soon.'

'Sure.' Prachand pointed her in the direction of the temple. That's when Vidya's phone rang. The shock on her face made Prachand snatch the phone. He heard static, then a garbled voice and then some more static.

'Damn this reception!' Prachand whacked the phone against his palm and pasted it back on his ear.

'Prachand Sa ... Prachand Sa...' was all he could hear from the other side.

'Arjunji? Is that you? What's the matter?'

'Come here please! Quick!'

'What is it?'

'It's your Dadi Sa. She has nabbed a ghost!'

CHAPTER 58

As they raced towards the haveli, Inspector Maya Gupta, a little out of breath, overtook them. 'You think you've heard it all, and then there's another phone call.'

There was utter mayhem awaiting them. While the technicians and daily wagers had vacated the premises with alacrity, some of the main cast and crew still seemed to be scrambling around for their things. However, the main act unfolding in the living room should have drawn a ticket price for what was on offer.

A bundled white sheet lay on the carpet. Ammaji, perched on the divan, had caught hold of a leg that was protruding from underneath and was beating the sheet like it was a carpet being relieved of years of dust.

'*Kambakht bhoot! Humka daraave chahat ho!*' Her whole body shook with indignation at the 'ghost' and her dentures took flight again.

This time, Bhushan caught them mid-air.

No one ventured near the suspicious white cloth. Rachna Tripathi, Bhushan, Chachu Tripathi and Yatish had stood and watched with trepidation. Vikas Kishen, meanwhile, had displayed some enviable scaling skills by climbing one of the ornate pillars that separated the hall from the dining area. Venky and Arjun Prajapati crouched behind Ammaji. Inspector Gupta cleared her throat. 'Get up and remove that cloth. Got lost, eh?'

Prachand followed her. 'On the contrary, I suspect this Bhoot Sa knows these surroundings like the back of his hand.'

'What are you mumbling on about, Prachand?' Vidya asked.

'Just wait.' Prachand's eyes twinkled as he yanked the cloth away and a ripple of gasps swept through the hall. It was Ramnarayan Rathod, scowling on the ground and clutching a pair of shoes.

'The custom-made size 9 shoes we have been looking for, I presume?' Prachand prodded. The captive man grunted and dusted himself as Arjun Prajapati, by force of conditioning, rushed to help his employer.

Ramnarayan Rathod shoved his hand away. '*Namak haram!* Stay away from me,' he said, leaving his faithful servant of years looking mortified.

Inspector Maya Gupta swooped in and carefully bagged the shoes. 'That's my evidence you're tampering with.'

'Hey!' Ramnarayan Rathod shot back petulantly. 'Those are my shoes.'

'Very much!' Inspector Gupta levelled with his gaze and stood clutching the shoes defiantly. 'Care to explain why you are sneaking around pretending to be a ghost? Did you come to get your shoes, or perhaps you're running away from another crime scene?'

'You're talking rubbish. What crime scene? I've been away on work these last few days,' he responded with a shrug, like a mulish child.

'Right. Away on work where no one could reach you, not even your wife. You stalk people and they turn up dead, you clean up after yourself, you traipse around the woods minutes after someone has been attacked, and here you are, collecting the shoes that connect you to the crime scene. You have a lot to explain.'

Ramnarayan Rathod's body sagged visibly, like a proud peacock turning into a pipsqueak after having sensed the futility of defiance. 'I will reiterate. I have no idea who has been attacked. As for everything else, I ... I did it for him,' he said and raised a quivering finger. All eyes turned to Paramveer Khattar who had just entered.

He looked surprised. 'What did I do now?'

'Your friend here was just about to tell us.' Inspector Gupta turned back to Ramnarayan Rathod. 'You were saying?'

'I don't know how to explain this.'

'You'll have to try. Now start talking.'

He took a deep, melodramatic breath and started. 'Life hasn't been kind to me, but I have fought back. My family and I, despite all the hard work, were always treated like dirt. I spent my childhood gawking at the glistening kothis, and when I was old and rich enough to show them what I was capable of, they still refused to accept me. They made fun of me, called me a blight on the name of the royals. A cheap imposter, a thug is what I was labelled. I'm tired of trying to prove myself, my choices and my way of life.'

The inspector shook her head in bewilderment. 'You and your friend deserve each other! Living your lives of privilege and then acting like victims of a cruel world.'

Yatish interjected impatiently. 'I agree with inspector Gupta! What is the connection between the murder and your sob story? Get on with it please.'

Ramnarayan Rathod's eyes flashed. 'Everything is connected. Param is the only person who gave me the respect, the love, the attention and the companionship that I deserve.'

'He sounds like he is talking about his girlfriend,' Rachna Tripathi whispered to Chachu Tripathi who glanced at the man of the hour. Paramveer Khattar had a quizzical look on his face.

Across the room, Vidya nudged Prachand. 'Is this going where I think it's going?'

Prachand patted her arm.

'I owed it to him. I had to protect him. I ...' Ramnarayan Rathod continued.

'Ram!' Paramveer Khattar piped up from across the room.

Ramnarayan Rathod looked at his friend, his temple pulsing. 'I'm sorry it had to come to this.' He looked searchingly at Inspector Maya Gupta for some support. 'You must understand that I had nothing against Ranjana Jha. She was just another spoilt brat working for my friend. That morning, she ...

'... saw you doing something you shouldn't have been doing?' Prachand completed his sentence. Ramnarayan Rathod's face fell.

'Yes. She saw me ... with ... with a young boy. It was harmless. I swear! But she misunderstood the situation and threatened to report me,' he balked at the look of disgust writ large on each face. 'You must believe me. She got the wrong idea.'

'You child predator! You are the worst kind of human being,' Vidya hissed. 'Your poor wife!'

'Don't get me started on my wife. She isn't the simpleton you make her out to be. She ...'

'The nerve! Now your wife has wronged you, is it? The inspector is right. You are plagued with a persecution complex.'

'Vidyaji, please,' Inspector Gupta said and held up her hand. 'Let's get back to the day of the murder.'

'Ranjana threatened me!' Ramnarayan Rathod roared. 'That's why I felt sick. The news getting out could ruin me. I kept an eye on her all day, even on the set, trying to steal a minute to speak with her, but she was never alone. I waited till after the storm and luckily found her leaving for a walk. I thought I finally had a chance. How could I possibly know I would find her ... dead!'

'So you're saying you found her dead?'

'Yes! I swear on all my ancestors. I stood by the well, saw her and froze. Then I started running back. That's when I saw someone else hurriedly making their way back to the mansion, just ahead of me.'

'Who was it?'

His head was hung low as he revealed the name. 'Param.'

CHAPTER 59

'You are the m … murderer! I knew it! I always had a ffff … feeling about this. How I've tortured myself over this for days. You scoundrel! Give me my d … dues before you are dragged to jail!' Aalok Kumar launched himself at Paramveer Khattar who was taken by surprise and knocked off his feet.

Bhushan, who was standing nearby, tried to intervene but was wedged between the two large men. He was soon reduced to performing the role of a cheese slice sandwiched between two pieces of toast. Inspector Brijesh jumped in, too, to pull them apart.

'Enough!' Inspector Maya Gupta thundered. 'Let the man speak.'

'If you could just let me explain,' Paramveer Khattar requested Inspector Gupta, but she dismissed him with a wave of her hand.

'You've had many chances over the last few days. Now let me listen to your friend.'

A weary Ramnarayan Rathod sat down heavily. 'Going by Param's body language, it was very clear to me that he was in trouble. When I got to the mansion, I realized that I was tracking muck. As had Param, while entering just before me. I really don't know how we missed seeing each other in the woods, but it could only have been minutes apart. Thankfully no one was in the hall. I realized I had to clear my trail, and my friend's too, so I immediately got Prajapati to clean up and take care of my shoes. Once everyone was asleep, I confronted Param, asking him what he had done. He swore that he, too, had only seen her body and not killed her, and that he had only stepped out for the drugs. I had no option but to believe him. That was also when I found out that he was dealing with my own driver, right under my nose, and I had no idea. Ever since, I've been tight-lipped. Only because I didn't want my ... my Param to get into trouble.'

'That explains the arguing voices I heard. I wasn't dreaming.' Prachand nodded at Inspector Gupta.

'You two scoundrels knew about the murder and still didn't call it in? You let a poor woman's body rot in the rain while you both were playing best buddies? Shame on you!' Yatish bristled in defence of the woman who could have been the queen of his lonely heart.

'Why do we run around scared of monsters we cannot see when the living ones are right here, amongst us!' Chachu Tripathi said and placed a comforting arm around his young friend's shoulder.

Paramveer Khattar crumpled to the ground, sobbing like a child. 'I didn't want her to die. We ... we were on the verge of ending things. She didn't agree; she thought I was her forever love. I tried my best to convince her that I wasn't. Yes, I've done bad things. I've lied to cover up my drug use, my affairs and I feel terrible about what happened to her, but I ... I swear on everything... on my father ... that I didn't kill her.'

'I'm never casting him. Such a bad actor!' Bhushan said, scowling.

'Oh, I don't think he is going to have any dates to spare. There's too much explaining to do. I have just enough evidence, and now a clear motive, to keep these heartless hounds in custody. That's all the time I need for a confession,' said Inspector Gupta, cracking her knuckles meaningfully as both men gulped.

That's when the lights started flickering again, with an intensity that made everyone want to cover their eyes. Almost as if they could sense the malevolence in the air. This was followed by a buzzing that kept getting louder, like from an attack of bees.

'What is going on?' Vidya turned to address Prachand. But Prachand had disappeared.

CHAPTER 60

Prachand hurried through the woods; his limbs were moving of their own volition. The wind howled and bit into his bones, and the brambles he was trundling into scraped against his legs. Amidst the flickering lights, he had had an epiphany. Driven by instinct, and possessed with an urgency, he dashed through the woods. A jackal howled in the distance as a stray rocket fired from the direction of the village lit up the sky. It highlighted the incongruity between Prachand's anxious state of mind and the innocent revelries nearby.

As he walked out of the trees, his eyes could discern the presence of an amorphous figure standing next to the well. He wanted to approach the shadowy figure, but every fibre of his body warned him against it. He finally found his voice.

'It really is the best place to dispose of murder weapons, isn't it? A bottomless well of death. Who would dare go in?'

'I had a niggling feeling that you would eventually find your way to me. But I had to try.' Prachand's chest constricted at hearing the raspy voice. It sounded both familiar and strange.

The figure moved in his direction. Without a clear visual and the moon playing hide-and-seek amidst the angry clouds, Prachand had to strain his eyes.

A torch came on, piercing the dark and illuminating what he had all along known as a beautiful face. In that moment, it was rendered hideous with the intent concealed in the eyes.

Prachand peered at Padmini Rathod, only she looked nothing like herself. Her eyes were swollen and she had blotches of what looked like blood on her cheek. The open hair lashed against her face in the cold wind.

'How did you know?' she asked in a tremulous voice.

'Honestly, I had never considered you, but there were certain comments and episodes that got me thinking. Slowly and steadily, all the little, invisible fragments of the puzzle start falling into place. Ammaji, made an innocuous comment the other day, something about how you were fussing over Paramveer Khattar. As I watched you, the intimate way in which you made such an everyday action so personal, the impossible possibility started taking shape. I watched you and realized how, in an odd way, you fit in as Paramveer Khattar's type. The dark and wavy hair, the height, the complexion. I can't believe I didn't see it earlier, how much you and Ranjana Jha looked alike. And, of course, I didn't know it at the time, but Preeti falls into that bracket as well!'

Padmini Rathod's eyes looked like cold, lifeless pebbles as the wind picked up and whistled about their ears. 'My grandmother used to tell me a story about a khejri tree in the desert that wanted to become a mango tree,' she said, speaking as if she hadn't registered a word Prachand had said. 'It wanted to forsake its roots, even the desert, and travel to a greener, better land. Many thirsty travellers rested in its shade and thanked it for its generosity, whispering fantastical stories in its ears. Soon, the tree, having its head filled, was so convinced that it could really be a mango tree that it requested a traveller to uproot it and carry it away. He did so. The tree lost all its vigour, dreaming of green pastures, mischievous raindrops and juicy fruits. I am no better. I dared to dream. Of becoming someone who could change the world; I dreamt of a happy life. I had my head turned by the man who was to become my husband. I uprooted myself from a life devoid of any happiness to another meaningless, loveless existence, where I was transported to a broken palace, a prison as broken as my dreams. Paramji was that one traveller who I was really meant to leave the desert with, but he came into my life too late. He made me forget that I was betrothed to another. He made me dream, coaxed me out of my shell and just when I had prepared myself to leave, I realized that he had a roving eye. But it wasn't his fault. It is the *fitrat* of the traveller to flirt with the changing winds and the dancing sand. I had to help him, free him from the clutches of someone who had him entranced and was standing in our way.'

'Ranjana Jha.' A voice emerged from the dark. Prachand turned with a start to see Vidya hurrying towards him. She slipped her hand into Prachand's, taking a firm grip.

Padmini Rathod was still rambling. 'I didn't hate her. I just knew she had to go. She was confusing my Param. I had to help him.'

'Help him?' Vidya spluttered. 'How can you be so obtuse? Can't you see that people like him can't be trusted? He is the one who has wronged you, driven you to this madness. You still don't see it?'

'You don't get it!' Padmini raised her voice, a duet of shadows and light playing on her face from the quivering torchlight. She took a deep breath and her voice levelled out again. 'She wouldn't let him go, even though he wanted to end things with her. How could she do that? I noticed how distressed Param looked and knew that I had to help.'

Vidya grunted out of frustration, held her tongue as Prachand squeezed her hand.

Padmini continued. 'I had realized a long time ago that the only way I could be with Param and build a life with him was if my husband released me, which would be impossible. I've been planning to kill him for so long. That's why I grew those plants. Only, I lacked the courage. I somehow couldn't get myself to take the final step. When I heard about the shoot I realized that it could be the perfect opportunity to execute my plan without getting caught. Little did I know that there were bigger obstacles fate had in store for me, including your involvement in the investigation. I had to change my plans and focus on the biggest impediment first, Ranjana Jha.'

Padmini was speaking fast, her initial reluctance replaced by some sort of urgency, as if she had been waiting to unburden herself. 'Since I knew the haveli so well, the flickering lights, the ransacked luggage and the handprints were all part of the paranormal distraction and easy for me to orchestrate, even though you almost caught me once. I found out that Ranjana had diabetes, and was extremely unhappy with the food on set. I promised her healthy food, especially prepared in my kitchen, and started drugging her a little every day. I don't even think she realized when the symptoms started developing.'

'Vidya did mention to me how you learnt a lot from a close relative who was a vaid. Your Digitalis concoction comes from the foxglove plants on your property, doesn't it? The cruder the extraction and distillation, the more potent the result?'

'How did you figure this out, Prachi?' Vidya looked at her husband in awe.

'Remember, I took a small detour in Jaisalmer? I went to meet a friend. He told me all about locally available plants. At the time it was only a hunch, but when I saw what was growing on the property and received a confirmation in Jaisalmer about the extraction of Digitalis from foxgloves, I deduced the culprit had to be someone with the knowledge and access to Ranjana.'

Padmini Rathod's expression was inscrutable. 'If you figured it out, why didn't you expose me?'

'I had no proof, Padminiji. Besides, there were other suspects. Aalok, Bhutaari Baba, Paramveer Khattar and even your husband, thanks to your craftiness. I was already on a sticky wicket with the inspector. Gut feeling is seldom construed as evidence,' Prachand said and stopped to think for a moment. 'Do you remember you gave me prasad, just before I left for Jaisalmer? I noticed then that you have really tiny hands for a grown-up, a size that could almost pass off for a child's. When I left for Jaisalmer, all I had to go on was an assumption about your affair with Paramveer Khattar, and the suspicion I had about you being the one behind those bloody handprints. But when I returned, it all started making sense—your never being around when something strange occurred, frequently taking ill and claiming to be in your room, and the lack of any chemistry with your husband. And the final confirmation came from the signature perfume that you brought back from Hotel Star Lovers, which you and your amour frequented. When I smelt it during our stay, it seemed familiar, but I couldn't place it. Initially, I thought it was Preeti, but then I realized you've worn it before, right here in Naveli Haveli.'

Padmini said nothing but started swaying imperceptibly.

Prachand spoke again in a halting voice. 'While you have said that you wanted Ranjana out of the way, I don't believe you meant to kill her as brutally as you did. It wasn't entirely pre-meditated, was it?'

Padmini Rathod shuddered visibly. 'It feels like a bad dream. She was just meant to go, to fade away from our lives. But ... the drug wasn't working fast enough. Perhaps I got the dosage wrong, or her body fought back. That night, after the downpour, I saw her stepping out and followed her. I suspect she was hallucinating or feeling sick because of the drug since I had added a very high dose to her lunch as a last-ditch effort. When I saw her fall to the ground, near the well, I ran to check, but she suddenly opened her eyes and said "It was you ... you've been making me sick." She then started pushing me away and collapsed, clutching her heart.'

A sob escaped Padmini's lips. 'I remember standing and watching her with terror seizing my heart, unable to grasp the finality of what I had done. Then ...' she looked away and said, 'I hit her on the head to be sure and disposed of the rock in the well.' Her gaze returned searchingly to Prachand's face 'I ... I had to make sure she was gone.'

At this point, her eyes were ablaze with a mix of tears and remorse. 'My plan had always been to disguise this whole episode under the veil of the curse. The best way to confirm the suspicion would have been to dump her body in the well, making it look like an accident by replicating what happened years ago. But my luck deserted me right then. As I dragged her body towards the well, I heard someone nearby ...'

'That was Aalok. He was startled by the noise he heard, possibly from when both of you were locked in a struggle, and threw a rock your way,' said Prachand.

Padmini Rathod nodded. 'I was petrified and barely missed the rock. That's when I decided I had to leave the body and run back to the haveli. I used a secret route only I know of, one that runs past the gate, from the other end.'

'That's when the little boy spotted you. He thought you were a daakan.'

Padmini Rathod gave Prachand a blank look. 'Strange, isn't it? The most deplorable thoughts seem justified when it comes to self-preservation. I remember that it struck me then. If only I could pin the murder on my husband, I would kill two birds with one stone. I would achieve what I had been meaning to do all these years, without his blood on my hands. Then Param and I would be free.'

'You're a cold-blooded murderer, Padmini Rathod. I'm ashamed to call you my friend,' Vidya spat, almost on the brink of tears.

Prachand implored his wife. 'Please don't do this right now, Viddu. I understand your feelings, but let her speak. She is not in the right frame of mind.' He then dropped his voice a notch and said, 'She is dangerous.'

'Dangerous! Hah! She has single-handedly destroyed her own life. It's like she poses the most danger to herself. She didn't even spare her husband. Yes, he is a perverted, pretentious fool, but how could she throw him to the dogs?'

'Don't you dare judge me!' Padmini Rathod thundered.

CHAPTER 61

Padmini Rathod's eyes were smouldering. 'Do you know what it is to live a half-life? To live in wait for something, someone, some twist of fate to set things right? If I hadn't married the wimpy, selfish man, my father would have sold me off to the highest bidder. Every night that I spent under the weight of his body felt like an assault on my soul. Over the years, as he finally lost interest in me, and I realized that his interests and sexual experiments amused him more than I ever could, we learnt to co-exist. As long as the facade of a happy marriage could be preserved, he remained busy with his own life,' she said.

By now, the clouds had parted and she was more visible in the diffused moonlight, pacing and wringing her hands. 'Paramji was the only one who could see how unhappy I was. He comforted me, gave me hope and made me want to live again. And to think that my cruel husband couldn't even let me have some happiness. The way he would obsess and fuss around Param! Oh it embarrassed me, but then I accepted it for what it was. Paramji has that effect on people. Still, what we had was special,' she laughed. '*Is* special. When you feel so strongly about something, the universe conspires for you to be together.'

'Isn't that a dialogue from *Om Shanti Om*?' Vidya inquired. Prachand immediately hushed her.

Padmini Rathod ignored Vidya. 'The film shoot was a great distraction, but whatever happened on that fateful night was the universe working in mysterious ways. I knew then that I was doing the right thing. All I had to do was propagate the curse theory and eliminate Ranjana Jha using it. Her walking into the woods, my husband's argument with her and following her there, bumping into Paramji, all of it had nothing to do with me. These were just pieces falling into place to help me. I was vigilant and took my chance when I could. Removing myself as his alibi helped move the needle of suspicion towards him. But when Paramji was pulled into the investigation, it broke my heart.'

'And it broke further when you figured out that Paramveer's next target was the stylist.' Prachand could see the impact of his statement on Padmini Rathod, as if she was re-living the despair and hopelessness that had washed over her. 'You heard about their rendezvous in Jaisalmer and it tipped you over. After all that you had done for him, here was a fresh obstacle.'

'Can you blame me? All I knew was that the shoot was ending and that it was my last chance to remove that chit of a girl from the picture. I entered from the back of the temple and stabbed her, but she elbowed me and ran into the light. I hoped the job was done. All I thought I had to do was get rid of the knife.'

'On one hand you speak of being blinded by love and compassion, but then you meticulously clear people from your path like a vacuum cleaner.' Vidya glowered at her former friend.

'You wanted to get rid of me as well,' Prachand added with a tinge of sadness. 'It was you, and not Bhutaari Baba, I assume? You made me sick.'

Padmini Rathod's eyes flashed. 'You were getting too close. I thought the glycerine was enough to keep you away, out of my way, but I underestimated you.'

Prachand shook his head. 'I just don't get it. Wouldn't you rather punish Paramveer Khattar? Can't you see that it is his philandering ways that have stood in the way of your happiness and not the people you attacked?'

She trained her piercing gaze on Prachand. 'How fierce is *your* love, Prachandji? What would you do to keep it? How far would you go? All I did was to protect what was mine. When you love someone, you love them with all your heart, with all their flaws. I knew that once all the distractions were gone, Paramji would see that he and I belong together forever.' The clarity and conviction of her erroneous belief was evident in her body language.

'You're impossible. How can you keep justifying what that man has done? He has turned you into a murderer. Are you truly oblivious to the fact that you will be going to jail for this man?' Vidya seemed even more agitated than Padmini Rathod.

'We are missing something, Viddu,' Prachand said.

Vidya looked at her husband. He had a peculiar expression on his face. 'Agreed that love births the most eager fools and the fiercest of warriors. But there is a part of this particular picture that is still unclear to me. For a person like her to be driven to murder, there has to be a bigger trigger. I am sure of it. Charm and Kamdev personified Paramveer Khattar might seem to women, but Padminiji would not have taken such extreme steps unless there was some kind of aggravation.'

Padmini Rathod's face remained impassive, her resolute lips set in a thin, straight line. Vidya's eyes widened. 'I know what the aggravation was, Prachi. She's pregnant.'

CHAPTER 62

The swaying trees, the pirouetting leaves and the doleful jackals all spoke in her stead, but Padmini Rathod placing a telltale hand on her womb confirmed Vidya's hypothesis.

'I must be daft to have missed it earlier. All those little signs that pave the way for a new life—the morning sickness, the clothes that got mixed up with mine, the ones she was trying to hide under the shawls she wore, the multitude of vitamins. Given Ma's consistent endeavours on the pregnancy front, I know those "essential" vitamins by heart,' Vidya's voice softened and she watched her friend's face intently. 'It was a critical juncture for the happily ever after you had envisioned; it pushed you off the edge. I know how badly you wanted a family of your own, a real family that you could love with all your heart, something you never had as a child.'

Even in the dim light, it was clear that Padmini Rathod was crying. A desperate wail escaped from her mouth. It was the most heart-rending sound, a mixture of anger, helplessness and longing. It gave goosebumps and also broke the gentle hearts of the two people who stood before her, feeling the full force of her suffering. They let her sob for a while, till she was only sniffing intermittently.

Prachand folded his hands before Padmini Rathod. 'Please listen to me. This is futile. Even with slim evidence, there's the knife in your hands, the poison trail leading back to you and the rock with blood stains somewhere in this well. They will make a solid case against you.'

Vidya took a step towards her. 'Think of your child. That inspector is a kind woman. Let me call her and ...'

Padmini Rathod leapt forward, like a caged tigress on guard. In the blink of an eye, she had Vidya in her grasp. One arm was locked around her neck and the other held a jewel-encrusted dagger.

Prachand's eyes widened with terror. 'Padminiji, what are you doing?'

'I'm sorry! I'm very sorry it has come to this.' She pointed her arm backwards. 'Just let me walk away. I'll find my passage through the ruins and go far away. I'll leave all this behind. Like the travellers. I'll travel so far that this moody desert, its whispering winds and these restless spirits will never find me.'

'You know I can't do that, Padminiji,' Prachand sighed.

Padmini Rathod was on the verge of hysteria. 'You're all the same! I thought you were kind. But in the end everyone turns on me.'

Prachand's response died on his lips as he noticed a peculiar movement on the tree under which Padmini Rathod held Vidya at knifepoint. A small form was crawling up the thickest branch. As the branch shook, Prachand balked at the face that peered back at him.

Bhushan Tripathi, determination writ large on his thin face, was trying his best to balance his highly unathletic body on the branch. Without a clue as to what his brother was trying to accomplish, Prachand only hoped this mission to save one wouldn't end up becoming a disaster for two.

Padmini Rathod had her eyes on Prachand who was trying his best to avoid looking at his brother. Bhushan had by now managed to reach the middle of the branch, his weak grip leaving him dangling like a langur. If his original mission had been to ambush Padmini Rathod and save his bhabhi, he had clearly spent very little time strategizing.

Prachand wanted to buy Bhushan some time. As he inched closer to Padmini Rathod, Vidya gasped. Padmini Rathod, even in her frazzled state, was as sharp as a needle. Fat drops of rain fell on the ground and a bolt of lightning ripped open the inky black sky. 'Something else has been troubling me, Padminiji. I must ask you. Have you ever met an old man in these ruins? Was he part of your plan to spook us?'

'I don't know of any old man,' Padmini Rathod said, as the rain picked up, spreading the smatterings of blood running down her face.

'But that's impossible! We spoke with him in the ruins. After that, Vidya almost fell into the well. That had to be you. There has to be an explanation.'

'Your wife has been the only beacon of light in my dreary world. I had nothing to do with whatever you just mentioned.'

Vidya, struggling in Padmini's grasp, laughed. 'Some beacon of light! And some friend you are, holding a knife to my neck! Now I realize that it was you who tried to frighten me when I came to visit you. It was you making that racket, wasn't it?'

Padmini Rathod smiled. It was the kind of blood-curdling smile that had you chanting the Lord's name with fervour. 'Then you both have felt them. I'm not mad.'

'You're the opposite of that, Padminiji. Which is what surprises me about your attempts to hide away what you did under the blanket of a fictional curse. You've admitted that you've gone to great lengths to try and frighten everyone. What I don't get is the bloody handprints on my mirror? What was the point?'

The soulless smile stayed on her face. 'Now you'll say that wasn't you either,' Prachand said.

But before he could continue, a bigger mystery charged at them from the clump of trees. Chachu Tripathi, clad only in his kurta, ran straight towards Padmini Rathod, arms raised. Right behind him was Inspector Maya Gupta, brandishing her revolver and holding a dhoti in her other hand. Bhushan decided to relinquish his feeble hold on the branch at the same time. As the trio descended on a startled Padmini Rathod, she let go of Vidya. Her body sagged to the wet ground, very close to where Ranjana Jha had breathed her last on a dark, cold night not very long ago.

CHAPTER 63

'There seems to be no man, woman, shrub or tree that wasn't in love with Paramveer Khattar. He is like some kalyug ka Kamdev,' Inspector Gupta said.

'Well, these little shrubs didn't,' Prachand replied and smiled at the inspector's feeble joke. He was prodding a cluster of shrubs and young trees with the wooden stick in his hand. 'They were poisoning Ranjana Jha in compliance with the wishes of their mistress, Padmini Rathod.'

Inspector Gupta squinted at the profile of the unassuming man from Kanpur who had brought the most confusing case she had ever worked on to closure. She felt a knot of regret in her stomach, knowing that he would be gone soon. 'You wanted it to be someone else, didn't you?'

Prachand drew a long breath. 'It might surprise you to hear this, Guptaji, but I root for the bad guys till the very end. In my books, there are no good or bad people, just happy or miserable ones. Take Padminiji for instance. Do you think she presents the picture of a stark, raving lunatic who belongs in a mental asylum? No. In her head, she did it all for love, to create the life she envisioned for herself, to finally stop running from her childhood and her marriage. And she decided to stop at nothing. She was as driven as someone who works relentlessly to feed their family, to protect them, to be with them. In her heart, she still thinks she did no wrong.'

'Even threatening to injure the friend who she claims was her only ray of happiness in the recent past?' Inspector Gupta shook her head with disgust.

'When Brijeshji was taking her away, she apologized profusely, saying she never meant to hurt Vidya,' Prachand offered.

Inspector Gupta picked up another stick from the ground and snapped it in half. 'If I had a rupee for every time some criminal said that to me! In fact, my whole life is littered with apologies from people who never meant to do what they did to me,' she said and averted her gaze when Prachand looked at her.

'Do you have enough evidence to make a case against her?'

'Well, this is a slippery slope, what with extrajudicial confessions always being looked upon with suspicion. But given the fact that she accepts what she has done and doesn't seem like she will retract her statement, we should be able to make a solid case with the thread of evidence we have.'

'I just hope they decide to be lenient with her, given her condition.' Prachand's heart ached with the knowledge that the compassionate, soft-spoken lady he had grown fond of would be spending the better part of her life in incarceration, and that her unborn child would also bear the brunt of it. But he was also sure that the kind inspector would do her best to help. 'Our empathy often blinds us. We both fell prey to it, not realizing amidst all the chaos that if her husband didn't have her as an alibi, she was unaccounted for as well.' He shrugged, looking up at the friendly trees that had looked so ominous just the night before. 'I can't even imagine what poor Ranjanaji felt on that cold night. Breathless, drugged, disoriented, wandering about the woods that would finally see the end of her.' Prachand shuddered and then continued. 'You know, Guptaji, I couldn't have done any of this without you. You supported me and allowed me the liberties I needed to take. Thank you for that. You're the most kind, intelligent and capable inspector I have ever worked with. And thanks for coming to our rescue.'

Inspector Gupta adjusted her belt self-consciously and tucked away a few stray curls back under her cap. 'Well, I had some help. I'm not sure what your brother was thinking he would accomplish by hanging from that tree, or why your uncle chose to streak through the woods to rescue you instead of alerting me, but it was brave of them to try. Apparently, Bhushan sensed something amiss and followed his bhabhi, and then your uncle followed him.' She laughed, thinking of something. 'When I saw your uncle rushing out of the haveli, I followed him. While crossing the woods, he was so terrified that when I called out to him, he thought I was a ghost. His dhoti got caught on a shrub and came undone, but he wouldn't even stop to retrieve it.'

Prachand was doubling up with laughter imagining the hilarious sight. 'That's why his dhoti was in your hands!'

Prachand and Inspector Gupta walked towards the haveli. 'So, when did you know for certain, without a doubt, that it was her?' Maya Gupta inquired.

'A few hours before the shoot, I went to visit the little boy who lives near the gate, the one who was touched inappropriately by Ramnarayan Rathod. He had earlier mentioned that having seen a witch run across the woods on the night of the murder. A child's imagination, on a gloomy, rainy night in the woods, can go far. When on a hunch, I happened to show a photograph of Padmini Rathod to him, he nodded his head vigorously. Clearly, she had paused long enough for him to have seen her face. He had recently moved here with his mother so had no idea who she was. That was enough of an identification for me, and that's when it all fell into place. I predicted that she would make another move soon, so I was alert and watchful. I just had no idea that she would go as far as ...'

'What you're trying to tell me is that *once again* you chose to withhold crucial information pertaining to the case from me. I thought I had clearly warned you that ...'

'Arey, Guptaji, why hold grudges now? All's well that ends well, right?' Prachand said and darted ahead without waiting for a response. He had a feeling that the inspector was speedily closing in on him.

CHAPTER 64

It took a few days for the police to take final statements, collect evidence and complete the legalities. This also meant that the Tripathis had to stay on. The lights and equipment were cleared out and the cast and crew was dispatched. While the mood was sombre, with a special pall of gloom hanging over Ramnarayan Rathod and Paramveer Khattar, the guests did their best to keep the atmosphere cheery. Rachna Tripathi took to the kitchen with a vengeance, helping in the only way she could, with a *karahi* in her hand. Vidya was unwillingly engaged as her sous-chef despite the cooks hovering around.

The day before their departure, Inspector Gupta and her team, Dr Behraam Wadia, and Dr Sisodia, were all invited for dinner. It took some effort to convince Dr Sisodia that this was a social call and that no one else had fainted or died at the haveli. All day long, the heritage structure hissed and sizzled with the heady aroma of frying and tadkas till the table was finally laden with aloo puri, kachoris, lauki ka kofta, chutney ke aloo, bharwa karela, paneer pasanda, samosa, shahi tukda, jalebi, kheer and mitha chawal. It was a feast! To celebrate ends and beginnings. Of course, the guests were delighted.

'Prachand, give two more puris to Inspector Madam. She needs some meat on her bones. *Sookhi kakdi lagti hai.*'

Prachand's face turned the shade of the beetroot sitting on the salad platter. He looked apologetically at Inspector Gupta, but she just laughed. 'Arey, Mataji, in my profession, it's better to be a *sookhi kakdi* than *moto taazo*, as they say in these parts. If I turn into a bharwa baingan, I'll be out of a job,' she said licking her fingers. 'I haven't eaten such delicious food in years!'

'Then come to Kanpur and you can have these treats every day. And wait till I take you for the *palak patte ki chaat* and the aloo chat. My mouth is watering just thinking about them,' Vidya said excitedly.

'It really does seem as if we have been here forever,' Yatish said, looking at the empty chairs that were usually occupied by the two best friends, their hosts who had excused themselves for the evening. 'I'm sure they can't wait to get rid of us either.'

A loud burp punctuated the conversation as Dr Wadia extended his arm and pointed at the jalebis. He picked up a handful and nestled them on top of the halwa. 'Excuse me! I've got so used to eating with dead people that my manners aren't quite what they used to be. My wife jokes that I could be eating intestines and I'd polish them off with relish.' His rattling laughter did nothing to assuage the horror on the faces around the table. Ammaji hurriedly placed the piece of paneer she was nibbling on back on to her plate and retired her dentures to the small potli on her waist.

In the main hall, as the grandfather clock struck seven, Arjun Prajapati darted out of a corner and started drawing the curtains and shutting the windows as per the evening custom.

'What are you doing, Arjunji?' Prachand called out to the man who was fidgeting with the windows, his limbs driven by some urgency. 'You no longer need to do that.'

Arjun Prajapati approached them with an incredulous look on his face. 'Prachand Sa, nothing has changed. You don't understand. Whatever happened was the doing of that child and his mother. Their spirits will never be at peace. Can't you see that Bhabhi Sa was possessed?'

'What nonsense!' Inspector Maya Gupta slammed her napkin on to the table. 'It's high time people took responsibility for their actions instead of blaming it all on superstitions and folklore!'

'Padminiji was a lonely and an intensely unhappy woman, that is all,' Vidya said with a note of asperity in her voice. 'Let's not dishonour her or Ranjana Jha by constantly dissecting the events.'

'This is why I keep telling your father to leave me alone and let me meet my friends in peace. What if I lose my mind and go on a rampage in Awadh Niwas?' Rachna Tripathi chose the most inopportune time to speak her mind.

'Who says you haven't lost your mind already?' Ammaji belched, announcing the end of the proceedings for the evening as far as she was concerned. She beckoned her youngest grandson to help her to the room.

Rachna Tripathi pressed a paan into her mouth. 'If I did go on a murderous rampage, can you guess the first person

I'll target?' she whispered conspiratorially to her brother-in-law with a sly look at Ammaji's retreating figure.

Prachand smiled. It felt like he was almost home. He couldn't wait to get back to Gwaltoli and stretch out on the charpoy in the aangan under the winter sun or sink into the comfy chair in his office.

Before long, Prachand was escorting the guests out. The other officers left in one jeep while Inspector Gupta offered to drop the doctors home. While the passengers settled in, she waited outside. Extending her arm to Prachand, she gave him a dazzling smile. 'You're certainly quite unforgettable, Mr Prachand Tripathi. Thank you. For everything.'

His hand was still in the lady's grasp when Vidya came running out with some pouches of paan. If Vidya had noticed, she didn't show it as she distributed the paan and then leaned in to hug Maya Gupta. 'My Kanpur offer stands. Come see us soon. And of course we will see you for the movie premiere!' she said to the policewoman.

Maya Gupta smiled in acknowledgement, slipped into her seat and drove away. Prachand darted a sideways glance at his wife, wondering if she would say anything. But she stayed quiet, watching the jeep disappear.

'Want to take a little walk with me, Prachi?' she asked, extending her hand. Prachand nodded and slipped his hand into hers.

He drew her close as they walked. 'It's a bit nippy, isn't it?'

There was no response. Prachand found it hard to decipher her expression in the dark. 'Are you all right, Viddu?'

'Yes. I'm fine.'

'So, where are we going?'

'You'll see.'

The ground was wet and the owls were hooting their stories into the night. Soon, they had crossed the entire path through the woods right up to the now-way-too-familiar clearing that housed the infamous well.

'Viddu, haven't we had enough of this place?' Prachand asked, his teeth chattering.

'Just a bit longer,' she said, almost dragging Prachand with her. As they reached the end of the clearing, the brick and mud exterior of the ruins loomed ahead. That's when he saw them.

Prachand's rational mind refused to acknowledge what his eyes were witnessing, but there they were. Young and old men, women and children, holding traditional hand torches, standing in between the dilapidated houses, sporting attire and expressions that did not belong to his world. Right in their midst was a familiar figure with a long white beard and a mirthless smile on his face, illuminated by the lantern he held.

'Bhutaari Baba?' Prachand could scarcely form the words.

'I told you, yet you never believed me. They are here. They will always be here. Go and solve this one, detective!'

'Viddu ... Viddu, this is ...' Prachand's heart was racing as he turned around wildly, looking for his wife, wanting her to infuse some logic and sense into the absurdity unfolding before his eyes. 'Bh ... bholenath.'

'Where are you, Viddu?'

He found her. Standing by the same well, replicating that terrifying afternoon. 'What are you doing, Viddu?'

Vidya turned to face him with an eerie smile. Right behind her stood a woman in a *ghagra choli*, her long hair encasing her like a shroud. She was holding on to a little boy who stared at Prachand, unblinking, yet knowingly.

That's when the sagacious, pragmatic and seasoned detective of Kanpur Khoofiya Pvt Ltd, non-believer of the supernatural, fainted and fell on to the mud of Kuldhara with a loud squelching sound.

GLOSSARY

Chapter 1

1. *Oye, bawlo!*: You fool!

Chapter 2

1. *Kulhad*: Disposable clay cups
2. *Aangan*: Courtyard
3. *Hirwa ke 'Khoofiya' Utpaad*: A line of products from Hirwa.
4. *Gau mutra*: Cow urine
5. *Kanda*: Cowpat
6. *Satyavadi Harish Chandra*: A great king of Ayodhya who never lied.
7. *Pota-poti kab khelenge aangan mein*: When will I see grandchildren playing in the courtyard?
8. *Phepdaas*: Lungs

Chapter 3

1. *Bholenath*: One of the names of Lord Shiva
2. *Kambakht! Lalchi lomdi!*: Greedy fellow!
3. *Neelam*: Blue sapphire
4. *Pukhraj*: Yellow sapphire
5. *Satsangi*: Spritiual
6. *Oye, baudam!*: absent minded.

Chapter 4

1. *Nausikhiya*: Newbie
2. *Jagratas*: Night-long vigils organized in honour of a deity

Chapter 5

1. *Choupal*: Community building or space in rural areas
2. *Ghar mein nahi hai daane, amma chali bhunaane*: With hungry mouths at home, she is off to do philanthropy
3. *Hamau ka thoda bhoon ke dei deo*: Fry something for me as well.
4. *Jab daant nahi tab doodh dayo, jab daant diye toh ann bhi dei hain*: When there were no teeth, He gave milk. If the Almighty has given teeth, he will provide food as well
5. *Suputra*: Son
6. *Firangi*: Foreigner

Chapter 6

1. *Khooni Haveli ka Khooni Rahasya*: The murderous secret of the murderous Mansion

Chapter 7

1. *Sabja beej*: Sweet basil seeds
2. *Barnis*: Glass Jars

Chapter 9

1. *Sher bachcha*: Lion-hearted child
2. *Dehen*: Burning
3. *Keval paagal pravesh karein*: Only idiots should enter

Chapter 10

1. *Panchmukhi hanuman kavach puja*: A special puja organized for protection
2. *Apshaguns*: Bad omens
3. *Koi maryaada nahin hai*: Such lack of decorum
4. *Dakshina*: Donation
5. *Jasoosgiri*: Detective work

Chapter 11

1. *Doosran ke phate mein taang mat daalna*: Don't meddle in other's problems
2. *Chintit*: Worried
3. *Ghani-ghani khamma! Atthe padhaaro sa*: Hallo and welcome

Chapter 12

1. *Bail buddhi*: Bull-headed
2. *Suprabhat*: Goodmorning

Chapter 13

1. *Baap-dadas*: Father and his predecessors
2. *Nada*: Drawstring

Chapter 14

1. *Zindagi jhand hai, phir bhi humein ghamand hai*: Life is in the pits, yet we retain our swagger

Chapter 15

1. *Jharokhas*: Stone windows projecting from the wall face of a building
2. *Chabootaras*: High platforms
3. *Naveli*: New

Chapter 16

1. *Pati hai ya pardada?*: Is he her husband or great grandfather?
2. *Thai bahut phutri laag riya ho*: You're looking lovely.
3. *Churan*: Sweet savoury balls for digestion/ digestive pills
4. *Aar parchi na baba*: I just can't take it any more!

Chapter 17

1. *Bhoot pisaach nikat nahi aave, Mahaveer jab naam sunave*: Paranormal entities stay away with the chanting of Mahaveer's name.

Chapter 19

2. *Bhootni*: A female ghost

Chapter 20

1. *Chhod do mujhe!*: Let me go!
2. *Theek hai, Beta*: Alright, my child.
3. *Tu dekh*: Wait and watch

Chapter 21

1. *Daakan*: Witch
2. *Maalish*: Massage
3. *Langots*: Wrestlers' underwear

Chapter 22

1. *Naari morcha*: Campaign for women's rights

Chapter 23

1. *Kahaan Raja Bhoj, kahaan Gangu Teli*: The difference in your status and mine is like the one between a king and a commoner.
2. *Ghor anarth hai yeh*: This is terribly inauspicious

Chapter 28

1. *Aate ka dabba*: Box used to store flour
2. *Baura gaye ho kya*: Have you gone insane!

Chapter 29

1. *Panchnama*: A record of witness testimony

Chapter 30

1. *Dikri*: Girl (In Parsi)

Chapter 31

1. *Gangajal*: Water from the Ganga, which is considered holy

Chapter 32

1. *Charan ki dhool*: The dust under your hallowed feet

Chapter 33

1. *Odhna*: Local Rajasthani term for dupatta, or a cloth to cover the head
2. *Nanire*: Maternal grandmother's house

Chapter 34

1. *Bholenath ki kripa hai*: Thanks to Bholenath
2. *Ek maa ki baddua hai*: It's a mother's curse

Chapter 35

1. *Karva Chauth*: A festival celebrated by women in India where they fast for a day to pray for their partner's long life

Chapter 36

1. *Charpai*: Variant spelling of charpoy

Chapter 37

1. *Matka*: Earthern pot
2. *Nirjala vrat*: A fast where no water is consumed

Chapter 38

1. *Yagya*: Religious ceremony performed using fire.
2. *Buri museebat ki naak ulte haath se pakdo*: Get to the bottom of a problem by thinking out of the box
3. *Vaid*: Local doctor, traditionally used to refer to a person who practices Ayurveda

Chapter 39

1. *Kabristan*: Graveyard

Chapter 40

1. *Aiyashi*: Debauchery

Chapter 41

1. *Kabhi baarish kabhi dhool*: Sometimes rain, sometimes dust storms
2. *Khaatas*: Accounts

Chapter 42

1. *Haklu*: A person who stammers
2. *Life ban jayegi*: Your life will be made
3. *Taash*: Cards

Chapter 43

1. *Mameri behen*: A cousin from the mother's side of the family.
2. *Kasam Bhairon Baba ki*: I swear by Bhairon Baba

Chapter 45

1. *Dhukariya ke tani kuch khaee ke de deo*: Can you feed this old lady?
2. *Hamaar bitwa!*: Our son!
3. *Khusur-phusur*: Whispering
4. *Bhabhuti*: Ash from the fire lit during a puja
5. *Khandahar*: Ruins

Chapter 46

1. *Mukhwas lao*: Get the mouth freshner

Chapter 47

1. *Kok hai ya anaaj ka bhandaar?*: Is it a womb or granary?
2. *Bitiya, jaun toka bhae, taun kar*: My child, do exactly as you please
3. *Yahan khoon hua hai, khoooon!*: A murder has been committed here!
4. *Kiski patloon?*: Whose trousers?
5. *Kuch ghooma phire jaike hai?*: Would you like an outing?

Chapter 48

1. *Hum na khaab*: I won't eat
2. *U ka khasam hain okey?*: Is that her husband?

Chapter 49

3. *Hum na jaab*: I won't go
4. *Humka kauna tarah oonth par dhar deo*: Get me a camel from somewhere
5. *Hamaar bahut icha baate*: It's a great desire of mine

Chapter 50

1. *Humka oonth par baithan deo*: I want to sit on a camel

Chapter 52

1. *Chokri aur pudiya bhi milegi*: I can get you a girl and drugs, too.
2. *Gadbad-ghotaala*: Objectionable activities

Chapter 54

1. *Chakkar*: Affair

Chapter 56

1. *O badmaas mil jaavego. Phikar na kar, bitwa*: I'm sure you'll catch him. Don't worry, Son.
2. *Prachand ki paheliyan Prachand hi jaane*: Only Prachand can decipher his own riddles.

Chapter 58

1. *Kambakht bhoot! Humka daraave chahat ho!*: You bloody ghost! You have the nerve to try and scare me!
2. *Namak haram*: Disloyal

Chapter 60

1. *Fitrat*: Nature

Chapter 63

1. *Kalyug ka Kamdev*: Modern-day god of love

Chapter 64

1. *Sookhi kakdi lagti hai*: She looks like a dried up cucumber
2. *Moto tazo*: Plump
3. *Bharwa baingan*: Stuffed brinjal

ACKNOWLEDGEMENT

Is this book going to be a bestseller?!

Don't like an author? Just walk up to them and pop this question. They'll turn purple in the face and disappear faster than jalebis at a dessert counter or a teenager from a room they've been ordered to clean up. It gives most of us the heebie-jeebies! I am not prescient enough to make these predictions either, but what I can tell you is that while writing this, I feel an indescribable euphoria that could possibly trump knowing that I've sold more books than..say, Ravinder Singh! (Alright. I know that's impossible.) Book 4. This can only mean that I have managed to surf the tidal and temperamental wave of countless words, myriad emotions ranging from hopelessness to immense gratitude, befriended strangers with the tales I have spun and had the privilege of watching my books glisten on bookshelves through tears of pride. If this isn't the best feeling in the world, I don't know what is. So here comes the next tide. Of gratitude and love, to the gentle winds, the gushing froth, the magnetic moons that have helped me on this journey.

Ravinder, you've had me waxing on across three books about how you've shaped my journey at every step, so I suppose you adequately get the gist by now, but the law of diminishing returns doesn't apply here! Thank you buddy, for everything and for finding multiple homes for my words. Here's to spending that day I've promised you, soaked in tea, coffee, bookstores, movies and endless chats (interspersed with singing and bhangra).

To the team at Harper. Swati, you're the coolest book binding, painting, knitting, puppy loving commissioning editor and guide anyone could ask for. Thanks for everything. Ananth, Aakriti, Prerna, Vikas, Rahul, Naveen, Hiren, Rajeshwar, Indranil, Asleha, Amit, Wasim and Sagiri. You guys are awesome and have helped me along in so many ways. Thank you Arcopol for doing what you do and rolling with the puns. Thanks Siddharth, for Story Ink and all for your efforts. You, your shiny office and your shoe collection are all incredible. First readers, cheerleaders, editors and research respondents never have it easy under my needy and watchful eyes. Thank you Anirban, Deepika (Vinkey di), Namita (Nitue), Didi and Papa for tolerating my whims and keeping me going, every single day. Can't do without even a single one of these vital organs. Thank you Manish Jijajee and Dr Neeraj Saraf, my forensic and medical superheroes. The fact that you are still conversing with me after I harangued you for so long about the living and the dead, is a testament to what stellar human beings you are. Yamini Singh Deo, the timeless tales of Vijaydan Detha, and all my Rajasthani friends, thank you for helping me see this historical and cultural wonder through your eyes. I couldn't have made this journey from the streets of Gwaltoli all the way to Kuldhara without the charming stories and memories you shared with me.

Ma, Baba, friends and family, all your love and support makes it easier for me to keep talking about my books and shove them onto your bookshelves. Mumma, I know you're the fire in my belly, the sinew in my hands and the very fibre of the words that help me connect with so many readers. I love you. Anika, you're my doll and my all. Banu, I've dedicated this book to you. You're not getting an entire paragraph this once.

Readers, Bookstagrammars, Bookclubs, fellow authors. You all come in different forms but leave me with one thought. That my words matter. Your kind words, emails, stories, posts and letters gratify me like nothing else. Thank you for your constant support.

Someone told me last year (I can't remember who, because I suffer from a cluttered mind syndrome. Everyday.) that the reason I included a paranormal element in this outing of the Tripathis was because of the horrors unfolding around us during the Pandemic. I can't really say. But what I do know is that while the world crashed about our ears and our hearts crumbled to dust, I needed a distraction and a glimmer of hope to cling on to. I wrote on, the world walked on, we held hands and marched our way out of the abyss. None of us were left unscathed but remember this, something Prachand Tripathi often tells me when I'm down and out.

You survived. You made it. Make it count. March on.

I hope you've enjoyed this new adventure and that you'll enjoy watching it on a screen even more. And before I waste any more space, one last time. Book 4. Yippee.

ABOUT THE AUTHOR

Richa S. Mukherjee is an award-winning writer, ex-journalist and advertising professional. She is the author of I Didn't Expect To Be Expecting, a candid take on accidental pregnancy and Kanpur Khoofiya Pvt Ltd, a humorous thriller that was procured for a screen adaptation. Her third book, Excess Baggage is also headed to the big screen. She has been a TOI Write India winner, is a blogger and travel writer and contributes to several platforms such as Womensweb, Momspresson and SheThePeopleTv. She is a Sheroes Champ and Blogchatter and Kool Kanya mentor. She has authored e-singles, anthologies and audio books. She lives in Mumbai and is often found in cozy coffee shops, eavesdropping intently for new book ideas.

You can reach her on Twitter (@richasmukherjee) Instagram (@mukherjeericha), email (richasmukherjee@yahoo.com) and website (www.richasmukherjee.com).